The Unseelie Court

THE WORLD BELOW BOOK THREE

VIVIENNE LEE FRASER

For all lovers of dragons, and for anyone who believes magic is real.

CHAPTER 1

There Be Dragon

Ed'rathe pushes off with his powerful hind legs, and we are airborne. The ground drops away and the wind whips at my face. We rise higher, and my stomach plummets as I watch the world fall away.

I bury my face in Snake's back and wrap my arms more tightly around him, holding on for grim death. It would be ironic if I fell and died minutes after embracing life again.

'Percival, are you okay?' Snake's voice drifts past me, and I struggle to catch his words as they're carried away on the wind.

'Yes,' I mumble into his back.

'Then can you ease off a little. I'd like to be able to breathe.'

I loosen my grip before immediately tightening it again as we climb higher still. As Ed'rathe banks I catch sight of the mountains of the World Between, the home of the dragons, just beyond the minotaur's maze.

I shudder. That maze tested Pris, Snake, and me to the very edge of our endurance. We were lucky to escape with our sanity and friendships intact.

We level out over the mountains, and I am able to make

out the edge of the Wyld Woods. My eyes are drawn to the home I have avoided for so many years. I am aware of the irony that now I do not want to leave it—not least of all because somewhere in the dense forest, our mother tree is sheltering my family while they mourn my father's passing.

Father and I were never close and were even less so after a curse turned me into something less than a sprite. However, I believe that in the end, he was proud of me.

I do not know why knowing that gives me solace. I thought I was past worrying what he, or anyone else, thought of me. Or maybe it is simply his prediction that I am integral to events happening in our world now has given me a purpose again—given me the motivation to act after so many years shying away from living—of allowing the shame of my actions and punishment to control my life.

Ed'rathe alters our course, and I shut my eyes, hoping this will help keep the food safely in my stomach. Riding on the back of a dragon is not how the legends tell it. It is not heroic. It is cold, uncomfortable, and quite terrifying. Still, if we are to reach the Unseelie Court tonight, I must endure this horror.

Of course, I have visited the court before with my friend Eleanora, and I know what to expect. No one has told Pris and Snake anything, so I fear this visit will try my companions even more than their adventure in the maze did.

This is where I can help. Some of the more senior members of his court are old friends of mine. They once played creature politics at the highest level. Their skills will be essential in the coming days if we are to save Queen Ariana and fix what is wrong with magic.

As the miles fall away and we draw closer to the portal between worlds, doubt begins to worm its way into my mind. Perhaps I have hidden myself from the worlds for too long. Will I be able to work with other creatures again? Or has my distance and isolation from the creature world changed me too much? What if they don't remember me? What if I am no longer able to influence them? Without that ability will I be of any help to Snake and Pris?

I straighten my spine and lecture myself. *Do not doubt yourself, Percival. Your friends will be happy to see you. They always are. Remember, you are one of the first lesser creatures to graduate university. You were part of the team that fought the blight and saved the worlds from disaster. You once stood up to the strongest governor in the land. You can be that person again.*

Perhaps my new sense of well-being is a result of the magic rolling off the dragon beneath me, or perhaps I have found my inner resolve. Whatever the cause, I am determined to hold on to this new-found confidence. I *can* help Pris and Snake convince the King of the Unseelie Court to visit the World Below. With his help I am certain we can restore Queen Ariana's health.

It was a shock seeing the Queen in the glass coffin held in stasis in the centre of the maze. She sleeps so the disease she caught does not have the chance to kill her. Even the dragons, the most powerful of magical beings, have not been able to save her.

The dragons believe the King of the Unseelie Court could awaken her, and together the two monarchs can restore the magical flow that has been waning for years. It must be something to do with the balance the dragons are so keen to maintain.

I hope they know what they are doing, because if they do not, then the World Below will be left without a monarch— and Bernais Baaronson and his cronies would just lap that up!

That want-to-be King would give anything to step in and take over from Queen Ariana so he could carry on his crusade to return the World Below to what they see as the glory days. If it were up to him, he would have lesser creatures like myself in virtual servitude in no time flat.

I shudder, and not just from the cold. We must convince the King to save the Queen and help restore magic. The alternative is too horrific to even contemplate.

The horizon draws closer, and I can sense a thrum of energy from the portal to the World Above. My head spins from the height and speed we are travelling. I take a peek around Snake, then immediately hide my face again. *Are we heading straight for a mountain?* My heart thumps in my chest, and I take another look and squint at the huge rock that looms in front of us, getting bigger and closer by the second. A tiny crack in the surface grabs my attention. There is a cave entrance, but we are going too fast to make that tiny pinprick of a hole—even with dragon magic.

As the portal draws closer and closer, I close my eyes, squeezing them tightly shut. If I block out the scene, I might be able to control the terror threatening to overwhelm me. I send a prayer up to the goddess for good measure and tell myself, *We will fly through the cave housing the portal and into the World Above. It will be no different than when I walk between the worlds at the Underground Ball Room.*

'No!' I wail, my eyes flying open as the consequences of moving between worlds hits me like a brick wall. *How could I have forgotten.... Above ground I will be a....*

The world around us drops away, sounds turning to echoes and white noise as we emerge from the darkness of the cave into dusk in the World Above. I have enough time to take in the grey depths of the water below us before my grip on Snake's back slips. I try to find purchase on the dragon's back, but the force of the wind is too much. I am falling, and the water is coming up fast. I hate water.

* * *

Adrenaline pumps through me as the World Below falls beneath us. My body wants to slump with exhaustion, but fear of falling keeps me upright and my knees locked. Ed'rathe's muscles move rhythmically beneath me in time with the beat of his wings.

I force myself to relax and admire the scenery, trying to keep my mind off the fact that those golden wings are the only thing keeping us in the air. The woods below may appear as a moss-green carpet from this height, but I'm sure it wouldn't feel like it when I hit those trees.

With that thought, my mind finally processes the fact that I'm flying on an honest-to-gods dragon. Me—Snake Fieth— on a dragon, just like the elves of old. I'm sure I have a stupid grin plastered all over my face.

Ed'rathe's voice rumbles through me. ***You are a natural flyer, Noble One. Perhaps when you and the princess join, you can request me as your dragon.***

'What?' The dragon's words jolt me from my reverie, and I play his words through again, trying to identify what had rung warning bells.

'We are not…. We have not….' I shake my head. What's the point of trying to explain what I don't understand myself?

Humph!

Did he just snort? Does he know something I don't? Can he see the future?

No, Noble One, but I can sense things.

'Oh.'

From the first moment I met Pris in the World Above, I was attracted to her. Since then, we have slowly built… something. Unfortunately, Pris and I have been so busy finding the key to the World Below and traipsing through the minotaur's maze, we haven't had a chance to find out what we are to each other.

I allow myself to remember the feel of her body against

mine in the minotaur's maze. Was that only a few minutes ago?

An uncomfortable heat sends my body tingling. I glance over at her flying beside us on Am'ratha, the dragon she is bonding with as a Princess of the Royal Blood—a princess in line to the throne of the Seelie Court.

Slumped across her dragon's neck, she looks as exhausted as I am and a little less comfortable on the back of her dragon.

That isn't surprising, really. We have been on the move for the last couple of weeks, which has been tiring enough. In addition to the physical stress, she has had to process a lot: that magic and magical creatures are real, that there is another world running parallel to the one she grew up in, and the fact that her family is elven—and royalty to boot.

After all of that, we thought we had reached the end of this nonsense when we made it to the end of the minotaur's maze, only to find the creatures who were supposedly helping us had their own agenda. They'd conspired to send us to convince the Unseelie King to rescue the Queen.

At the Midnight Ball it was obvious we were being manipulated by the unscrupulous elf, Bernais, and his faction of the council. Now the supposed good guys had joined in. We had to play along if we wanted to keep everyone safe.

Pris and I kept telling ourselves we would find the time to spend with each other—time to figure out what we are to each other—once we got to the centre of the minotaur's maze. Now we'll have to wait again.

I turn my head and glance back at the maze, now not much bigger than a pinprick in the distance. It was a dirty trick, luring us there only to let us into the secret being kept from the rest of the magical world.

How can they believe the three of us will have enough influence to change the King's mind? Yet the Queen's dragon was adamant that we are the only creatures who can, and that was the excuse they used for deceiving us.

'Are you all right, Snake?' Percival's muffled voice comes from behind me. 'You seem a little tense.'

I bark out a laugh. 'A little tense? No, I'm a lot angry. Every time we think we have done enough to free our parents, someone puts up another barrier. I'm a tired of being a pawn in someone else's game.'

I force out a breath and try to release the building tension. Pris, Percival, and I had agreed we would go to the Unseelie Court and do our best to convince the King to perform his duty. Allowing my emotions to get the better of me will not make the experience any more pleasant.

I hope there are decent showers at the court. Clean clothes and a soft bed would also be great. At the thought of bed, my eyes drift to Pris, and the memory of our kiss in the maze brings a smile to my lips. Maybe tonight we will find time to explore what we mean to each other?

Beneath me, Ed'rathe shifts, altering our course, and I watch as Am'ratha does the same. Pris ducks lower on her dragon's back. The mountain's surface splits, making way for the cave, as we enter the portal between worlds. Her white hair streams behind her, making her look every inch the elven princess she is.

We are plunged into darkness, and the magical barrier clings to me as Ed'rathe forces his way through. We emerge into evening in the World Above, and Pris is once again the girl I first met, bronze skinned with black curly hair—very human, but no less regal.

I smile at the vision she makes riding her dragon over Loch Ness. For the first time since we've taken to the air, Percival's grasp finally loosens, allowing me to breathe. Suddenly, I don't feel him at all.

I turn in my seat only to find a black cat staring at me with wide, frightened eyes. I grab for it, but I am too late. The cat slips and plummets towards the depths of Loch Ness.

⋅⋆˚⋆˚⋅

As Percival and Snake swoop ahead of us, I try to focus on anything but my fear of falling. I use Am'ratha's wingbeats to measure my breathing. Eventually it works, and I have almost convinced myself that travelling by dragon is normal.

My eyes droop, exhaustion weighing heavy on my mind and body as I lie against Am'ratha's neck. I shake my head, trying to clear the fog. Is it possible I'm dozing while flying on the back of a dragon? I should be excited at the very least, but all I can think is, I hope I don't fall asleep and end up plummeting to the ground.

Don't worry, Royal One, I will protect you. My magic will keep you on my back. Am'ratha has directed her voice into my head, and I know this conversation is for me alone. Still, "Royal One" is new.

What's with the formalities?

Am'ratha snorts. ***The Dragon Queen has warned me to follow the rules. That means I can only talk with creatures who are titled royal, noble, or dragon friend.***

So, since I'm royal, you can talk to me. Can you talk to Snake and Percival?

Snake is your consort, so he is noble.

It's my turn to snort. *Consort?* ***You're getting a little ahead of things.***

Am'ratha chooses to ignore me. ***Also, he is the son of one of the Seelie Queen's advisors, which also confers this status.***

Was she teasing me? I'm not quite sure, but I think she was.

Percival has long been a friend of the dragons.
What? Now that's interesting. **How come?**
That is a long story, Royal One, and is perhaps best saved for another day.

If flying on the back of a mythical beast isn't mind-bending enough, I'm having telepathic conversations with a freaking dragon, and she's winding me up about Snake. _If only my friends could see me now!_

It's hard to believe it was only a couple of weeks ago that a boy burst into my home, announced he was a gnome, and informed me my parents had been taken to some magical world.

I've come a long way from being the girl who lived a sheltered life in London, far from the magical world my parents grew up in. Now I ride dragons, travel with a sprite and a gnome, and have almost accepted that I'm an elven princess who could one day be Queen of that magical world.

No, that'll never happen. I may have taken on their stupid quest and agreed to be their emissary to the Unseelie Court, but I will never be Queen. I have not chosen this, and I have to draw the line somewhere, or I fear this magical world will take over my life.

Before all of this, I was going to be a human rights lawyer, but that was before I found my parents had hidden this whole world from me. Now my future path is not so clear. Could I forget all of this and go back to my real life, to being a university student, and perhaps dating Snake in the real world?

Will he be able to go back and take up his position studying physics at university? Or has finding out he is part elf changed what he wants for the future? Certainly, if I were him, I'd be annoyed at how the other creatures treated me and my family, and I would want to do something about it. That's me. I haven't had a chance to ask Snake how he feels about it all. Maybe when we arrive at the Unseelie Court, we'll be able to make some time to talk.

As we speed towards an opening in the mountain, I keep low over my dragon's back. I tighten my grip as the world around us goes absent of sight or sound, temporarily shocking my senses as we fly through the film of the magical portal. I hold my breath until Am'ratha stretches her wings over a lake. I catch sight of a derelict castle on the shore and wonder if this is Loch Ness.

Now that we have successfully made it back to my world, it occurs to me Snake and I may not even be able to choose our own futures. If the Queen is not placed back on her throne, will Bernais ever let us leave the World Below? Or will he send us to the World Above and prevent us from ever returning?

I resist the urge to close my eyes and hide from the overwhelming uncertainty that question invokes. There are too many variables and so little we can control.

I shiver as the cold air sends icy fingers through my clothes. Actually, the thing I want most at the moment is a hot bath, or even a shower will do, and to fall into a blissfully warm bed.

'Percival!'

The shout jolts me from my dreams of soft sheets, heat, and cleanliness in time to watch a cat falling toward the loch below.

Poor friend Percival. Of course he would return to cat form when we left the World Below, Am'ratha purrs inside my head.

'He returned to what?'

I am sorry for the intrusion, my Queen, but we forgot about Percival's curse.

'Who are you talking to?'

Shh, Royal One. There is no time for explanations.

A new voice enters the conversation.

You may use magic to stay the curse for seven days. If

the deed cannot be done by then, the curse will be returned.

Thank you, my Queen.

The cat is still falling towards the water as if in slow motion. As it is about to plummet into the icy water, it turns into Percival. He pinwheels his arms and legs chaotically, desperate to slow his descent, and my heart practically burst out of my chest in panic and fear for my friend.

His terror-filled scream rips through the air, just as a dark silver dragon leaps from the water, catching the semi-wet sprite on his back. Crisis averted, I let out a breath, relaxing against Am'ratha's back as the three dragons head to the ruins of an old castle at the edge of the lake.

Just when I am getting used to things in my new life, another twist throws me off-balance.

When we are all safely on the ground, I ask, 'Am'ratha, why is Percival a cat in the World Above?'

Shh. My uncle speaks.

If the dark dragon who emerged from the loch had eyebrows, they would be raised. Instead his thoughts in my head are laced with skepticism. *These are the ones our Queen believes will persuade King Maddox to do his duty?*

They are, Uncle.

My jaw clenches as I let go of Am'ratha's scales and rise to my full height. *Who is he to judge us?* At the same time, the full force of the magnificent dragon's presence hits me, and I have to stop myself from bowing before this creature.

They are our last hope, Am'ratha says before I can tell the dragon exactly what I think. *The Queen believes the King will listen to these three.*

As the dragons talk, Percival dries himself with magic before climbing back onto Ed'rathe. He appears unhurt, but he won't meet my eye. Something is not quite right with him.

How fares the world here, Uncle? Am'ratha asks.

Already the lack of magic is being felt, youngling. Weather patterns are changing and crops are failing. If we do not fix this soon, both worlds will suffer beyond repair.

No pressure, I think, and the new dragon raises his head to look at me. Of course he is reading my mind.

Royal One, this is no time for larking about.

I tamp down the anger beginning to surge within me. I'm tired of being both underestimated and used by creatures in the magical world, but an angry outburst will get me nowhere.

Ignoring the older dragon, I direct my thoughts to Am'ratha. *Why is Percival a cat in the World Above?*

He has not told you? The curse is part of his punishment for unknowingly spreading the blight centuries ago. In the World Below, he takes human form, and in The World Above, he takes the form of a cat. In neither world can he be his true self.

It takes a moment for her words to sink in, then it hits me like a freight train as I begin to understand the burden Percival has been under. *You're joking, aren't you? He has endured centuries of punishment for something he did unknowingly—how barbaric.*

It is worse than that. As I understand it, he can no longer commune with the trees or be with his soulmate. Their story has touched the heart of many a bard, and he features in many of our favourite tunes. Many dragons hope he will save your Queen and have his punishment lifted.

I'm stunned into silence, and believe me, this does not happen often. My heart breaks as contemplate Percival's agony at being separated from his soulmate, and, worse than that, he can never truly be himself. Suddenly all my worries pale into insignificance. Percival chooses that moment to look towards me. He takes in my expression and frowns.

'What are we waiting for?' he asks.

Good luck, the Loch Ness dragon says as Am'ratha leaps for the sky. ***I fear you will need it.***

Shivering with bone-chilling cold, I grip Snake tightly as Ed'rathe prepares to follow his sister into the sky. The dragon takes pity on me and sends waves of heat through my body until my shaking subsides.

Although I am now warm, my arms still tremble with fear. Returning to cat form was bad enough. Doing it while on the back of a dragon above a lake shocked me out of my complacency. I had become so comfortable being in human form, it did not occur to me I would transform as soon as we left the World Below.

And that look Pris gave me. She is clearly aware of my past, and she pities me. Her dragon must have told her everything. No doubt Ed'rathe will tell Snake as well. How will I be able to face them as an equal, let alone a guide, now?

Are you ready to leave now, Dragon Friend? Ed'rathe asks me, doing me a great honour by speaking directly to my mind.

'I am.'

The dragon from the loch turns his intense gaze in my direction, and his golden eyes narrow to slits. ***Our Queen has*** *given you seven days in this form before the curse will return, Dragon Friend. The graveness of the situation is the only reason she allowed us to do this.*

Could you not have done something sooner? Sprites hate water. I lash out as my shame burns.

The air by the loch stills, and it is like the whole world holds its breath at my audacity. The water dragon throws back its massive scaled head and laughs.

You are either very stupid or very brave, Percival. Let us hope it is the latter because you will need it if you are to help sort things out at the Unseelie Court.

'What do you mean by that?' Snake asks, and I feel another wave of shame at finding out he has been included in the conversation all along.

It is not my place to tell, Noble One. Besides, you will find out soon enough.

I am tired of the games and the half-truths. I want to be on our way. The sun is setting, and the air is cold. All I desire is to curl up beside a blazing fire. Snake does not seem to feel the same way.

He points at the ruins of Urquhart Castle. 'Is that where we're going?'

No, young creature. The court once resided in Urquhart Castle because kings of old preferred to be close to the portal. The new King prefers human amenities, so he moved his court to a city and set up a guard post here.

'I guess it is a bit of a ruin, but I thought... you know, that the court might be hidden.'

The crumbling stone is indeed an illusion. The gate-keepers and their family reside in the castle.

'Ah, I thought the ruins were veiled in a shimmer of magic.' Snake shifts in his seat so he can face the dragon. 'Which city did the court move to?'

'It is in Inverness, Snake,' I say, unable to keep the impatience from my voice. 'And I would like to go there if you have finished your history lesson.'

My companion's body tenses, and I expect him to snap back, but he does not.

'Yes, we're all tired, and we've dealt with a lot these last few days.' His voice is calm and controlled as he smooths things over.

And you should not linger too much longer because our glamour will fade, the Loch Ness dragon says. *Once it does, people will talk of the monster in the loch. There are always some who can pierce the glamour we place to hide our presence, but those individuals are often treated as if they are crazy. If a whole busload of people was to see us, there would be nothing less than total chaos.*

Taking a deep breath, I force my voice directly into the large water dragon's mind. *I am sorry I was so rude to you. I appreciate you saving me from drowning.*

The dragon holds my gaze as if he is assessing the weight of my words. *It has been a difficult road in life for you, Percival. You have paid so much for your youthful mistake. Do not fail in this chance to end your suffering.*

As far as pep talks go, it's a little lacking. I have to remind myself that for a dragon to show even a little empathy for a creature is way out of character. Acknowledging the favour he has bestowed on me, I bow my head.

Not wanting to dwell on my embarrassment, I turn my thoughts elsewhere. Until I fell from the dragon, I was looking forward to returning to the Unseelie Court. I thought I could contribute something towards Pris and Snake's efforts to persuade the King to return to the World Below. Dropping from Ed'rathe's back put an end to that.

All my doubts and fears are back, and they are fighting for

space in my mind. I cannot continue like this. If I cannot control my doubts, I may as well stay here and wait for my young friends to return.

Ed'rathe bunches his muscles, preparing to take off. 'Ed'ruven, can you tell us anything else that might help us at court?'

The dragon who had emerged from the water shakes his head. *The court is not how you remember it, Percival, and the change has not been for the better. Tread carefully and rely on your old friends to guide you.*

I duck back behind Snake to avoid the cold night air as we take to the sky. The dragon's cryptic comment replays in my head as we travel towards Inverness. Is there more to the King's reluctance to help solve this problem than Fairburn, the head of the Queen's Guard, had let on when he sent us on this mission?

I push aside all my self-doubts, and I begin to worry about what sort of mess we are walking into.

· · ✦ ☾ ✦ · ·

Ed'rathe pushes off, taking us upwards before levelling out and following his sister. The pressure of Percival against my back raises my anxiety levels. I'm still not over the shock of seeing a cat falling towards the loch, and I'm still getting my head around the idea that the cat was Percival. I'm now wishing I put him in front of me for this leg of the journey. The loch dragon assured us he won't turn back into a cat, but still... better to be safe.

The fact that Percival is a cat in the World Above is still a surprise—and a black cat at that. A black cat? I saw a number of black cats when Pris and I were in the World Above, including the one at Eleanora's place....

'Percival?'

'Yes?' His voice is muffled, as if he is pressing his face into my body.

'It wasn't a coincidence that Pris and I kept seeing black cats on our journey to the World Below, was it?'

I wait for a response and am thinking he probably won't answer me when his voice drifts forward, tentative and reedy.

'It was me. Eleanora sent me to protect the two of you.'

'It must be so cool to shape-shift.' The words slip out before I engage my brain.

'It might be if I were able to actually decide when I wanted to shift.' Percival's voice is tight and controlled.

I sense a story there but one Percival is perhaps not quite ready to tell.

His body tenses and relaxes, as if he is sighing. 'I was transformed as a punishment for spreading blight when I was around your age.'

Surely I didn't hear right. 'Transformed? Into a cat?'

Percival doesn't answer for a few wingbeats. 'Yes. It was partially reversed, so I am human in the World Below and a cat in the World Above'

'Don't you mean you're a sprite in the creature realm?'

'I am no longer fully sprite.'

Percival's words are a whisper on the wind but filled with such pain. I take in the enormity of his revelation, and I'm shocked to the core. Transformation of a creature is forbidden and is punished more severely than murder.

'By who? I mean, who would impose such a horrific sentence?'

'Magnus Baaronson.' Percival spits the name out like it's a vile taste in his mouth, and those two words rock my world.

'Baaronson? Bernais is a Baaronson.'

'Yes, he is. Magnus is his father, and he also happens to be governor of the region where Eleanora and I grew up.'

'But that's monstrous. Transformation has been outlawed for hundreds of years.'

Percival's body tenses against my back, telling me this conversation is difficult for him. 'I am aware of that. I was the last to be punished that way. Your great-uncle, Drow, and I worked together to ensure a law was passed that prevents other creatures from going through the physical and emotional trauma I endured.'

So many questions swirl around in my head as anger and sorrow war for a place in my heart. Percival was the sprite who made history by taking a governor to court and making sure no lesser creatures would be punished by an imposed transformation. It was one of the early steps that led to equality for lesser creatures. My great-uncle was a part of it? Percival knew my great-uncle?

'Hold on, how old are you...? You must be old if you've been this way for over a couple of hundred years. One small mistake changed the course of your whole life?'

Wow, Snake, way to go. You could have handled that better.

'I deserved some form of retribution for spreading the blight. You need to understand how big a deal the blight was at the time.'

This is Percival as I have never heard him—meek and uncertain. It's like he's reverted back to the boy he once was. This is so out of character.

'Percival, I can't see you doing something like that to the forest.'

'I would never.... Not on purpose. It was an accident, but I deserved to be punished because I was a thoughtless young sprite.'

'Okay, I get that. But really, overkill much?'

We are silent as Ed'rathe transports us towards the lights of a city. Then another thought hits me.

'You had a decision to make when we were in the minotaur's maze. In the end, you chose to stop being an advisor and join our quest. Did you do that because the Queen might be persuaded to commute your sentence if you help redress the balance between worlds?'

'Perhaps,' Percival agrees. 'Yes. But mostly I am doing this because, before he died, my father convinced me something big is going on here. Something even bigger than the blight.'

I'm struggling to remember my history of those years, and how Percival, now that I know he's *that* sprite, might have fitted in.

'Didn't you work with Princess Petunia and some others to stop the blight's spread? Wasn't that enough to earn you a commuted sentence?'

'Apparently not. I don't want to talk about it anymore.'

In the short time I've known Percival, I've found that when he decides something, he can't be moved. I try another tactic.

'Percival, my family doesn't talk much about Drow. Wasn't he banished?'

'Yes—well, no. He left along with most of Princess Petunia's court when she was exiled, but I don't believe he was ever formally banished.'

We fall silent, both lost in our own thoughts until Ed'rathe interrupts us.

We are almost there, Noble One, Dragon's Friend. When we land, you must depart quickly, as there is not enough magic to hold our glamour for long,

Soon we are swooping over a city, and Inverness Castle comes into sight. The dragons circle the castle by the river, giving us a bird's-eye view of the historic city of Inverness as darkness falls. I want to be excited about the view and landing in the courtyard in front of the castle while riding a dragon. In reality, though, I'm so tired, I can barely keep my eyes open.

As Ed'rathe's wings fold inwards, Percival holds himself away from me, stiff and formal. I think it's because he is a private creature. He's done sharing his past and he wants things to go back to the way they were.

'Percival, what we just talked about….'

He is silent, almost as if he is holding his breath.

'It can stay between us, but… if you ever want to talk about it, I'm here.'

The silence continues, and I wonder if he has heard me.

'Thank you,' he eventually says, and perhaps that's all he is capable of saying given the circumstances.

Ed'rathe lies down to allow us to dismount. When my feet hit solid ground, I reach up, stretching out my back. Then I take a couple of steps, making sure everything still moves. I catch a whiff of something foul and scan the courtyard for the source—perhaps an open sewer or drain. Sniffing again, I realise it's me. My nose wrinkles in distaste. Boy, I need a shower, and the sooner, the better.

By the time we arrive at Inverness, the sky is dark and the town is a twinkle of lights below. We fly over the city, and I marvel at how the modern town blends with the old. The castle stands as a beacon on a rise beside the river, which Am'ratha informs me is the Ness.

Welcome to the Unseelie Court, Royal One.

Inverness Castle is the court? It's a traditional Norman structure—not at all what I expected. I can't believe they have it out in the open like this. The World Below is so secretive, and all about not showing magic to humans.

Am'ratha snorts, something I'm beginning to notice she does when she thinks I'm saying, or thinking, something stupid. ***This is simply the doorway to the court. Like the Underground Ballroom through which you entered the World Below, the Unseelie Court is held slightly out of the World Above. Creatures can come and go through the special entrance, but few in the World Above know it is here.***

Magic is so cool, and kinda scary because it's existed right beside me for my whole life, and I never realised.

With the court so close, butterflies begin to flutter in my stomach. In the maze, I had been so certain that I, a Princess of the Royal Blood, would be able to talk the King into doing what others were unable to persuade him to do. Now that I'm actually here, I begin to wonder, what help can I be? I've never spoken to royalty, so why would a king listen to me?

Then, it's like my anxiety is on a roll. My concerns pop into my head one after another before I have time to fully process them. I've never been to court. How should I behave? If I'm royalty, will they expect me to conduct myself as if I am? I mean, I only found out I was an elf a few days ago. Oh, and will they use magic? I'm still quite bad at controlling mine.

Suddenly the war cry I owned when I formed my first magical flame—I'm a freaking elf princess—sounds so hollow. I couldn't convince a trumped-up court to release my parents. How will I ever be able to convince the King of a magical court to do something he so obviously doesn't want to? I tighten my grip on Am'ratha's scales. Perhaps she can fly me back to London—to normalcy.

Being expected to be a princess isn't the only thing that worries me. Always there's that nagging doubt that I haven't been told everything about who I am. My parents kept everything from me, and each new revelation hits like a punch to the gut.

I'm not sure they will ever reveal the full truth. I only uncovered my magical heritage because Mum and Dad were taken to face Bernais's charges of using magic for their personal gain in the World Above.

My mother is a princess, a niece of the Queen of the Seelie Court. No one will tell me why she and my father live in the World Above, denying their heritage and lying to me. Everyone else knows what happened, but they say I must wait for my parents to tell me.

Straightening my spine, I imagine my father telling me, 'Focus on the things you can control and influence, Pris, everything else is a wasted effort.' Now more than ever his words ring true.

As Am'ratha drops down so I can dismount, I think I might throw up.

You are a Princess of the Royal Blood and way stronger than you are letting yourself believe at the moment. Enter the court and do us both proud.

I wish you'd stop reading my mind.

Perhaps I will when you stop broadcasting your thoughts so loudly.

Although I don't like that she invades my head, her words bolster me. I slide from my dragon friend's back and stare up at the sandstone walls of the castle and the steps that lead to the enormous wooden door. No lights shine through the thick glass windows. It looks deserted, as though it's been locked up for the night. What if no one's home?

Go knock on the main door. I have sent a message of your imminent arrival. Someone will come for you.

Suddenly I don't want Am'ratha to leave. I am stronger by her side. *Can you stay until they do?*

You have Snake and Percival. Besides, there is not

enough magic around for me to stay shrouded for much longer. Ed'rathe and I will find a place to hide near Loch Ness. If you need me, just call.

How will you be able to hear me? I ask, as much to delay her departure as wanting to find out the answer.

You are talking to me now.

So distance doesn't matter?

She drops her head to look me in the eye. *Sometimes it is easy to forget how little you know of our world. No, my princess, distance does not matter. We are linked, you and I, and we can talk to each other anywhere.*

Oh. Oh! That might be something to keep in mind next time I kiss Snake.

Don't worry. That is private, and I would never intrude. We dragons place strict boundaries on our links, and I would appreciate it if you followed them too.

My face heats up, and I try to change the subject.

Won't you be bored waiting around for us?

No, Ed'rathe and I enjoy playing around and scaring the humans who come to Loch Ness searching for monsters. We will be fine for a few days.

She steps away from me and prepares to leap. I'm almost toppled over by the force of the wind her wings create as she and her brother take off, leaving us to face the Unseelie Court alone.

CHAPTER 3

Welcome to Inverness Castle

Snake and Percival join me at the foot of the stairs, watching the dragons as they fly off into the night. Moments later they disappear, their glamour hiding them from sight. We're left standing in the empty courtyard in front of the foreboding locked wooden doors of the deserted castle.

The chilly evening air seeps through my clothing and into my bones, and I shiver. After the balmy weather in the maze, it's a shock to the system. Trying to ignore my growing unease, I take a step forward. Snake moves with me, dropping an arm over my shoulders. I lean into him, enjoying the shared warmth of our bodies.

'What now?' he asks.

Percival has not moved. 'Is he all right?' I ask, nodding towards our friend.

'I think so. The cat thing was a shock, and for his story to come out that way.... Well, it can't have been comfortable.'

'He knows it makes no difference to us, doesn't he?'

'He can hear you,' Percival says sharply. Then adds a little more softly, 'But thank you. I appreciate that.'

Snake chuckles. 'Yeah, he's okay. So, any ideas on how we get in?'

'Am'ratha said she told them we are coming. So, I guess we knock.'

Percival takes a step forward and says over his shoulder, 'Well, we certainly cannot stand around here all night, chit-chatting. We will catch our deaths in this cold.'

We follow him up the stairs and wait while he pounds on the door. The sound echoes in the night air. We wait. No one answers. Exhausted, I snuggle closer to Snake and as I do I remember our kiss in the maze. I nuzzle into his neck, and he pulls me closer.

Percival kicks the door, and this time the wood shimmers as a smaller entrance appears within the larger door seconds before it opens, throwing a shaft of light across us.

A female voice sounds from within. 'Show some patience. It takes time to deactivate the wards.'

I blink a couple of times and tense. Is that our au pair, Susan? Leaving Snake's protective embrace, I step through the opening and find myself staring into her familiar grey-green eyes. When she disappeared at the same time as my parents, I'd worried I might never see her again.

She steps towards me as if to wrap me in a hug before stopping short. My face must have shown my confusion at her being here. Not to mention the hurt and anger her abandonment had caused. Now I add betrayal to the list. For her to be here in the Unseelie Court means that she must have known what my parents hid from me for all those years.

'Susan, I didn't expect to see you here.' I try to keep my voice even, but my tone is chilly.

She flinches a little, but her eyes shine with sympathy and understanding. 'You are upset with me. I would expect no less from you.'

'So, what are you doing here?' I ask. My words are as

clipped and unemotional as I can make them, hopefully masking my shock at her presence.

'I am a member of the Unseelie Court. When I found out your parents had been taken, I came to report to the King and also to beg him to help as was my duty.'

'Was it also your duty to lie to me about who I was?' Another thought occurs to me. 'Were you also spying on us for the King?'

'Never spying, only guarding.' She opens her mouth as if she is about to say more, then closes it. She settles the mask of polite host on her face and says, 'It is cold and late. Come inside. Rooms have been prepared for you all,' before lowering her voice and saying only to me, 'We can talk about all this later.'

'Indeed we will,' I mutter under my breath.

Snake slips his hand into mine, giving it a gentle squeeze. 'Is that your nanny? The one who left us that amazing lasagna.'

I don't want to be reminded that Susan thought to make sure I had food before she disappeared, leaving me to face the last couple of weeks on my own. Focusing on her lies and betrayal allows me to retain my animosity.

'Yes, it is. And it appears she's always been an agent from the Unseelie Court.'

'That's interesting,' Snake says as Susan leads us along the corridor, Percival in her wake. 'I wonder if she's friend or foe?'

My eyes narrow as they latch on to Susan's back. 'I'm not sure, but I aim to find out.'

Our footsteps echo in the empty building as we follow Susan through a cold, dark castle. I expected sumptuous furnishings and great works of art covering the walls, but everything is stripped bare. Soon our journey takes us past scaffolding and plastic sheets, indicating that this part of the castle is undergoing restoration, which explains the sparse decorations.

We stop in front of a white plastered recess that looks as though it was once a door to somewhere. Susan walks through the wall and disappears. Percival follows. Snake and I look at each other.

'Shall we?' he asks.

I take a deep breath, then nod. Together we step through the wall, and I shiver as the familiar chill of a magical portal washes over me. On the other side, we find ourselves in a luscious castle hallway that is everything I'd imagined a castle would be. I turn slowly, taking everything in.

If I had to describe it, I would say it was over the top turn of the 19th century—all wood and stone and wall tapestries—but it was a whole other level. It was luxury gone mad.

'Impressive,' Snake understates as he studies the surroundings.

'When Huntley remodelled Inverness Castle in the World Above in the 1850s, the old King of the Unseelie Court took the opportunity to build a parallel building,' Susan tells us as we regroup. 'The new King finished the work, expanding the court to house hundreds of creatures. Lately we have been having problems with magic in the World Above, so some of the courtiers returned to their homes, and the King placed part of the court in storage.'

'In storage? What does that even mean,' I mutter.

Susan taps her index finger on her lips. 'How do I explain this? The central court is attached to physical elements of Inverness Castle—the portals, the windows we look out of, and the like. The King uses magic to set this up, but once it is there, it takes very little effort from the King to maintain, and maintenance creatures are used to keep the barrier between us and Inverness Castle strong.'

She cocks her head to the side as if waiting for something. Ah, she's waiting for me.

'I'm with you so far.'

'Good. Now, the King is then able to extend the court from that core by using magic to make rooms larger, add on floors, and even extend beyond the boundaries of Inverness Castle.'

I think back to my magic lessons in the minotaur's maze. Particle magic allows things to be changed by adding stray particles in the air to what you already have, making it bigger or changing shape. I have used it to change small items, but.... My eyes widen, and Susan grins.

'I see you understand now. It takes a great deal of magical strength, a high concentration of magic, and a large number of extra particles to keep the larger court operational. As magic has decreased, the King has been forced to reduce the size of the court.'

Snake asks, 'So you're saying it's more like a country house than a castle now?'

Susan chuckles. 'Hardly. At full capacity the court is more like a small village. At the moment we still have enough creatures attending for the castle to be full. In fact, with you arriving, we are a little pressed for space.'

I send Snake a questioning glance, wondering if he caught her comment about the problem with magic. He shrugs, and I lean in to whisper, 'If they're already aware of the magic problem and it's impacting them, why isn't the King leaping at the chance to help fix it?'

'It is odd,' he says, stifling a yawn.

I yawn myself in response, and suddenly remember how bone tired I am. I tug on Snake's hand, and we catch Susan up.

'Is it far to our rooms?' I ask her. 'We've had a long day, and all we want to do is wash up and get some sleep.'

Susan pauses a moment and studies us in the light, a slight

frown drawing her brows together. We must make a sad picture.

'Of course. Your dragon did warn us that you were in no state to be presented at court immediately, although I had hoped to tidy you up and at least introduce you to the King tonight.'

She pauses again, and I wonder if she is waiting for us to say we would like to meet the King. None of us moves. I suspect Snake and Percival are as exhausted as I am after our experience in the minotaur's maze, and none of us are in a state to make a good first impression on the King.

Susan's shoulders rise in a shrug. 'I will arrange time with the King tomorrow, so you can rest tonight. I have done the best I can with your accommodation given the short notice and—'

'The problem with space,' I offer.

Turning on her heel, Susan leads our motley crew down the rest of the corridor and around the corner. If we had thought the corridor opulent, we were mistaken. We find ourselves in the entrance hall of the Unseelie castle, and it is spectacular.

Chandeliers send light up the three floors of the building, bathing the sweeping polished wooden staircase in a dappled spotlight. The parquet floor below reflects the sparkling lights above, and the walls are almost completely covered in portraits and scenes of the World Below.

Susan sweeps up the stairs, not giving us much of a chance to take in the scenery. After hustling her along, I can't ask her to wait while I gawp at the room like a tourist in a National Trust museum.

As we reach the middle floor, Susan turns left, and we head away from the river. At any moment I expect to run into another creature or for the sounds of dining and dancing or something to fill the air. All I hear is our muffled footsteps. Are magical courts supposed to be this deserted?

·· ⁎ 🌙 ⁎ ··

I'm not sure I was expecting a warm welcome to the Unseelie Court, but I certainly wasn't expecting empty corridors and an almost eerie silence, especially as the court is supposed to be full. Pris keeps her hand in mine while Percival walks almost stoically in front of us. Our procession reminds me of a death march.

I glance sideways at Pris. Her eyes bore into Susan's back. She is not as angry as she was when she found her former au pair answering the door, but she isn't quite happy with the situation either.

I understand where she's coming from. I only recently found out that my mother had not exactly been truthful with my heritage and that my grandmother was an elf. Inter-creature relationships are frowned upon in the World Below, and mixed-race children are often shunned. So, while I get why she didn't tell me, it still hurts.

Pris's parents' betrayal is so much more comprehensive. They kept her entire family and her magical heritage from her. Then to find out that the one other person you trusted your whole life was part of that deception—it's gotta hurt.

The silence is oppressive, and I feel the need to break it. 'Where is everyone?' My voice sounds loud in the too-quiet hallway.

Susan doesn't break stride as she answers. 'They're at dinner in the dining hall on the ground floor. I had thought you might be able to change and join them, but as you're all so tired and, well, you smell like you haven't bathed for a week, I will have food sent up for you.'

Percival glares at our host, and she obviously feels the burn, as she turns and says, 'That last comment doesn't apply to you, Percival. You are as immaculate as always.'

Percival preens, and I can't help but smile.

'Thank you,' he says. 'And thank you also for understanding that we are far too tired to make polite conversation with strangers tonight. We have had rather a trying time these past few days.'

As I consider the option of dinner, my stomach rumbles, and my cheeks heat up.

Susan half turns, eyeing my stomach as it continues to grumble. 'Perhaps I had better make food a priority.'

I nod, too embarrassed to speak. At the end of the passage, we turn right and find ourselves in a guarded corridor. Pris's eyes widen as she clocks the guards, and Percival stops moving.

'I have never seen guards in the residential suites before,' he mutters.

'Why are the soldiers here, Susan?' Pris asks, her voice wary.

Susan closes her eyes momentarily before answering, and I fear we're trying her patience. 'Strange things have been happening in the court lately. So, the King believes we can't be too careful with security when strangers arrive unexpectedly in the night.'

'Are they here to protect us or protect others from us?' Pris attempts to clarify.

'Here we are. This is the suite of rooms you will be sharing.' Susan looks at Percival and me as she reaches for the handle, avoiding answering Pris altogether.

The doors swing open, revealing a sitting room with two chairs and a sofa arranged around a fire. By the window sits a table with four chairs. Four doors break up the walls on either side of the room—two on the right and two on the left.

'The guest bedrooms are through the doors on the left,' Susan informs us. 'There is a shared bathroom between. Thank goodness the new King arranged to have the plumbing modernised so you can have a bath without someone having to haul water up for you.'

'I was kinda hoping for a shower,' I say, too tired to hide my disappointment.

Susan laughs. 'We are getting there, but we're not that modern yet. I see you arrived without a change of clothes. I'm sure the Royal Wardrobe will have something for you. I will arrange for clothes to be brought up while you bathe.'

'Two guest rooms?' Pris raises an eyebrow. 'Where will Percival be? We would like him to be accommodated with us.'

'I'm sorry, Princess, I haven't been quite clear. Snake Fieth and Percival of the Wyld Woods have been invited to stay here by the suite's occupants. You are to stay in the royal quarters.'

Pris drops my hand and glares at Susan. This isn't going to be pretty.

'I want to stay here with the others.'

Susan is clearly used to dealing with Pris in her demanding mode. 'I'm afraid that is not only not possible, but it's inappropriate.'

'So what do I have to do to make it possible and "appropriate"?' Pris air quotes appropriate, underlining the sarcasm dripping from her words.

'When the King heard who was in your party, he arranged where you were to stay himself. I am unable to go against his wishes, Pris, no matter how much it annoys you.'

Annoyed is a bit of an understatement. Anger is rolling off Pris in waves.

'So, let's go talk with him and arrange something more suitable.'

Susan sends Pris a hard stare. 'This is the Unseelie Court, Priscilla, and you do not go barging in and demanding the King cater your every whim—especially not when you are dressed like a navvy.'

The door swings open as if to punctuate Susan's words, and a guard's head appears. 'Do we have a problem here, Lady Susan?'

Susan doesn't respond, as she and Pris are locked in a battle of wills.

I take Pris's hand. 'Pris, it's only for tonight. We shouldn't make waves before we've even met the King.' I lean in closer and whisper, 'Besides, we have waited this long to spend time alone together. We can wait a little longer.'

A smile curls the corner of her lips. 'Or I could just sneak back here later,' she whispers, her breath tickling my ear.

I lean my forehead against hers for a moment, simply enjoying her being close, then pull away.

'Percival, look after Snake and see he doesn't cause any mischief,' Pris says, brushing past the guard as she leaves the room.

Susan barks out a laugh. 'I don't think Snake's the one we should be worrying about.'

The door closes, and I almost collapse on the floor. Percival eyes me critically, and his nose wrinkles in distaste.

'You take the first bath. I wouldn't want to upset our hosts with your odour if they arrive before we are clean.'

'I'll try not to be offended by that,' I tell him, but without malice. If I'm honest, I'm so relieved to be bathing, it's all I can think about.

I head for the closest guest bedroom and make my way to the adjoining bathroom before Percival changes his mind. Compared to the public areas of the castle, it's relatively modern with blindingly white subway tiles and an enormous claw-footed bath. I turn the taps, and the water runs hot, steam gently filling the room. I groan as my muscles tremble in anticipation.

Quickly stripping out of my dirty clothes, I leave them in a pile behind the door. Finally, I slip into the water, emerging myself fully before leaning back and half lying down, allowing the glorious heat to soothe my body and soul. I've a lot to think about, and maybe even a lot to plan for, but I clear my mind and sink beneath the surface again, blocking everything out.

* * *

The last time I visited the Unseelie Court with Eleanora, the hallways were packed with courtiers and their hangers-on. To arrive and find everything so quiet is strange and quite unsettling. Given my experiences on the way here, I do not need anything else to throw me off balance.

When we walk through the portal, not a single sound emanates from the staterooms, where no doubt everyone is eating. No music, no laughter, and no sounds of fun being had? I will admit, I was a cat last time I was here, and so my hearing was a little more acute, but this is still way too quiet.

I wander over to the fire, and I add another log before taking a seat in the chair closest to the blaze. What was I thinking? I should have asked to speak with Eleanora's sister, Euphemia. She is the witch responsible for creature care in the north of the World Above.

She always has her finger on the pulse. Effie would be able to fill me in with what is going on, because, make no mistake, there is something other than the failure of magic turning the court into a shadow of its former self.

Agitated by my thoughts, I wander over to the window.

Leaning my forehead against the lower pane, I watch the activity in the streets of Inverness below. It is early evening, and the humans are heading for their homes, or perhaps they are leaving for an evening out. The scene is so normal, it only serves to accentuate the uncanny atmosphere in here.

The Unseelie Court uses the windows of Inverness Castle to view the outside world, but the glass shimmers if you look closely. That slight distortion tells me the court's wards are operational, keeping us all just out of time and space. The wards are still working, which is a relief, so it must be something else. A light tap sounds at the door, and I pull myself away from the view.

'Come in.'

Moments later a female servant—a brownie, judging from her slight form—enters dressed in a floor-length black dress and white apron. She bobs a curtsey before carrying a covered tray over to the table. I barely have time to say thank you before she backs out of the room.

The scent of spices sets my mouth watering. I lean over the trays and lift a cover. Haggis and mashed potatoes—excellent. On another plate, the bread is still warm enough for the butter to be melting through. Lovely.

Another knock on the door has me dropping the cover back on the dish.

'Come in,' I say again.

A new servant enters with clothes draped over her arm.

'Where do you want these, sir?' she asks.

'The smaller set in the farthest guest room and the larger in the other.'

She silently distributes the clothes and leaves without making another sound, and I am once again alone. I debate whether to start eating without Snake. After all, I do not want the food to get cold. Good manners win out over abject hunger, but I will not wait forever.

I knock on the door to Snake's room and say loudly, 'Food has arrived. I give you five minutes to dress before I start eating.'

My stomach rumbles, and I must admit, I am sorely tempted to start without my friend. I also want a distraction to keep my mind off the feelings of inadequacy and shame transforming into a cat stirred up. The whole experience shook my resolve to help Snake and Pris, reminding me of how out of practice I am at taking action.

To fill the time, I open the door to our suite and step into the corridor. A guard is beside me before I can leave the shadow of the doorway.

'Can I help you with something, sir?' he asks. His tone is polite, but I am under no illusion—he will not let me take another step further.

'Yes. If you could, would you please send a message to Lady Euphemia? Let her know that Percival would like to speak with her as soon as she is free.'

'I am sure I can arrange that. Now, if you would please step back inside.' He pushes the door open behind me.

For some reason, even though he is being polite, his gesture irritates me more than his words. 'And would it also be possible to have some tea and cakes sent up?'

He presses his lips together at my request, the only sign my treating him as a servant has annoyed him. 'Of course, sir,' he replies, his tone somewhat less polite than before.

'Thank you.' I smile smugly and return to the room. The guard shuts the door firmly behind me.

Snake is standing by the fire, wrapped only in a towel. 'Have you eaten all the food, or did you leave some for me?' he asks.

'I have not even started, and I am sure I can wait until you get dressed.'

'Dressed?' he asks. 'In what?'

I draw in a breath and call on what little reserves of patience I have. In some ways my travelling companions are so capable, but every now and again, I find myself behaving like their parent.

'A maid brought clothes up. They should be in your room.'

He stares at me as if I am mad.

'I walked through there and didn't see anything.' He glances over at the food as if he is expecting me to say that we should eat and he can dress later.

Instead I open the door to his bedroom and point at the clothes laid out on the bed. 'Those clothes? Yes, I can see how you would miss them.'

Snake mutters something under his breath as he holds up the shirt. He slumps on the bed. 'You may want to start dinner. It might take me a while to get into these.'

'I know they look too small, but this is a magical court, after all.'

He stares blankly back at me, clearly not his usual self.

'Take your time,' I tell him. 'I will have my bath and will heat up the food for us when I am done.'

He nods, and I slip into the bathroom. While the bath fills, I reach through the portal in the pocket of my trousers to find my own suit of clothes from my room at Eleanora's.

I bathe quickly and then find myself having to wait for Snake. To fill the time, I wander around the living room, trying to work out whose rooms we are occupying. I do not find much in the way of ornamentation except for a couple of books on creature history beside one of the chairs, so I am guessing the inhabitants are most likely male, or perhaps they, like us, are only here temporarily.

From my previous visits to court, I know we are in the royal followers wing of the castle. Eleanora and I generally stay with Euphemia, so I have spent little time here. The witch is a great friend of Princess Petunia, the sister of Queen Ariana, and her rooms are in the royal wing, close to the princess's.

The best I can do is hope that we have been placed with friends rather than foes and that they will be prepared to help us convince the King to join us in the World Below.

If we can do that before I turn back into a cat, all the better.

CHAPTER 4

Family Reunions

Snake picks at the food on his plate, eats a forkful of mashed potato, then raises his eyes, his fork hovering over the haggis. 'What's this?'

'It's oats, and spices, and meat.' What I don't tell him is that the meat is mostly offal. I mean, the boy needs to eat, and I see no reason to put him off his food.

He takes a mouthful, chews thoughtfully, then smiles. He follows it with another. I stop watching after those initial mouthfuls because the way he is shovelling food into his mouth will surely quell even the most ravenous appetite. Taking a sip of water, I am surprised to find it's spring water. It refreshes me and is almost as good as a glass of wine—almost.

Before he has even cleared his plate, Snake's head is drooping.

'You should get some rest.'

He jolts awake. 'I thought Pris might come back,' he tells me as his face flushes red. 'For some planning,' he adds.

'Of course,' I agree, but I am not fooled. 'I will be awake a while longer. I can wake you when she arrives.'

'If you think—'

'Go. You are no good to anyone like this.'

He stands and reaches up in a stretch before tidying his plate and mug onto the serving platter. As he does so, there is another knock at the door, and Snake is suddenly alert.

'Come in.' I watch the door expectantly.

Snake smiles hopefully as the door slowly pushes open, and a servant enters with a plate of small cakes and a carafe of wine. No tea though, but I am sure the wine will do very nicely. A crestfallen Snake grabs a couple of cakes from the plate before disappearing into his bedroom.

'The Lady Euphemia sends her regards and says she will join you soon. She also suggested wine would be better for your conversation this night instead of tea.'

'She might well be right,' I say dryly, but the servant has already left the room.

I finish eating my meal and tidy the dishes before scanning the bookshelves on either side of the fire for a readable volume of something. I'm pleasantly surprised to find some modern fiction has made its way onto the shelves. As I choose my book, I wonder if these belong to the room's inhabitants.

With a copy of *Great Expectations* balancing the plate of cakes and a goblet of wine in my other hand, I make my way to a chair by the fire. With the food and wine settled on a table within easy reach, I curl up with my book. The red wine is delicious and goes well with the cinnamon cake. I am well into Pip's tale when the door creaks open.

'Did you not hear me knock?' a female voice asks. Euphemia, or Effie to her friends, is a slightly older, curvier, miniature version of Eleanora. She has the same startling green eyes and black-brown hair, but whereas Ellie is statuesque, Effie is petite. She also exudes the warmth of a witch with their power based firmly in the earth.

She is wearing an off-the-shoulder, full-length evening dress complete with crinoline undergarments that would not have been out of place in the late 19th century. This is not surprising, as the Unseelie Court never moved with the times —Victoriana has been the fashion here for as long as I can remember.

I struggle to uncurl my legs, my muscles complaining at being asked to move.

'Percival, please, do not get up. It is so good to see you, my old friend—I mean to see *you*, and not you the cat.'

Effie's smile is warm and welcoming, but there is a shade of sadness there as she mentions my usual form. She perches herself on the edge of the chair opposite, arranges her skirts, and pours herself a goblet of wine.

'You could have changed into something more comfortable,' I tell her. 'I would have waited.'

She smiles as she takes a sip. 'I am used to this,' she says, sweeping her hand above her dress. 'Besides, I am only here for a minute or two. I am sure you are tired. We can have a proper catch up tomorrow.'

'I am afraid we may not have time for that. Our mission is time critical, and we do not have long to achieve it—only seven days, in fact. So, if you have time now, I would like to find out what is going on with the court.' I place my book on the table. Untangling my legs from under me, I sit properly on the chair.

'Seven days?' She raises an eyebrow in the same way Eleanora does, and I want to smile, but the bitterness of my next sentence stops me short.

'I am here with two others at the request of Queen Ariana and the dragons. The Dragon Queen has granted me a stay of punishment for seven days to allow me to complete my task.'

'Oh, Percival,' Effie says, covering her mouth with the hand not holding the goblet. 'How we all have failed you over the years.'

I shake my head, not wanting to dwell on this particular aspect of our mission. 'We haven't time for this now.'

She drops her head a fraction, accepting my words. 'Are you able to tell me why you are here? Rumour has it you have two very interesting companions.'

'I am sure I can tell you a little. My role is more that of an assistant to my companions, Snake of the Fieth Clan and... well... Princess Priscilla.'

Effie's eyes widen as she recognises the name, and she leans forward in excitement. 'Well, this is a turn up for the books. You really must tell how this came about.'

Sitting by a warm fire, a drink in hand, I want to unburden myself, to tell my old friend everything, just like I would have in the old days. However, I am conscious that not all of this is my story to tell.

'While I want to tell you everything, Effie, Princess Priscilla is the emissary on this mission, and we have not yet spoken with the King....'

Effie studies me for a moment before asking rather shrewdly, 'So I take it Cecily and Malachi still insist on keeping Priscilla in the dark about our world?'

I nod.

'All right. I will wait and find out what is going on with everyone else tomorrow. So, how can I help you now?'

'Thank you for understanding,' I say, then take a gulp of wine. I require fortification before approaching what has been worrying me since I entered the building. 'Effie, what is going on here? I mean, the Unseelie Court is subdued. We are aware there is an issue with magic, but that cannot be the only reason why a court once so flamboyant and full to bursting with creatures is now virtually a ghost town.'

'Ah, so you noticed?' she chuckles. 'Then again, how could you not?'

'So this is not only about reducing the size of the court because of the lack of magic?' I prompt.

She twirls the goblet between her fingers. Why is she so reluctant to answer me?

'Effie?'

'There have been attacks on members of the Unseelie Court,' she says, tears welling in her eyes.

I wait for her to continue, but she says nothing. 'Members of the Unseelie Court have always been prone to attacks,' I say, hoping she will elaborate.

She shakes her head. 'These attacks are different. This is not just a small group of crazies having a go at those who are different. These are co-ordinated, targeted attacks aimed to kill or, at the very least, maim creatures.'

A gasp escapes my lips. 'Who would do that?'

She tilts her head to the left, and the expression of her eyes turns from sorrowful to flinty steel. 'Really, Percival, you have to ask?'

'No, Effie, you must be wrong. Magnus, Bernais, and their cronies may be purists, but so long as the Unseelie stay above ground, they leave them alone.'

Effie nods. 'They did... until they decided to make a bid for power. They were not able to gather enough followers by using the usual tactics, so they turned to the tried-and-true method of finding a target for everyone to hate. After all, hate bands people together to fight a common enemy, and the Baaronsons chose to use our court as their target. The attacks have been so violent, court members have been reluctant to return from their homes for some months now.'

I stare at Effie, not quite able to believe what she is saying, but at the same time, her words resonate with what I know to be true.

My friend still will not meet my eyes, so I am guessing there is more to come.

'Then, a little over a month ago, the King's consort was returning from a visit with his family when he was brutally attacked. He managed to make it back here, but when he arrived, he was barely breathing. The poor creature did not last the night.'

'But... but he was so young.... Only a little over 200 years old.'

'As I said, the attack was brutal. He was not meant to survive.'

'How did we not hear of this?' I ask, still stunned and unable to comprehend what this means to our mission.

'I guess you could say the King and the court went into immediate mourning. We battened down the hatches and withdrew into ourselves. None of us have any idea how to respond to creatures who have such malicious intent against us, and, until we do, we will remain in hiding.'

I study Effie as she stares into her wine. It is only now I notice the tightness around her lips and the fine lines around her eyes that were not there when I last saw her six months ago.

She takes a deep breath before continuing. 'A couple of weeks or so ago, Lady Susan arrived with the news that Prince Malachi and Princess Cecily were taken to face charges in the World Below. Priscilla disappeared soon after. The King panicked and sent his men to bring Princess Petunia to court, worried she might be a target too. Few people have come or gone since then, and under the circumstances, it is difficult to be joyful when we live under such a dark cloud.'

'Oh, Effie, if only we had—'

'You would not have been able to do anything. Nor would Ellie or Eugenia. Still, you are here now, and I cannot help but think that your mission is somehow tied to all of this.'

We drink our wine in silence as I attempt to fit all this new information into my picture of the worlds.

'Effie, I am not sure how all this goes together, but I am sure we have the right people here to figure it out. We have overcome these creatures before, and we will do so again.'

Even as I try to boost her morale, my words sound hollow to my own ears. Last time we faced the traditionalist in our world, we had the Queen standing by our side. Now we are alone.

A door opens, and a fully dressed Snake pops his head into the room before his body follows.

'I heard voices. I thought perhaps Pris....' His smile slips as he catches sight of Effie.

'Snake Fieth, may I introduce you to my friend, Lady Euphemia.'

Snake blinks a couple of times, his eyes adjusting to the light.

'Pleased to meet you,' he says politely, but he is clearly distracted. 'I think I'm going to find Pris. I hate that she is alone, and she said she'd be here.'

I rise to my feet. 'Snake, you cannot. The guards will not let you.'

As I take a step towards him to put a restraining hand on his arm, the door crashes open, and a booming voice announces, 'I see our guests have arrived. Perhaps we can stir up a party in here, since no one in the dining hall wanted to join in.'

⸱⸱⸳⸱☽⸳⸱⸳⸱

Standing in the middle of the room, shaking my head slowly from side to side, I feel like I've lost it. I must look that way too. Overtired and restless, I thought I heard a female voice next door. To be fair, I did hear a woman speaking, but it wasn't who I expected it to be. Instead of finding Pris, I find a mini-Eleanora.

Part of me wants to make polite conversation because that is what is expected in these situations. The bigger part of me wants to find Pris and make sure she's okay. As I tried to sleep, my anxiety levels rose as I managed to convince myself something was wrong. If she was all right, she would've found a way to come to me.

At that moment the door flings open, and someone whose face I have only seen in a picture is standing in the doorway. A little worse for wear and sporting what appears to be an alcohol-fuelled grin, but he's recognisable as my grandfather nonetheless.

My grandfather's eyes slide over me, dismissing me as unimportant.

'Percival, me old mate, great to see you in the flesh, so to speak.'

He attempts to stagger forward, and the creature holding him up struggles to prevent him from falling. 'Heart tried to single-handedly motivate the court into a singalong,' the other creature tells the room.

The gnome leads my grandfather to the sofa and helps him to sit, then moves the carafe of wine away before grandfather can take a drink. When the gnome guard sits down, he seems to be protecting the wine.

I am frozen in place, but I force myself to turn and face the creatures seated by the fire. Percival is eyeing me warily, as is the creature who arrived with my grandfather. He too looks strangely familiar, but all my attention is for the creature trying to keep himself upright while grinning stupidly at Percival.

'You're not a cat.'

Percival presses his lips together as if he is trying to stop himself from saying something. Unable to keep quiet, he says, 'No, I am not.'

My grandfather doesn't even have the wits to ask why. He stumbles on. 'So you are staying here with us? Excellent. And you can use a guest room rather than curling up by the fire.'

'You? You are here?' The words slip out as a whisper. 'You were in the World Above the whole time.'

The eyes my grandfather turns to me are cold and rather more focused than those of someone who is completely blotto. He leans forwards and peers at me before dismissing me again.

With his attention back on the others, he says, 'Euphemia, I might have known you'd be here, gossiping, no doubt. I could have used your help jollying everyone along.'

'Heart, you do know that you are a bard and not the court jester, do you not?' she asks dourly.

For a moment the creature's face clouds over. 'I know better than anyone that you cannot wallow in self-pity when you have lost the love of your life. So what are the two of you doing here? Catching up on the family news?'

Percival takes a deep breath. 'Actually, Heart, you could say we have been catching up on some of your family... ah... news.'

'What? Percival, why are you staring at me like that? And Drow, you look like you have just discovered a miracle, or at least something very interesting in one of your books. Why have you all gone quiet? And you have not introduced me to your young friend. I am sure he would love to meet the famous bard of the Unseelie Court.'

'Mmm,' Percival starts, his voice dry. 'He might have, had you not made such an ass of yourself.'

I remain where I am, not believing this is happening to me right here, right now.

Percival stands up, takes a step forward, and says, 'Snake Fieth, may I present your grandfather, Breaker of Hearts, called Heart by his friends. And this is your great-uncle, Drow Fieth.'

If I was shocked by my grandfather's appearance, he was more shocked when Percival introduced me. He mumbles something, stands up, sways, grins at me, steps forward as if to catch me in an embrace, stumbles, then collapses back into the chair.

I follow his actions, unable to move as a war rages inside me. Once the initial shock at finding Heart here at the court settles, little waves of anger travel through me, taking its place. He lived so close and could have helped my mother and me, and he didn't. This thought is followed by gut-wrenching hurt because none of this appears to be a big deal to him.

My grandfather was living in Scotland while my mother and I struggled in the World Above, not even knowing he was here. In the end, anger wins out, and I take a step backwards. Heart makes to stand again, but Drow, perhaps reading the room, stands up and lays a restraining hand on his shoulder.

'If you were in this world, why didn't you help Mum and me? How could you leave us to fend for ourselves like that?' The words tumble out, and my voice cracks with pent up emotion.

Heart stares at me, and I watch his face as he sobers. Was his drunken babbling all an act? I fear it might have been, because there's no sign of it in his voice as he says to me, 'Your mother worked so hard to distance herself from me and from the Unseelie Court.'

He stares down at his hands for a moment, as if gathering his thoughts. 'She ignored my letters and did not answer my calls. After a while I stopped trying to contact her and let her drift away.'

He pauses and runs a hand through his hair. 'Once her mother died, she wanted to be seen as a gnome. She did not enjoy being in the spotlight, and she did not want to join our fight for creature equality. She would not be a part of this court, and, after all we had been through together, I could not desert my friends. We were at an impasse, so I decided to let her live her life her way. I promised not to contact you or her directly but always thought she would relent.'

He glances up at me, and I glare back.

He blinks back tears and attempts a smile. 'Over the years Eleanora kept me updated on what your mother was up to. It was through her I learnt that you were born. When your father left, I sent money to ease your path a little, and Eleanora saw that you got it.' He stares me straight in the eyes as he tells me, 'I always hoped you would find me when you were old enough, and now you have.'

Astonishment and anger are now joined by confusion, and they are vying for dominance in my head.

'How would I find you?' I choke out. 'I didn't even know you existed until a couple of days ago.'

I expect him to say that was my mum's decision, but Drow interrupts. 'Many see our court members as outcasts, and it is easier to ignore our presence than face our existence. I am afraid your mother was one of those. And to be fair to her, I think she always wanted Heart to choose her rather than us. It cannot have been easy for her to stay behind.'

'I couldn't stay,' Heart's voice breaks, and this time he lets the tears run freely down his face. 'To stay with her required me to deny her mother, and I could no sooner do that than pluck out my own heart.'

Families are complicated. I don't know where the thought comes from, but it pops into my head anyway. Perhaps I was better off not knowing who mine are?

'Whatever your reason for being here, I am happy you are here now,' Heart says, giving me a look of such hope, I find the ice around my heart begin to melt.

Still, I'm not ready to forgive him, and I remain rooted to the spot.

'Well,' Percival says into the awkward silence. 'Fun though this is, we are not exactly here for a social call.'

At this Drow's attention moves back to the sprite, but Heart still holds my gaze.

'We are here to present a royal petition to the King,' Percival finishes.

Drow's eyes crinkle with a smile. 'So, once again you and I must work together to petition royalty, old friend. Let us hope we are just as successful this time.'

It is then I remember that it had been Drow who worked with Percival to have transformation banned as a form of punishment. Pulling my gaze from Heart, I study the creature who is my father's uncle.

'Will you help us?' I ask him.

Euphemia learns forward in her chair. 'It is perhaps more pertinent to ask, will the King allow him to help?'

To be honest, I had almost forgotten she was in the room.

Drow raises his eyebrows. 'I do not see how he can deny me time with my family and friends. If we happen to spend that time working in the library....'

The room falls silent again. I want to say so much more, but where do I start?

Euphemia stands up and stretches. 'Come now, it is late. We are all tired, and we should perhaps start afresh in the morning.'

I turn to the door. 'But I was—'

'Going back to bed,' Percival finishes for me. 'I don't think now is the time to take on the court guards and rock the boat.'

'What had you planned?' Drow asks me, his eyes narrowing.

'The other member of our party is a female,' Percival says, and Drow nods understandingly.

'Look, Snake, sneaking round corridors for illicit liaisons is not the way to make an impression on the King, and I am sure your friend's chaperone is telling her the same. Best you get a good night's sleep. Tomorrow is not that far away, and you will see her again then,' my uncle counsels.

I'm not sure which of my newfound family members I prefer. Heart, who wears his heart on his sleeve, or Drow, who is coolly practical. If I am honest, at this moment, I wish, instead of meeting either of them, I were well on my way to finding Pris.

'All right,' I say. 'I bow to your superior knowledge—this time. Good night, everyone.'

Heart stands up to do... I don't know what. Fortunately, Percival intervenes. 'Let me have a word with him, Heart. This has come as a bit of a shock to him. Besides, there will be plenty of time to build bridges tomorrow.'

I sense rather than see Percival follow me into my room. He shuts the door behind him, blocking out the tangle of trouble in the room next door.

'I know this is difficult. If I had known we were staying with your family, I could have warned you.'

I flop down onto the bed. 'It's not that.'

'I know, you want to make sure Pris is all right. I understand, but please believe me when I say that what I learnt about the Unseelie Court tonight.... Well, let me just say, it is best if we do not break any of the rules.'

I sit up and study Percival. He is so serious and clearly worried about something, and he has not led us astray yet. 'This is why you are here with us, isn't it. Not only do you know these people, but you're here to make sure we don't do anything stupid.'

Percival laughs, and the sound eases some of my tension. 'I guess I might be, at that.'

'All right. But if Pris is angry with me, I expect you to back me up and tell her how you virtually locked me in my room.'

'Deal,' Percival says. 'Now, get some sleep. We have a lot of work to do tomorrow.'

He closes the door, and I crawl beneath the blankets, still in my clothes, planning to wait until everyone is in bed before I go find Pris. I'm asleep before my head even touches the pillow.

· · ✦ 🌙 ✦ · ·

I want to scream, 'Just leave me alone for a minute'. There are so many creatures dressed in maid uniforms from some bad gothic movie crowding me, all vying for attention, asking if I need this or that. I don't want anything except some peace and quiet.

I frantically scour the room and finally find Susan. I send a silent plea to her, and she nods once before ushering the others not only out of the bathroom, but out of the entire suite.

'I'm out here if you need me.' Susan closes the door behind her, leaving me in blissful silence.

I strip off my filthy clothing, and I leave them in a puddle on the floor before stepping into the steaming hot bath. I shiver as I slip under the mass of lavender-scented bubbles, then I relax and allow the water to work its magic, easing away my stress while cleaning the dirt from my skin.

The bath is the most enormous claw-footed affair I've ever seen. It is so large, I can lie back with my legs stretched out and still not touch the end. All right, I am not as tall as I am in the World Below, but I'm not short in my human form either.

I curl a strand of black hair around my finger and am surprised I kind of miss the white it turns when I'm in my true form in the World Below. One thing I don't miss is my pointy ears. It's disconcerting enough to grow a couple of inches and have white hair without my ears changing shape as well. That transformation is so much more... personal.

Enough self-indulgence. I need to plan a way to get to Snake. I sink a little lower under the bubbles, leaving only my face exposed, and begin to plot. This corridor may not have guards placed at either end, but there is the gaggle of maids who I'm sure have not gone far. I'll have to dodge them if I'm to meet up with him.

The door handle rattles, and I shift so I can growl at the maid who has dared to interrupt me. I catch a glimpse of pink floral silk—this isn't a servant. Closing my mouth, I warily eye the door.

The woman who enters is dressed in a silver-and-pink off-the-shoulder gown with an impossibly slim-fitting bodice flaring out to a skirt caught up at the back, making her bum look enormous. Her auburn hair is swept into an elaborate bun held by a sparkling comb. My eyes widen. Are those real diamonds in the comb? And in the drop earrings and the choker around her neck? She could buy a small country with that set.

This woman is so put together and has such presence, I'm suddenly all too aware I'm lying naked in a bath. Thank goodness for the modesty-saving bubbles.

Without saying a word, my visitor glides over and perches on the rim of the bath before studying me, her face not giving anything away.

'So you are Cecily's daughter,' she says, her voice a rich purr.

I nod.

'And the rumour amongst the maids is that you have come to petition the King on behalf of Queen Ariana?'

I nod again, not quite sure where my voice has gone.

Somehow this woman's imposing presence has robbed me of the power of speech.

'My sister has sent numerous creatures begging for his help, and he has sent them all away. But perhaps you might stand a chance where others have failed.'

I stare warily at the creature beside me as my brain puts together the breadcrumbs she has dropped. She is the Queen's sister, Princess Petunia. Princess Petunia is Mum's mother... and my grandmother. This woman is my grandmother. These thoughts flood my brain as a more practical part considers her comment. What does she mean, 'I might stand a chance where others have failed'?

'Do you speak, child? Because it will be difficult to petition the King if you cannot.'

Her tone is tart, and she gives no indication that she knows who I am or that I'm part of her family. Or does she speak like this to everyone? Holding her gaze with what I hope is defiance, I order myself not to apologise because the sudden appearance of a family member I only found out existed today is throwing me off my game.

Slowly my brain kicks back into gear. Is this what Fairchild was hiding from me in the maze? That my grandmother is here? Was that what I overheard Percival asking him to tell me?

Princess Petunia watches my face, still waiting for me to speak as I process what is going on. In my most sarcastic tone, I say, 'You'll have to excuse me. I'm not used to complete strangers barging in on me when I'm in the bath.'

The princess's blue eyes flash. 'I am hardly a stranger. I am your grandmother.'

Anger bubbles inside me so quick and so white hot, it's a wonder the water isn't boiling. 'I don't know how it works in your world—I couldn't, of course, because it was kept a secret from me—but someone you have never met is a stranger where I come from, even when they are a blood relative.'

A flash of something crosses the princess's face. Is it pain? It is gone in an instant, replaced by the mask Petunia arrived with. The silence after my outburst is heavy, and I wait for a haughty putdown. Then her face softens as she laughs. It's a full, throaty chuckle of pure mirth, giving me the merest glimpse of the person beneath the princess mask.

'Yes, Priscilla, you and I are going to get along just fine. For a minute I thought you would crumble under the weight of your responsibility, but I should have realised Cecily's daughter would have a backbone of steel and a whip-sharp tongue to go with it.'

I don't quite know what to say to that or how to take this creature. I'm saved from having to respond by the entrance of a maid carrying a bundle of clothing draped over her arm.

'No way,' I mutter as I catch sight of what I assume are a bustle and a corset. 'I am not wearing those.'

Rescue comes from a surprising quarter. 'Goodness, girl, do you have no common sense? The princess is not going anywhere tonight. Bring her a nightgown and robe.'

Minutes later when the maid returns with the requested items, my grandmother rises, takes them from the trembling girl, and places them on the chair in the corner.

'We shall speak more when you are dressed,' my grand-mother says as she leaves the room.

Not wanting to keep the princess waiting, I drag myself from the now cooling water, regretting that I had so little time to enjoy my long-awaited bath. I dress quickly and plait my hair loosely, hoping it won't frizz too much.

The clothing is silky and smooth, and it completely covers me, but I'm reluctant to leave the bathroom, feeling somewhat exposed without undergarments. A part of me appreciates that this is normal for the period in history the court appears to be stuck in, but still, it feels odd. I'm about to slide my feet into slippers when there is a knock on the door.

'Yes?'

Susan enters, her modern clothing now changed for a dress appropriate to the period the court prefers. She hands me a plastic packet. 'Many of us here prefer some of the comforts of the outside world.'

I look down and find a multi-pack of underwear.

'When the shops open tomorrow, I'll send someone to buy a selection in your size.'

I smile at Susan, her thoughtful kindness breaking through the wall of ice around my heart. 'Thank you.'

'No worries.' She smiles as she leaves me alone.

I slip on a pair of knickers before slumping into the chair behind the door. It's the underwear that does me in. A wave of homesickness washes through me, and I wish I was home in my own bed. I'm tired of this adventure. I want some normalcy, and I want Snake.

To be honest, what I want most is to walk out of here and find Snake lying on my bed. To then lie beside him and have him wrap his arms around me and tell me we will make it through this. And I would believe him because the two of us can do anything together.

Tears well in my eyes, and I let them run down my cheeks. The door opens, and my grandmother, now in bedclothes herself, enters. I hastily brush the tears away.

'Come, child, I have ordered some soup and bread. You will feel better after you eat.'

She leads me to the sitting room, which is between what I now believe is her bedroom and mine. The fire is blazing and the chair comfortable. She places a bowl of soup in my hands, and at the smell of chicken, my hunger returns, and I almost inhale the liquid.

Once I am finished and the soup has been replaced with a mug of tea, the princess asks, 'So, granddaughter, how did you come to be sent on this mission? Last I heard, your parents were taken and you had disappeared.'

I tell her about the trumped-up charge of using magic for personal gain in the World Above, which saw Mum and Dad taken to the World Below. Recounting how I met Snake brings a smile to my lips, and I'm sure the eagle-eyed creature in front of me has noted that down.

In an attempt to distract her, I reveal that Snake's mother had been taken for the same reason, and we had decided to work together to save them. Then I recount our journey to the Midnight Ball to speak up for our parents and how Bernais had tricked us into the quest in the minotaur's maze to retrieve what was in the middle.

Princess Petunia is quiet as I speak, although minute changes in her facial expressions give me an idea of what she is thinking. She refills my empty cup and asks me to go on.

'When we finally made our way through the maze, we found Queen Ariana held in stasis at the centre. She was what we needed to retrieve, only to remove her, we have to convince the King to return with us because only he can heal her. Then they can fix magic, and the Queen can return home.'

I stop suddenly. Have I said too much? Should I have saved this for the King? While I'm berating myself for over-sharing, Princess Petunia is sitting quite still.

'My sister is so ill, the dragons have placed her in stasis?'

Her lip trembles, and I think she might cry, but her face again returns to what I'm beginning to realise is the public mask she hides behind.

'Things have become more precarious than we thought. And with the Queen out of the Capitol, that explains the boldness of the attacks we have been experiencing. We must take care how we introduce you to King Maddox tomorrow. It is important he understands the severity of the situation, and that is why they have sent you in particular as an envoy.'

'Me and my friends,' I correct her. 'Snake and Percival have a role to play here. The dragons were insistent.'

The princess frowns before saying, 'Well, I am not sure they will have the same impact as you, but yes, your friends as well. Now, I can see you are exhausted. Time for bed. You need to be at your best tomorrow.'

I want to say I am fine, but the combination of food and tea and unburdening myself has worn me out. The princess leads me to a room with an honest-to-god four-poster bed in the centre. As I slip between crisp sheets smelling of roses, my feet touch something warm—someone has put a hot-water bottle down there. I'm so tired, I'm dozing before I can fully appreciate the gesture.

CHAPTER 5

Family Commitments

Stretching my limbs between the sheets, I marvel at how strange it feels to sleep in a bed. It has been well over a hundred years since I have spent the night in one. I slept well, but cramps in my arms and legs tell me I slept curled up in a ball as I have every night for centuries now.

Rubbing the sleep from my eyes, I sit up and resist the urge to arch my back and stretch. A sharp knock on the door has me shooting back under the covers.

'Yes,' I say tentatively.

At my bidding, a maid enters. 'Sir, Princess Petunia requests your company for a light breakfast in her rooms.'

Now, this is interesting.

'All right. I'll join her as soon as I am able,' I tell her.

Her cheeks turn red. 'Begging your pardon, but I am to wait and escort you.'

A summons, not a request. Even more interesting.

What can Petunia want to talk to me about this early in the morning? I doubt very much that it is a social call. After dressing in my usual black, I check my appearance in the full-length mirror. Satisfied with my presentation, I allow the maid to lead me along the corridor and up a set of stairs to the royal suites.

Not only am I surprised the corridor is no more richly furnished than ours, but that Princess Petunia's suite is smaller than ours. Although keeping with the style of the court, every-thing is plush and comfortable. I wonder if the furnishings are modern reproductions. The windows face out over the Ness, framing a cloud-laden sky.

Petunia and Effie are already seated at a table overflowing with breakfast options. At the smell of freshly baked muffins, my stomach rumbles.

'Come, Percival, join us,' Petunia says, never one for formalities.

As I take a seat, she pours me a cup of tea just the way I like it and pushes it towards me. I fill my plate with blueberry muffins and toast and jam. She waits to speak until I am done choosing.

'I spoke with my granddaughter last night. She has had quite an adventure.'

Do I hear a gentle rebuke in that comment? No, Petunia is not usually that subtle.

'She has, and she has shown herself to be a capable young woman,' I say neutrally, wondering where this is leading.

'Creature,' Petunia corrects me.

I pause before responding, wanting to frame this comment as inoffensively as possible. 'I am not sure she yet sees herself as one of us, Petunia. She was brought up human and only recently learned of her true heritage.'

The princess looks down her nose at me, and I feel a lecture coming. 'I am aware of her history, but she is a crea-ture, no matter how she identifies herself, and a high ranking one at that.'

I take a bite of muffin and chew. It is not worth arguing

with Petunia over this. Still, until she sees Pris for who she is, our mission is going to be made more difficult.

'Petunia, you did not bring Percival here to discuss your granddaughter,' Effie prompts.

'Indeed I did not. We need to plan, and to do that, you and your new friends need to be made aware of everything going on here.'

I pause, a muffin halfway to my mouth. I glance at it reluctantly before placing it back on the plate. 'Pris and Snake should be here for this,' I tell my old friends.

'I do not know my granddaughter or this Snake. You I do know and trust, and I can speak openly with you,' Petunia says.

I could tell her she can trust Snake and Pris, but experience has taught me that when Petunia makes up her mind about something, it takes time to change it—time we do not have.

'All right, but when we are done here, I will tell them everything we discuss.'

Petunia slowly inclines her head in an almost nod, indicating this is an acceptable compromise.

She places her cup on the table and folds her hands in her lap. 'Over the last few months, we have experienced an increase of attacks against the Unseelie Court. The increase is both in number and severity.'

'Substantially more than normal?' I ask. There have always been people in our world who see the court as unnatural for accepting things Seelie high society would not.

She nods. 'I believe this is a campaign of activity targeted at destabilising the court.'

Effie leans forward, resting her arms on the table. 'Many of us believe it is a result of higher creatures working to regain their positions of power in the World Below.'

'I fear Effie is right, Percival. Things are changing in the

World Below, and it is seeping into what was our haven here. Priscilla told—'

I wince. 'She prefers Pris,' I tell the princess.

She arches an eyebrow. 'Really?'

'Yes,' I confirm, undaunted by her display of hauteur.

Petunia's eyes flash, but she chooses not to question me, which is out of character. My senses go on high alert. Something is wrong—very wrong.

'When Priscilla told me about the Queen's absence from court, I knew it had to be Magnus and that son of his, Bernais, at the centre of these attacks. They are trying once again to twist society to their vision of what it should be.'

'To make matters worse, magic is waning both in the Unseelie Court and in the rest of the World Above. There has been little I can do to help the King keep it strong,' Effie adds.

Just as we get to the nitty-gritty, the door behind Petunia opens, and Pris emerges, her face set in morning grumpy mode. I brace for a bumpy ride.

'Ah, Priscilla, good of you to join us,' Petunia greets her.

Pris pulls out a chair, and Effie beams at her. 'It is such a pleasure to meet you, Princess. How like both your mother and father you are.'

'How nice it is to be continuously spoken to as though people know me well.' Pris reaches for a muffin, pulls an edge off, and pops it into her mouth.

'Priscilla, that is unforgivably rude. Apologise at once.' Petunia's tone is steely, and I am surprised when Pris does not react to it one bit.

Effie regards Pris for a moment, her gentle eyes showing warmth and concern. She places a hand on Petunia's arm. 'Blunt though she may be, Pris is right. Her parents chose to keep her away from our world while they themselves continued to visit us. We've watched Pris grow from afar, and it is as if we have known her her whole life.' She turns to Pris.

'How irritating and hurtful it must be to have been left out, then suddenly treated as if you have been a part of this world all along.'

I expect Pris to say something about being spoken about as if she is not here. Instead, she stares at Effie, an unreadable expression on her face. Her eyes fill with tears. She opens her mouth as if to speak, then pushes back her chair before rushing to her bedroom. For a moment no one moves.

'Well, I thought she would have more backbone than that,' Petunia says breaking the silence.

'Petunia, have some heart. She is young and a long way from home in so many ways. And think of all she has been through in the last couple of weeks,' Effie scolds.

As I stand up to go check on Pris, her door swings opens and she re-emerges. Although her eyes are red, she has clearly got herself back under control. She returns to the table and calmly carries on eating as if nothing has happened.

'I am sorry, Priscilla, I should have introduced you. This one of my dearest friends—the Witch of Westhill, Euphemia of the Wyld Woods.'

'And, as you already know, I am delighted to finally get to know you, my dear,' Effie says.

Pris raises her eyes and forces a smile. Her eyes widen and she says, 'You look just like—'

'An older, frumpier version of Ellie?' Effie supplies.

'Ellie?' Pris splutters, and Effie laughs.

'Oh, she's still doing the Eleanora thing, is she? She can be imposing when she pulls that one. I find it difficult to see her that way. I remember her as a scrawny, grass-stained youngster playing with Percival in the woods all day.'

Effie always knows the right tone to put creatures at ease. She would say it is because of her strong connection to the earth, but I think it is because she grew up having to navigate her way through the stormy waters Eleanora and Euphemia left in their wake. As the middle sister, she was often the glue that held them together.

Pris's shoulders relax, and she smiles at me. 'Were you and Eleanora childhood friends?' she asks.

'Hard to believe, but yes, we were,' I say as I return to my seat.

Pris helps herself to coffee and fruit, and, ignoring her grandmother, she half turns to Effie. 'Did I hear you say this court accepts... well, outcasts?'

'Yes. For instance, although your grandmother is wed to an elf, many of their friends have mixed marriages. When given the choice of denouncing them or being exiled.... Well, as you can see, she is here now.'

Pris's eyes widen. 'My grandfather is here? In the castle?'

Petunia returns her cup to the saucer before answering. 'Sadly not. He is at our property near Loch Ness—Urquhart Castle. We are the first port of call for people changing courts, so someone must remain to ensure a smooth transition.'

'Oh.' Pris manages to inject so much disappointment into that single word.

Petunia plows on though, refusing as ever to give in to the negative. 'There are other creatures here I would like you to meet. Your travelling companion—Snake, is it?—is break-fasting with his grandfather and his great-uncle. They are old friends of mine too. Drow in particular will be able to help with preparing you to meet with the King.'

'Snake's grandmother was an elf, I believe,' Pris says, turning to her grandmother.

Petunia seems to hesitate, her eyes glistening with tears. 'Yes, she was a good friend of mine. I still miss her every day.'

Pris gaze softens a little at Petunia's display of emotion. Then she has to go and ruin the moment by saying, 'If I am to meet the King today, can you tell me more about him? Like, has the crown been in his family for long? Is he happy, grumpy, evenhanded?'

I sit forward in my chair. 'Pris, there is something you should know about the King—'

'He lost his husband a couple of months ago,' Petunia interrupts, 'and he has not been the same since. He became closed off, and this once vivacious court has been in prolonged mourning ever since.'

The room is silent for a moment. I had no idea about the depth of the King's despair, and I try to imagine Maddox as a creature withdrawn from society, but it is difficult. All I see is his smiling face and his personality bringing to life any room he enters.

'Another thing you should know,' Effie adds. 'The line of Unseelie Kings does not go from father to son, but often from uncle to nephew, and sometimes passes to non-family members.'

Pris does not respond for a moment. 'Why, are the kings unable to have children?'

Effie nods. 'In a manner of speaking.'

I shake my head. 'Effie, stop beating around the bush. Pris is from the modern world, and her generation discusses differences in people more openly.' I turn to my travelling companion. 'The Unseelie Court was founded when the doors to the world were closed in medieval times. The brother of the Queen of the Seelie Court decided not to return below because he would not have been able to live with his male partner there. Because the King had no heirs, he established the tradition of passing the crown on to a male member of the court.'

'Except in 1482 when King Eron's niece became Queen,' Petunia interjects.

Pris's brow furrows. 'So the court accepts creatures who are outcasts from the Seelie Court but doesn't have queens?'

'Yes, except for that one blip in history, due to the fact that no faction would support any of the male candidates,' Effie explains.

I interrupt. 'We have gotten a little off track. Pris does not need the details of various successions in order to represent the Queen. A simple outline will suffice—although I must confess, I am interested how you found all this out.'

'Drow and I have been looking into court succession,' Effie says.

Drow has been spending time on succession? I cannot help but frown as I consider this new piece of information. He is one of the great legal minds of our time. What is going on here?

I keep my mouth shut and carry on eating breakfast while Petunia and Effie discuss what Pris should wear for her court presentation.

· · ✴ · 🌙 · ✴ · ·

So, something is going on at court. Big surprise. Why would I have thought it would be otherwise. Nothing has been easy since I found my parents had disappeared, so why should it start now?

I wish Snake were here so we could share our disdain at all this courtly stuff. Last night I was strongly discouraged from finding him. This morning he is with his family as I am with mine. It's as if now that we have found each other, fate is doing its best to keep us apart.

We will be together at court, at least. That is if he can recognise me after I've been primped into someone acceptable of being presented. As Grandmother and her friend chat, I turn imploring eyes to Percival.

'Percival, they want me to wear some monstrosity of a dress.... A pink dress. Can't you get me out of this?'

Percival deftly sidesteps the issue. 'I am sorry, Pris, but female creature fashion is not my area of expertise.'

'The dress is blush,' my grandmother interrupts, 'and it is quite the fashion at the moment.'

I'm not sure what to make of my grandmother. Sometimes she is quite friendly, and at others she is tart enough to sour cream.

When I don't respond, Euphemia says, 'The fashions have not changed since the court was set up. However, within reason, we can accommodate something a little more to your tastes, can we not, Petunia?'

Why isn't she my grandmother? She is much less... prickly.

'All right.' Petunia pushes herself to her feet. 'Come this way, Priscilla. We shall check my wardrobe.'

'If you are dressing, I will say my good-byes.' Percival stands up, and his gaze follows us as Euphemia and I trail after my grandmother.

I throw a 'save me' glance over my shoulder at Percival. He smiles and waves his fingers before slipping out the door. How I wish I were going with him.

Grandmother's room is decorated in pinks, but no frills, and is actually quite comfortable. When she opens her wardrobe, it is a different matter. There are frills and sparkles and all manner of bling and bows. Now, don't get me wrong, I don't mind a little bling when the occasion calls for it, but this is over the top. My thoughts must be written on my face.

'We have not kept up with the times, have we? Not much has changed here since I was a girl of your age,' Grandmother says.

I force myself to smile. 'I mean, it's all beautiful, and I am sure you turn heads all the time. They're just not... me.'

'So, let us find a compromise. Court rules dictate legs must be covered at all times. During daylight hours, so must arms and shoulders. That is non-negotiable.'

'Do I have to wear a dress for this appearance?'

She raises an eyebrow.

'All right, it has to be a dress, but no corset.' I'm adamant on that. 'And I don't want one of those.' I point at what I think is a bustle that makes her bum look enormous.

'That is a shame, because they do highlight womanly attributes, and you certainly have those.'

'So fat shaming is a thing here as well,' I say in a dry monotone, well aware that my figure will never meet the waiflike standard of fashion models, nor would I want it to.

'My dear, you are not fat. In fact there is not an ounce on you. I am merely commenting that you have a shapely figure, and it would be a shame to hide it.'

I place my hands on my hips. 'It would be an even bigger shame to believe I must meet some physical standard to be taken seriously.'

My grandmother glares back at me.

Effie steps between us. 'It would also be a shame to flout conventions simply to make a point when you want to get the King on your side. There must be a middle ground.'

Grandmother closes her eyes, and I can almost hear her mentally saying, 'Goddess give me strength.' She pushes some clothes aside.

'Thank goodness this is a formal court, not your debutante ball. Mmm.... Something with no corset or bustle, how about a day dress?'

I stare at my grandmother's and my reflections in the mirror. With her petite stature and slim figure, she is tiny beside my more athletic build. How are her dresses ever going to fit me?

She chooses a muslin number with capped sleeves. When

she holds it up for me, I notice it's lightly gathered under the bust and has a skirt intended to fall to the floor.

More my style, but instead of saying that, I blurt out, 'It's pink.'

Grandmother purses her lips. 'What colour would suit you, Princess?'

'Purple,' I say, scanning the wardrobe for any hint of my favourite colour.

Before my eyes, the flowers on the creme dress change to lavenders and purples and greens. It is very pretty, perhaps a little too pretty, but better than before. It also appears to have grown to a size that will most likely fit me.

'Thank you,' I manage to force out, grateful she has tried to meet me halfway.

'We are not done yet. We will have to "pimp it up," as you young people say, for the court. Effie, I believe Lady Susan left some underclothes out for Priscilla. Would you mind getting them while I look for some accessories?'

A few minutes later, I'm pulling on the dress, which might have come right out of a Jane Austen movie.

'Now, to make it suitable for court,' my grandmother says.

Feeling a little like a rabbit in the headlights, I attempt to reason with her. 'It's beautiful as it is. I'm happy to go like this.'

The two older creatures turn to each other, then to me, shock written on their faces.

'My dear, I cannot let my granddaughter turn up to court so unadorned. It would be an insult to the King as well as reflect poorly on me and the Seelie Court. You must make the appropriate first impression.'

Okay, this is not a battle I'm going to win. If I'm honest, although I don't like it, my job will be easier if my clothes meet local expectations.

Grandmother produces a rose-coloured underskirt that

she proceeds to turn lilac. I slip it underneath the dress, and she kneels in front of me. With practiced ease, she uses two small flower broaches to gather two front sections of the skirt so the underskirt can be seen.

Euphemia stands back and studies the dress, chin in hand, a frown forming between her brows. Honestly, they're taking this dressing thing way too seriously.

'I think the dress needs to be darker, Petunia. What do you think?'

Grandmother joins her, mutters something, and the dress shifts as if a breeze has caught it. Now when I look in the mirror, the fabric is cream raw silk with embroidered flowers. This is too much. Or apparently not. Effie and my grandmother are beaming.

Grandmother nods once. 'There, much better. Now for some jewellery.'

She strides to a dressing table and opens a box and rummages around before returning with a pouch.

'Put these on once Lady Susan has done you hair and makeup.'

On autopilot, I take the heavy velvet bag from her.

'Do not just stand there gawping. I still have to dress, and Lady Susan is waiting for you. No, wait a minute. Tell Susan to put your hair up, and I will bring in a tiara.'

I'm jolted out of my stupor. I've reached the end of my patience.

'No tiara,' I say.

Grandmother stifles a sigh, as if realising she has gone as far as I will allow her to. 'All right, there are enough pearls in there for her to do something appropriate with your hair. Now go finish getting ready.'

This time I'm bundled out the door, followed closely by Euphemia, who tells me, 'I must get ready too. I wouldn't miss court today for anything.' She sends me a wink before leaving, and I'm left wondering why she finds this whole thing amusing.

Susan meets me in my room and sits me in front of the oval mirror.

'Just something simple,' I tell her, and she snorts.

'I have instructions from Princess Petunia and, to be honest, she is way scarier than you.'

I meet her gaze in the mirror and smile. 'You're right. But can you somehow manage to keep me looking like myself rather than some painted doll?'

Susan smiles back at me. 'That I think I can do.'

After arranging my hair on top of my head, Susan threads some pearls through the front so it mimics a tiara but is way less flashy before pulling some curls down around my face. She completes the outfit with a pearl choker and some pearl drop earrings.

I turn so she can do my makeup. Normally I would just whip on some mascara and lip gloss, so I'm grateful for her expertise. When she turns me back around, I survey her handiwork. My eyes are outlined in smoky purple and framed in black. Something she has done has given me cheekbones, and my lips are a subtle dark pink gloss. It's me, but not me. It's kind of like when I change in the World Below.

'Thank you,' I say to Susan as the door opens. A maid enters carrying a pair of low-heeled purple pumps. The shoes don't appear to be big enough for my feet, but like everything in this strange world, they manage to fit perfectly.

'I feel... strange,' I say, slipping the shoes on and then standing up. 'And over-dressed.'

'Yes, I bet you do.' Susan laughs. 'You aren't used to all this finery. Unfortunately, here, as in your world, it is important to make the right first impression.'

I shrug. 'And what does all this say?' I ask. 'That I am a girl to be dressed up and preened?'

Susan shakes her head. 'No one there will be dressed like you today. They will all be shiny silks and glittering jewels trying to stand out from the crowd and be noticed. What all of this says is, 'I see your rules and I have made them my own. I acknowledge your conventions, but I am me.'

'Oh' is all I can think to say as tears of gratitude prick at my eyes.

'And most of all, it says, "I am an ambassador of the Seelie Court, and I am someone to be listened to."'

I stare at myself in the mirror, trying to see what Susan does. Dressing like this is like putting on armour for battle. I nod—ambassador me will do. She can pull off a regal show at the Unseelie Court, and she won't have butterflies swooping in her stomach, making her feel ill.

'Now, there are a few things we need to go over—can you curtsey?' Susan asks.

I frown. 'What? Curtsey?'

'When the King enters, you curtsey, and you do not rise until he is seated.'

I curtsey as I had been shown in etiquette class. Somehow it feels easier in this dress.

'All right, not bad. Now, you do not approach the King or speak to him unless he gives you leave. You never, ever initiate a conversation.'

I turn and face Susan. 'What if he chooses never to speak to me? How will I be able to plead our case?'

Susan raises an eyebrow as she always does when she thinks I am overthinking something. 'I am sure he will want to speak with you. If for some reason he does not, or if he does not appear for the court session this morning, then you will need to petition his secretary for a private audience.'

'What about my grandmother? Can she arrange an audience for us?'

Susan gives me a strange look. 'She is the disinherited sister of the Queen of the Seelie Court. In this court, you have more standing than she does.'

I process this for a moment, then realise it is likely because I am still in line for the throne. 'Oh, this is going to take some getting used to.'

Before I have time to ask anything else, my grandmother appears in all her pink frills and finery.

'We should go, or we will not be able to make our entrance before the King arrives.'

Her tone is commanding. For a moment I consider disobeying her, then change my mind—being with her is better than making my entrance to the court alone.

· · * 🌙 · * · ·

I tug at the ruffle collar around my neck. It is choking me. Grandfather frowns.

'It's hot in here, and this coat is making me sweat.' I resist the urge to tug at the green brocade tailed jacket. At least my tight-fitting trousers and boots are comfortable.

'Just be grateful you are not a woman,' he whispers and nods towards a group standing by the window.

In fancy dresses lifted from goodness knows what period drama, they're like a gaggle of peacocks. I have to admit, I wouldn't like to be wearing all of that. Still, this collar has to go.

I undo the fastening and slip it from around my neck before realising the only pockets I have are in the trousers. These trousers are tight enough for the collar to make an unsightly bulge. I sidle a little closer to the potted tree and drop the offending item under the foliage.

'Hey, that's Drow's second-best collar,' Heart says, rocking his own even more frilled collar like a second skin.

'I'll come back and get it later,' I tell him.

'But you look so... plain.'

'But I'm not choking.' I smile. 'For that alone I am happy to have just a simple Mandarin collar.'

'Well, it is too late to do anything about it now,' Heart says as he schools his face into a neutral mask.

After spending breakfast with my grandfather, I still don't know how to take the gnome. During the meal he was polite and asked questions about mine and Mum's life but revealed very little about his own.

Every now and then, I would tell him something, and he would relax and smile and really engage. Then he would stop, and the mask would be back. It was as though he didn't want me to meet the real him. The atmosphere remained awkward until Drow joined us.

Drow is different to anyone I've ever met. He loves the law and works tirelessly to change things to be more egalitarian. I would have thought we would have gotten on better given that we have so many ideals in common, but he is awkward and difficult to like.

I make sure no one is close enough to overhear us, then lean close to my grandfather and ask, 'Heart, why Drow is so hard to talk to?'

'Ah, I believe it's because he is married to his cause and has forgotten how to be with people.'

'That's sad.'

My grandfather nods. 'Indeed it is.'

'Still, he had some great tips on how to deal with the King.'

Drow had helped me outline a draft petition. When I was happy with what we'd done, he advised me the court today was not the time to present the details. We would need to request a private meeting to do that.

'What is today for, then?' I asked.

'For the King to meet you and for you to be accepted into the court,' Drow explained.

Court protocol is so complex, I'm relieved we have people to help us navigate it.

I scan the fifty or so courtiers in the room while I wait for Pris to arrive. The one time I tried to leave our rooms this morning to find her, a guard persuaded me it was in my best interests to remain in the suite.

Percival has assured me she is fine with her grandmother. Still, we are meant to be doing this together, and I would be less nervous with her by my side.

The room is cavernous, with windows down one side and chandeliers hanging from the ceiling in line with each one. Standing alone in front of the dais, I feel isolated and alone. All right, Heart is here, but it's not the same.

Where are Percival and Pris? Finally my scanning pays off. The crowds part, and I glimpse Euphemia, dressed in emerald green. It must be a family favourite, I think, remembering Eleanora's slinky green number at the Midnight Ball. Like her sister that night, Euphemia is escorted by Percival, who is dressed all in black and not a frill or any adornment to be seen. How does he get away with that?

Walking behind them is a petite woman decked out in pink, and looming over her is Pris. My heart literally leaps at the sight of her, and not because she looks amazing. I mean, she is stunning, but it's because it is her, and she is here.

Her dress is simple compared to others in the room but all the more stunning for it. And I for one appreciate the amount of her... um... chest peeking above the neckline. I thought she looked amazing when we dressed for the Midnight Ball, but this is a whole other level.

I take a step to join her, but Heart grabs my arm. I glare at him, and he nods towards the dais. Drow and a tall, gaunt elf have appeared. When they are standing on either side of the small wooden throne, a young elf dressed in royal colours announces that the King is ready to hold court.

Everyone bows or curtsies, and I rush to copy them. They're all so stately, I feel like a country bumpkin who has no idea what he's doing—largely because I don't.

We have been down so long, my back starts to cramp. Heart nudges me, and I straighten up to find that the whole room is not only silent, but is caught up in a drama playing out before them.

The elf who entered is standing in front of the throne. I do a double-take—he is a mirror image of Pris's father. Then it hits me, and I look from Pris to him and back again.

She is staring at the King of the Unseelie Court. Her eyes flicker. She must be putting together the same puzzle I have. I know the exact moment she realises why everyone believes she might be able to tip the scales in the Seelie Court's favour.

Pulling my eyes away from Pris, I turn back to face the King, who is now seated on the throne.

'I see the Seelie Court has seen fit to surprise me with their newest envoy,' the King chuckles. The rest of the room joins him, easing the tension somewhat.

Pris is standing still, and I thread my way through the courtiers until I am by her side. Who knows what rules of etiquette I'm breaking, but I don't care. The only thing I care about is being here to support Pris. Her hand is trembling as I place it in the crook of my arm.

'Come on,' I whisper into her ear. 'We've got this.'

She leans her head against mine for a moment, then stands tall as the King nods, and the petite pink-clad woman leads our party forward.

'Princess Petunia,' the deep voice booms in the hall. 'Can you please introduce the emissaries from your sister's court?'

'Your Majesty, may I present: Percival of The Wyld Woods, Snake of Clan Fieth, and Princess Priscilla Crown as envoys from my sister, Queen Ariana.'

The King ignores Percival and me, his focus turning directly from Princess Petunia to Pris.

'Hello, niece. Welcome to my court.'

CHAPTER 6

The Surprises Keep Coming

That's it? Welcome to my court.

I'm trembling with resentment as the reality of why it is important for me personally to be here hits me. It is not just because I am the Queen's niece, but because I am also the King's.

King Maddox is still talking. I can see his lips moving, but I can't hear what he is saying for the pressure building in my head.

Why didn't they tell me? And why haven't I met this man before. Scotland isn't so very far away from London. After all, he paid for my education and my extra karate lessons....

I stand there shaking while the fragments of my life click into place. Members of the Unseelie Court have been attacked over the years—I have too. They weren't random like my father told me. Snake suspected as much, and I wasn't quite sure I'd believed him. Now I'm certain they were because I'm related to the King of the unpopular Unseelie Court.

Did Snake know? I turn accusing eyes on him, but either he is a good actor, or he is as stunned by all of this as I am.

As if sensing my gaze, he squeezes my hand and whispers, 'Pris, are you okay? The King is waiting for an answer.'

'I... I....'

I have dealt with so much. My parents going missing. Finding out about the magical realm. Being hoodwinked into a quest. Finding out I'm a potential heir to the throne of the Seelie Court. Now this—my uncle is the King of the Unseelie Court.

Each piece of solid ground I fight to gain shifts beneath my feet, sending me hurtling towards another truth from my past. Only this time I fear I can't find a way forward.

It's all too much. I shake myself free of Snake and spin around, the other court attendees appearing as a kaleidoscope of colours through my tears. When I entered, there had been so much expectation on those faces—so much hope that I'm here to save them. I'm not up to this.

'Pris?' The concern in Snake's voice and the murmurs of the crowd follow me as I run from the room.

I've no idea where I'm going, except that I want to be away from here. Paintings rush past as I run along corridor after corridor until I reach a dead end. Turning back the way I had come, I stop to catch my breath, unsure of where I am.

Further along the hallway, a maid is carrying a laundry basket. As she disappears around the corner, I push myself off the wall and rush after her. Taking the same left turn she did, I feel the slimy coolness of a portal and find myself outside in the World Above.

A few feet away, a couple of tour groups are assembling in front of the castle. They turn to stare at me as I emerge from the portal, surprise showing on their faces. I can't tell if it's because of the way I'm dressed or because I appeared from nowhere—and I don't really care. Ignoring them all and blocking out their startled comments, I hurtle down the grass bank leading to the river. My heart pounds in my chest. Once I reach the pathway running alongside the Ness, I halt, unsure what to do next.

All I can do is replay the scene in the audience chamber over and over. Why didn't anyone tell me the King is my uncle? Why did they allow me to make a fool of myself like that? Is there more they're not telling me? All the while tears stream down my face, and the Ness swirls and roils as if nothing in the world has changed.

I shake my head to clear my thoughts. This is not me. I don't stand by while things happen. I'm a planner. I am calm. I process facts and come up with a strategy. Only how can I do that if the facts keep changing? There is only one creature who I can trust. One creature who can take me away from this mess.

Am'ratha, please come and take me home.

I choke back a sob as I wait for her to answer. Can she even hear me? She said I could talk to her from anywhere.

Am'ratha?

I pick up my skirts and start walking along the river, away from town, looking for a space where Am'ratha might land.

I hear you, Royal One.

Relief floods through me.

Thank goodness! Can you come and take me away? I can't be here anymore.

Silence again.

I am sorry, Princess, but it is daylight, and too many people wander the grounds of the castle. I cannot risk them seeing me.

Biting back another sob, I tell myself I won't break down here, dressed like some flaming historic heroine, in front of all these people.

Tonight? I send.

Perhaps. I will have to consult with my Queen.

I stare out across the churning waters, frustrated and

alone. Okay, so I can't rely on anyone to take me away from here. I stare down at my clothes. Damn, I can't very well head back to London dressed like this. I don't have any money, or a credit card, or any identification. Who can I call? I can't even do that because my phone is still in the World Below.

'Are you all right dearie?,' an elderly woman asks, and I stare at her with unseeing eyes, my brain unable to process her words.

'It's okay, she had a bit of an upset. We're doing a photo shoot up at the castle and, well... photographers can be a bit... abrupt,' a familiar voice answers for me, and if I weren't so sad, I'd be grateful for his quick thinking.

The woman pats my arm. 'Dinnae let the buggers get ya down, lassie.'

I force my lips into a smile, and she walks off, muttering something about the pressure people put on young girls nowadays.

Resisting the urge to follow her, I turn to Snake, ready to face the music. Instead of leading me back to the court, he wraps his arms around me and pulls me into the circle of his embrace. For a moment I try to stay strong, to make like I don't need his comfort. When he leans his cheek against mine, the dam breaks.

The tears flow, and they flow, and they flow again, along with huge sobs that wrack my body. I can't remember a time when I've cried so long and so hard. And as I bawl, Snake holds me in his arms and says nothing.

I've no idea how long we stand there, or how long I cry for, but after a while, the tears stop flowing, and I simply lean into Snake, allowing myself a chance to recover. Finally, I take a deep breath and step back. Snake's arms release me, and he steadies me as I turn to lean on the barrier.

'You're not going to jump?' he asks, only half-joking.

I give him a watery smile. 'Not yet, but one more revelation like that, and who knows what I might do.'

A group of girls walk past, gape at me, and huddle together before bursting out laughing.

'I must look like a drowned rat,' I say, and Snake smiles.

'You're always beautiful to me. And maybe raccoon eyes will catch on.'

This time the smile I give him is genuine as he uses his thumbs to gently clear away the worst of my makeup.

'Wanna go back?' he asks when he is done.

'Can we just stay here for a bit so I can pull myself together?'

'We can stay as long as you need.'

I lean against his shoulder and watch the river flow by, satisfied I do have someone who will help save me after all.

· ·⋆· ☽ ·⋆· ·

Standing with Pris, leaning our arms on the wall overlooking the river, I try to imagine what she's going through. It was difficult enough finding out she was in the line of succession to the throne of the Seelie Court. Then to find out that the King of the Unseelie court is her uncle....

That is not what's bothering her though. It's the fact that everyone who knew just let her walk into the room without saying a word. How can you do that to someone? And how can Pris trust them after that?

I slip my arm over her shoulder, and she leans against me.

'I had no idea he was your uncle.'

She doesn't respond, and I worry she may believe someone had told me. Or, worse still, that I've always known.

'Believe me, if I'd found that out, I would have fought my way through heaven and hell to you to tell you.'

'That's a bit dramatic,' she says.

'And this from the creature who just ran out on the entire Unseelie Court?'

She chuckles, but the sound is still hollow.

'I understand, you know. Your family and mine seem to be expanding by the minute.'

Pris faces me and places a hand on my chest. 'Oh, Snake, I've been so wrapped up in my own problems, I haven't spared a thought for you. How are you getting on with your new family?'

I shake my head. 'My grandfather is an enigma, and my great-uncle is.... I'm not sure how to describe him other than extremely serious. How about you? What do you think of your new grandma?'

She chuckles softly, and a smile tugs at her lips. 'After having no one but Mum and Dad, I now have a clutch of royal relations—a pink princess, and a Scottish king right out of Othello.'

'You think that's bad. I've gained a rebel bard and a revolutionary.'

Now she is laughing for real, and I join her.

Finally, I say, 'What do you want us to do now, Pris? You say the word, and we're out of here.'

She shakes her head. 'I already thought of that. My credit card and both our IDs are back in your family home in the World Below. And we're not going far in these clothes.'

I'm a little surprised she has actually considered running away already.

'What about the dragons? Can they take us back to the World Below?'

She shakes her head again. 'Not in the daylight.'

Okay, even more surprised she'd attempted to call her dragon.

'So, we can wait until tonight and have the dragons spirit us away, or we can go back to the Unseelie Court and finish what we started—that is, if I haven't screwed everything up by being such a drama queen.'

I hug her closer. 'If it were me alone, I would choose option two. I originally started out trying to save our parents, so I would focus on that. However, now that we've found out why you're really here, I can't ask that of you.'

She leans into me, hiding her face so I can't tell what she's thinking.

Her voice is muffled when she asks, 'Do you think my being his niece will make the King change his mind about helping Queen Ariana?'

Part of me wants to tell her, yes, of course it will, and we'll be one step closer to getting our parents out of Bernais's clutches. I can't do it though. Too many people have put their needs before Pris's, and they've hurt her too much.

'Honestly, Pris, I have no idea. He may listen to you, but he may not. I spoke with Drow this morning, and he was helping me draft out a request based on creature law and history. Perhaps if we can combine that with your family connections....'

'How long would it take to pull a full petition together?'

'I'm not sure. Drow spends most of his time with the King and his other advisors, but he did say that Percival would be able to guide us. Did you know Drow and Percival are famous for bringing a compelling case to the Seelie Court that changed the law forever?'

Pris pulls away from me, her face stony. 'I can't work with Percival. He knew the King is my uncle. I thought I could trust him.'

'I think you still can. When you left the court, Percival

literally went ballistic at your grandmother. Apparently he would have told you today, but the princess changed the subject.'

Pris closes her eyes before nodding. 'I think he might have tried.'

'Whether he did or not, he was telling her she should have listened to him and that they all should have told you the truth because you finding out this way was unfair.'

Pris is so still, and her jaw is tense. Time to lighten things up again.

'Then he paced about, saying, did they listen to him—no, they didn't. He finished by going into a rant, saying that for all their friendship, they still treated him as a lesser creature, and from now on his allegiance was to you and you alone, and the others could go to hell for all he cared. It was all very intense, and he was kinda bad-ass.'

'Percival ranted?' she asks, and this time she manages a full-on smile.

'And that's what you chose to take from all of that.' I'm relieved I've got her back.

The smile has now reached her eyes. 'So you, Percival, and I really are a team?'

'I believe so.'

'Save the world to save our parents?'

'Yep.'

'No,' she says so quietly, I almost don't catch it.

'No?' I ask, wondering what she's planning now.

'Save the world, save Percival, and our parents.'

I grin. This is something I can get on board with. Pris's eyes turn fierce—she has more to say.

'Then, once they're free, I'm going to kill my parents for not telling me about all of this.'

I know how she feels. I'm only now realising how much my mother kept from me. All families have secrets, but this is getting beyond a joke. Somehow holding Pris in my arms makes it less hurtful. A couple passes by, rubbernecking, but they avert their gaze when I glare back at them.

'Pris, we're getting a few stares out here. Do you think we could head back inside?'

She smiles. 'Lucky we're in human form. How would they take the white hair and pointed ears?'

'Perhaps, but then again, there are so many fantasy programmes being filmed now, we might actually be more accepted.'

Pris sighs. 'Can't we stay out here? Maybe find a cafe and talk? Just the two of us, without this... mess?'

How tempting that sounds, and for a moment, I consider taking her somewhere for a coffee so we can pretend to be two normal people on a date for a while. Then I remember our clothes. 'Another time, when we're more appropriately dressed.'

I hold her for a moment longer before leading us back inside. We head for the portal Susan took us through last night, but there are too many people around for us to enter.

We go back outside and eventually find the entrance Pris had come through. As we wait for a tour party to pass so we can enter, Pris leans her head on my shoulder, and says, 'I missed you last night.'

'I missed you too.'

We step through to the other side, and Pris touches my arm as I move towards the main entrance. 'Wait.'

The hesitancy in her voice makes me pause.

'I can't go back to the court just yet,' she says. 'Not until I've processed this and regrouped.'

Her eyes are filled with pain, and all I want to do is take her away from here. Unfortunately, the stakes are too high for us to simply run away. So, I slip her hand through the crook of my arm.

'Let's go to my rooms. The notes Drow and I were working on for the petition are there, and we can go over them if you like.'

Her hand slides down my arm until we are palm to palm, and she entwines her fingers with mine. 'That sounds perfect.'

Anger is not an emotion I give into often. In fact, over the years since my curse, I have buried most of my feelings so deep, it would take years to uncover them. Perhaps it is because I have decided to fight to return to my old life, or perhaps it is because I have watched that poor Pris being battered emotionally—because others wish to have their secrets—that I am consumed with rage.

As I berate them all for not telling Pris about her heritage, I am aware someone has cleared most of the courtiers from the room. I punctuate each point I make by banging my hand into my fist, but that is not enough to work off my agitation.

I pace in front of them as I list the way my so-called friends have let Pris down and then patted themselves on the back for doing what her father wanted. What about Pris? Why should she pay for her parents' decisions?

Normally I would worry that I was putting on a show, preferring to keep my opinions to myself. I would melt into the background. At the moment all I can think of is how hurt Pris must be and of how we... *I* have let her down.

My rant goes on for a while, but no one can sustain that high a level of emotion forever, and I soon find myself slowing down and taking a breath. When I finally run out of steam, I finish with a final blow. 'I warned them not to do this, that this would go better if you told her who she is. And look how it has turned out.'

I glare at the group left around me: Petunia, Effie, and Heart. The King and his first advisor are still on the dais, with Drow at their side. King Maddox's eyes bore into me as if he is testing the truthfulness of my words, and I quickly turn away from his gaze, hoping I have not angered him.

'It was her father's wish that she not be told about any of her heritage unless he and Cecily were doing the telling. It was in her best interests not to say anything,' says Petunia.

I find I still have some anger left, and I snap, 'You do not even know her. How could you make that call? She was bound to find out—everyone can see Maddox and Malachi look alike.'

Petunia presses her lips together and glares at me. 'I was simply adhering to his request, as I have done since she was born.'

'And that was fine when she had no idea any of this existed. How do you think she has felt, finding out she is fey and part of a magical world before being told she is in the line of succession for the throne in the World Below, and all of that in the space of a couple of weeks? And she had to find this out from other creatures, not her parents. How was not telling her the King of the Unseelie Court is her uncle the best course of action?'

'If she did not come to take her rightful place in our world, why is she here?'

King Maddox's voice comes from behind me, and I jump before turning to face him, surprised he's joined our group.

I step back so I can see his face when I answer, 'She has come because she believes this is the only way her parents will be released.'

'So, she has come to ask for me to intervene with the Seelie

Court, and in return someone will release Malachi and Cecily?'

I shake my head. 'No, she has come to petition you to help Queen Ariana so the Queen can release her parents.'

The King glances away but not quickly enough to hide the disappointment in his eyes.

Petunia rubs King Maddox's arm. 'Oh, Maddox, can you not see? Until she saw you, she had no idea she was related to you. She came to meet with the King, not her uncle. Now that she is aware of who you are, that might change.'

King Maddox's face when he looks at Petunia is schooled back into the royal mask. When he speaks, his voice is a monotone. 'Oh, I understand. Malachi has not relented and told her about me.'

Giving his arm a gentle squeeze, Petunia says, 'You know the plan was to bring her to Scotland on a family holiday in a month and then to bring her to court to meet us. Unfortunately, Malachi and Cecily were taken to the World Below before that happened.'

King Maddox's eyes slide to the window. 'So she came as an envoy?'

'I am sorry, sire, that is correct,' I tell him.

The King sucks in some air and lets it out before returning to his throne. 'That is disappointing, but it changes very little. You—' He points at me. '—go find my niece and bring her to me.'

I bow to the King, and back out of the reception hall. When the doors close behind me, I relax, but only for a moment. The King wants me to bring Pris. He will not wait long, and I have no idea where she is.

Snake went after her, this much I know. Where would he take her? Not back to Petunia's suite of rooms, that is for sure. Perhaps the music room? No, I am sure I have not mentioned there is one, let alone where it is. Ah, there is only one place he would take her—our rooms.

I walk up the flight of stairs and follow the corridors until I reach the one our rooms are on. The guards have been removed, so I guess that is something. As I reach for the handle to open the door, I hear voices inside. I blow out a breath, relieved they were so easily tracked down.

Inside, I find the two of them at the table, their heads bent over some papers.

I announce my presence. 'Ah-hem.'

Two heads rise, and I am pinned with two pairs of eyes. Pris smiles. 'Great timing, Percival. Have you seen this?' She gestures at the papers.

I am relieved Pris appears to be all right, but the knot of my own guilt sits heavy on my stomach. 'Ah, no, but—'

'You should come and take a look. Drow and Snake have been drafting our petition.'

'I am sorry, Pris. I should have said something. I tried, but—'

She grins at me. 'Snake said you gave our families a roasting, and in front of the king too.'

I look at my feet, suddenly embarrassed about my outburst. 'Um, yes, I was perhaps a little too vocal.'

'As I see it, you were probably about vocal enough, and I appreciate it. Now, come look at this.' She points at the paper.

'Ah, thank you, I think. The King has requested you return to the court, so perhaps we should....'

Pris's face turns hard as stone. 'Tough. I am not ready to go back yet.'

Snake drapes an arm over her shoulders and whispers something in her ear. If it is possible, her face hardens even more than before.

'I'm tired of being sent here and there by everyone else. I will go to him, but in *my* time.'

Snake stares at me. He is asking something of me, but I am not sure what it is. I shrug, unsure what to say. Pris needs to take some control of things, but what can I do against a king?

'Is it possible that you might take a little time finding Pris?' Snake suggests.

Ah, I understand. 'Of course, it is unlikely I would find her in the first place I search, so I have time to peruse the petition before we head back to court.'

Pris relaxes, her face softening once again. She and Snake make room for me at the table so I can join them and the document. I can see Drow's fingerprints all over it. He has started by outlining the history of co-operation between the two courts and their commitment to keeping the flow of magic between the worlds. Then he moves on to the issues caused by the Queen overtaxing herself and finishes with outlining the potential impact on both worlds of not resolving this issue as soon as possible.

Under each section is a list of supporting documents and references that should be found in the library to fill out the argument and support our case. Reading this reminds me of the last time Drow and I petitioned a court.

It should bring back happy memories of our friendship, but instead it has my stomach churning. This time, as with the last, my future relies on the success of a petition. Last time I only got part of what I asked for. This time I need everything to go well so I can finally be free of the curse that keeps me from being a sprite.

'It is thorough. Then again, I would expect nothing less from Drow.'

'How long do you think it would take to pull this together if we all work on it?' Pris asks.

I rub my chin and try to remember how long it took Drow and me last time. 'Will Drow be helping?'

Snake shakes his head. 'He's offered to review what we do, but he's pretty tied up with the King.'

'Then two, perhaps three days,' I say.

Pris smiles. 'That's what we thought. So, let's get started.'

I hate to say it, but I must remind Pris we still have to face the King. 'Perhaps we can drop Snake at the library on our way back to court, and he can make a start.'

Pris sets her jaw, and I sense a fight brewing. Then Snake says, 'The sooner you get this over and done with, the sooner you can concentrate on why we are here.'

For a moment I think Pris is going to refuse. Then she closes her eyes, and when she opens them, our Pris is back.

'Come on, Percival, let's go and meet with my uncle.'

CHAPTER 7

Pleased to Make Your Acquaintance

Percival takes my hand as we walk down the stairs. He gives it one last squeeze before we turn left and find ourselves outside the court reception room. I'm touched by his concern but also worried because he thinks I need the extra support.

'King Maddox is in his study, Princess.' The guard on duty nods to a smaller door to the left of the huge double doors of the public room.

Percival and I step forward, but the guard places himself in front of us. 'Just Princess Priscilla,' he says, moving his body to cut Percival out.

I lean around the guard, trying to catch Percival's eye. Instead I watch my friend puff out his chest and say, 'I am the princess's advisor. Where she goes, I go.'

I grin at his cheek—I'm loving this new, improved Percival.

However, the guard is not so impressed. He folds his arms across his chest. 'I am informed this is a family meeting, not a state affair, so advisors are not required.'

'It's all right, Percival,' I say, preventing any further arguments. 'Go back to the library, and I'll meet you and Snake there once I'm done.'

Percival opens his mouth as if to object, glares at the guard, then looks at me. 'I will wait here for you.' His pronouncement made, he walks over to one of the chairs dotting the walls, sits down, and crosses his arms, not taking his eyes off the guard.

Stepping between them, I smile at Percival. 'I'll call for you if I need to. Hopefully this won't take too long.'

He waves his hand in a shooing motion, and I take the hint. The guard escorts me to the door and knocks. At some sort of signal only he can hear, he opens it and announces, 'Princess Priscilla for you, sire.'

'Send her in,' a voice barks from within.

The guard steps aside, and I pause for a moment to settle the butterflies dancing in my stomach, then enter. My eyes are immediately drawn to the figure seated behind a desk which dominates the room. His head is bent as he writes. He no longer wears his crown, but he is still dressed in his formal court clothes. I stand just inside the door, waiting for him to notice I'm here.

The guard takes pity on me and says under his breath, 'Go stand in front of the desk and curtsy. He will command you to rise when he is ready.'

I slide a glance at him, checking whether or not he is joking. No, he's not. Thinking it best to follow his advice, I stand in front of the desk and drop into a curtsey. Unfortunately for me, adhering to protocol does not gain the King's attention.

'You may leave us,' he says without raising his head.

Soon after the latch clicks, so I assume he is talking to the guard and not me. I continue to stand, knees bent and head lowered, waiting to be acknowledged. When the King still doesn't stop working, I decide I've had enough of this, and stand up.

The King is still engrossed in whatever it is he's doing, so I take the opportunity to study my surroundings. The room is narrow, with the King's desk opposite the door I entered. To his left is another doorway that I assume opens into the court's reception room. Running along the top of that wall are some narrow windows letting in some natural light from next door.

The opposite wall is lined with shelves that are overflowing with books and papers and folders all shoved in haphazardly. I suspect this is the space where the running of the Unseelie Court occurs.

I drag my eyes back to the figure behind the desk to find a pair of almost-black eyes studying me.

'So, you do not curtsey before your King?' he asks, his face deadpan.

I can't tell if he's being sarcastic or not. Either way, I dismiss his comment, thrown off balance by how much this man resembles my father. Not only could they pass as twins, but his voice is the same rich baritone. Hearing it sends a jolt of pain through my heart as I think about the position my father is in.

I'm speechless, but only for a minute. Then the rage from earlier rears back to life. I'm angry at my grandmother, angry at him, and angry at my parents for keeping secrets from me all these years. This rage is much more empowering than the fear that overwhelmed me by the Ness. My fury allows me to express myself, and I channel it all into my voice when I respond.

'I did, but you chose not to acknowledge me, and it was getting a little uncomfortable.'

Something flashes in his eyes. It could be amusement, but it disappears so quickly, I'm not 100 hundred percent sure.

'I will let it go this time, but in future you should remain in position until I see fit to release you.' He leans his elbows on the desk and steeples his fingers.

I hold his gaze and say nothing. I will not agree to this, but I'm smart enough not to say so. We stay like this for what seems like minutes but at a guess is probably only a few seconds. Eventually he relents and sweeps a hand towards one of the two seats in front of the desk.

'You may sit.'

I take up his offer but choose the other seat. It's petty, but I'm tired of being ordered around.

'So, we finally meet, Priscilla. Your parents have told me so much about you that I feel like I know you already.'

Everyone here knows me, or so they think. Rage bubbles almost to a boiling point in my veins, but I keep it under control. 'Funny, because I know nothing at all about you. And I prefer Pris.'

He shoots me a dark look, then sighs. I can almost hear him saying, 'So, this is how it is going to be.'

'All right, niece, I get your point. I do not know you, I know about you. And you know very little about your family. These are facts we cannot change, and we must move past them.'

Well played, Your Majesty. 'I suppose we must if I am to do what was asked of me. I am here as an envoy from the World Below, and I request a time to formally petition you on their behalf.'

He rests his chin in the palm of one hand and studies me... really studies me, and for a moment he seems almost human.

'So, you will not accept your role in *my* family, but you will represent your family from the World Below in my court.'

Why is he so annoyed? He's not the one who's been kept in the dark and shunted around to meet other's needs. I'm seething, but I don't want to show weakness in front of him, so I keep my next words clipped and precise.

'To be fair, when I agreed to this, I'd only just found out I was important enough in the Seelie Court to be considered suitable for a role. Secondly, Snake Fieth and Percival of the Wyld Woods are also part of this delegation. Thirdly, I had no idea my mysterious uncle would even be here, let alone rule the Unseelie Court.' I force myself to relax and try to keep the tremor from my voice. 'And finally, I believed I had no option but to come here if I ever want to see my mum and dad safe again.'

He doesn't respond immediately, giving the impression that he is choosing his next words carefully. 'Fair enough. I want my brother and his wife safe as well.'

If you do, you have a strange way of showing it.

'If that's true, why have you refused requests to help Queen Ariana?' The words tumble out before I have a chance to parse them.

The flash of anger on the King's face has me immediately regretting my lack of control. I wish Snake or Percival were here to help me keep a check on my temper.

'I am King. I have to put the needs of my people first.' It is King Maddox, not my uncle speaking now.

I wait for more, but he says nothing. Closing my eyes, I breathe deeply until I have my emotions under control and I can speak as dispassionately as he did. 'This is important. If you won't help because it's the right thing to do, or for your brother and his wife, then you should do it because if you don't, magic will fail.'

The King's eyes are now like black ice, and his fists pound the arm of his chair. Surprisingly, his voice is all controlled fury when he responds. 'The Seelie Court despises us, and your father rejected a position here. I have enough magic to protect the Unseelie Court, so why should I put myself out to help those who would rather we did not exist?'

I lean forward, making eye contact and trying to reach the

heart of this foreboding man. 'You won't lift a hand to save your own brother? What happened that you would cast him adrift like that?'

He runs a hand through his hair before leaning back in his chair. 'Our history is complex. When your father and I arrived at the Seelie Court of Britain as goodwill ambassadors from the Court of Africa, royal elves in our own right, they rejected us because of our skin colour. While I was fighting for a place in their world, Malachi was falling in love with their princess —foolish boy that he was.'

He pauses, and I wonder if he's going to say anything else. He shifts in his chair and clasps his hands on the desk in front of him. 'When I left to come to the Unseelie Court where I knew we would be accepted, he stayed with your mother. They were so in love, they made that stupid pact to renounce everything and live in the World Above—all so they could stay together.'

Although the King's voice is monotone, his eyes are heavy with sadness. A twinge of sympathy wriggles into my heart but not enough to take his side over my parents.

'What was so wrong about them choosing to stay together?'

'It is not that. They did not have to be alone. They could have come with me, and their marriage would have been accepted here.'

His words pierce my heart. Could they have? My life would have been very different if they had made that choice, I would have known my family and who I was. No, they must have had a good reason to do what they did. I would reserve judgment until I had a chance to talk with them.

'I believe they did the best they could to protect themselves at the time,' I say stubbornly.

'What good did it do them? In the end they came to me anyway. When you, the fruit of their union, began to experience attacks from creatures who didn't like your dark skin—or perhaps they didn't like me—either way, Malachi turned to me. I paid for your fancy school with high security and your fighting lessons, but they still only visited once a year. And they kept you away from the court—away from me.'

I shuffle forward on the seat as my uncle speaks, the hurt and loneliness in his voice drawing me in. Had he wanted a relationship with me? To be a part of my life when I was growing up?

King Maddox rubs a hand across his forehead and draws in a deep breath. 'None of that matters now. You were to come and meet me in a month or so anyway, but it is better you are here now. It is a this time of great disruption, and I need someone by my side to help keep the court running. With Tomas gone, that will fall to you.'

'What?' I am so cut up by the loss underpinning my uncle's words, I'm sure I misheard what he said.

'My deal with your father was that when you were finished with school, you would abdicate from the Seelie Court line of succession and join my court. You are here now, and I expect you to remain by my side.'

My jaw drops, and I stare at him. He can't be serious. Does he expect me to go along with some deal he and Dad made when I was a kid? No way is that happening!

'I'm thankful for you helping Mum and Dad out when I needed protection, I really am. But all this magical world stuff is new to me, and I'm not sure where I fit and what, if anything, I want to do about my family affiliations in either court.'

The royal mask falls back over King Maddox's face, hiding the man underneath. 'It makes no difference what you want. Your parents and I already agreed.'

'I don't care what you all agreed. I'm an adult now, and I'll make my own choices.'

Our eyes lock, and this time neither of us is prepared to give way. Tension is sucking the air from the room. I'm shaking, and I don't know whether it's from disappointment or anger. Either way, I won't back down. I'm tired of being pushed this way and that to meet others' needs. There is no way this unknown uncle will dictate my future.

King Maddox's lips draw into a grin, and it sends shivers down my spine.

'You will choose to stand beside me at court, or I will refuse to accept your petition.'

Is he seriously blackmailing me? Using the fact that my parents are in danger to force me into something I don't want to accept? I search his face, looking for any sign that this might be some sick sort of joke. He stares back, not giving away anything.

King Maddox has backed me into a corner, and he thinks he has won because there is no way I can say no when my parents' lives are at stake.

I rise to my feet and turn my back on the King, vaguely aware there is some protocol about leaving the monarch's presence but not actually caring if I've insulted him.

'I have not given you leave to depart.' King Maddox's voice is a low rumble as it follows me to the exit.

'Go to hell,' I growl as I slam the door behind me.

·˙*❥.*˙·

As I drop the books I've gathered onto the table, a grin lifts my mouth as they send a resounding thump through the room. It was easy enough to find most of the volumes Drow suggested for background details and legal precedents. Now all I have to do is search for the correct information, copy it out, and reference it.

'Just like a school assignment,' I say out loud as I take a seat.

I'm about to open the first book when the library door is flung open so hard, it thuds against the wall, then bounces back. Pris pushes it aside as she storms in, followed by an almost running Percival, and slumps into the chair opposite me. I wait for her to speak, but when she says nothing, I turn to the sprite.

'So I take it the meeting didn't go so well?'

He shakes his head as he tries to catch his breath. 'I do not know,' he manages to say. 'She won't tell me anything.'

Percival pulls out the chair beside Pris and sits. We both eye her hesitantly.

She stands up and begins pacing. 'If he thinks I'm going to fall into line because of some deal he made with my parents, then he's got another think coming.'

I turn to Percival, but he shakes his head again. He has no idea what she is talking about either.

'But if I don't, he won't hear our petition. And I can't have that.'

'Pris?'

She carries on pacing as if she hasn't heard me, so I stand up and grab hold of her arm. She stops and glares at me. As her eyes focus, her glare softens, and tears well in her eyes. I gather her into a hug.

'Come on, Pris, talk to us. We're a team, remember?'

She nods against my shoulder, and I lead her back to a seat. Sitting beside her, I take her hand in mine.

Pris draws in a couple of deep breaths. 'My uncle, the King, wants me to lead the Unseelie Court with him because of some deal he made with my parents. He says if I don't, he won't allow us to present our petition.'

A punch to the gut couldn't have taken the wind from my sails this quickly. Luckily, Percival is on the ball.

'What did he say when he asked you to lead the court with him? Are you to be his heir? Or just his consort, a ceremonial Tomas replacement?'

Pris's voice is so quiet, I almost miss what she says. 'The second, I think.'

'That's a shame because if he said heir, we could argue that there has never been a Queen of the Unseelie Court.'

I look from Percival to Pris and back to Percival. 'So, are you saying we can't do anything about the other one?'

Percival's brows draw together in a frown. 'What exactly did the King say to you, Pris?'

Pris draws her bottom lip between her teeth. 'He said I should give up my claim to the Seelie Court throne, join his court, and be by his side.'

'Interesting. And if you don't do this, we won't be able to petition the King?'

Pris nods.

'This is whacked!' I explode, and the others turn to me with identical quizzical looks. 'Your own uncle is blackmailing you.'

'I'm aware of that,' Pris says. 'We're discussing this because I want some ideas on what to do about it.'

She looks hopefully at me, and I have nothing—no ideas on how to avoid this. Nor has she. A thought tickles the back of my brain, and I wait for it to form. When it emerges, it's something else. All I have to do now is persuade Pris.

'Well, obviously you have to do it.' *Okay, perhaps not the best start.*

Pris blanches, and I see the hurt in her eyes. 'You want me to do as he says? Give in to blackmail?'

I squeeze her hand. 'Sometimes you have to give a little to get what you want. Then once you have it...'

I nod at her, willing her to catch on. She just stares back, her eyes still full of hurt.

'I think what Snake is trying to say is, you agree with what the King wants until we have presented the petition,' Percival pipes up. 'Or, worst-case scenario, until he leaves for the World Below.'

Her expression changes from hurt to hopeful. 'When can you have a somewhat reasonable petition ready?' she asks.

'If we work through the night, I think by lunchtime tomorrow,' I tell her.

'Percival, do you think you could ask Drow to give it a quick check tomorrow morning?'

The sprite nods.

'Okay,' Pris says, her eyes narrowing. 'Percival, how do I renounce my claim to the Seelie Court throne?'

'You have to attend the court and announce it to all those assembled. After it is noted in the official records, it is done.'

Pris grins. 'I can't do that at the moment, but I can hint that I will in the future. I'll tell my uncle later today and endure an evening and morning of being a court follower until we present our petition. Then I'm home free.'

The air feels lighter, and Pris laughs.

'At some stage, though, you will have to make this right with your uncle,' Percival says. 'He is not a bad man, just one who is feeling alone.'

The light fades from Pris's eyes. 'I know, and I will. But before I tell him, we have to sort out the Queen, fix the decline of magic, and get our parents freed.'

'Agreed,' I say, but I'm not as happy as Pris about all of this. With all the family complications we've run into, I'm finding it's no longer easy to see what Pris's and my futures will be when this is over. She has royal responsibilities, and I'm being slowly drawn into my own family issues.

Some of my turmoil must have shown on my face, because

Pris places her hand over mine and says, 'Hey, it's only play-acting and only for a couple of days. How hard can it be?'

I force myself to smile. 'Now you've gone and jinxed it.'

'You may believe this will be easy,' Percival says, 'but do not underestimate the King or his advisors. Drow may be able to keep his opinions on the depth of your commitment to himself, but I doubt Chancellor Rimould will. He is the King's man through and through. If he senses any deception, he will go straight to the King.'

'He's right, Pris. If you do this, you must do it properly. No sneaking away, no snide comments—'

I stop talking when I see a smile tugging at Pris's lips.

'You don't think I can do it, do you?' She moves so she can include Percival. 'Either of you?'

I'm shaking my head when the castle shudders. Pris's eyes go wide, and the building rocks again. I brace myself, gripping the table as books tumble from their shelves and bits of plaster fall from the ceiling.

'What the—?'

'I think.... I think someone is attacking the castle... with magic.' Percival sounds like he can hardly believe what he's saying. 'Perhaps we should take cover under the table.' His eyes dart around the room, a little panicked.

'Or in a doorway,' Pris suggests, 'like in an earthquake?'

A loud *crack* sounds, and we all dive under the solid oak table as the castle shakes again.

We huddle together, and I reach for Pris's hand, gripping it tight. Shouts and the sounds of footsteps running ring out from the hallway, but there is no more shaking. We wait a good few minutes to make sure whatever it was has stopped before emerging from the table's protection. Pris heads straight for the window.

'I would not stay there,' Percival tells her. 'The windows are the weakest part of the castle's protections.'

Pris appears not to have heard. I move to her side. 'Come on, Pris, we need to find out what is going on.'

'Look,' she says, pointing at a figure running down the street. 'Isn't that—'

'Grossman Green,' I say before she does. 'What is that slimy rat doing here?'

My lips curl back into a snarl. I have not forgiven him for selling us out in Wiseman's Woods or for taking part in the plot against our parents. Now he's here during a magical attack on the court. It can't be a coincidence.

I drop an arm over Pris's shoulder and lead her away. 'Come on, there's nothing we can do about him, but we may be able to help with repairs or something.'

I lead Pris to the door, with Percival following behind. Before I can open it, a guard enters.

'Is everyone all right in here?'

We all nod, but his attention is on Pris.

'Good. We have experienced a direct magical attack. The King has ordered all the entrances and exits closed until we find the culprits.'

Pris's hands clench at her sides, and she leans into me and whispers, 'Great. The enemy is in town, we can't leave, and I have to play princess—'

I hold up my hand. 'Please don't say it. You've already jinxed us enough for one day.'

Pris chuckles softly, and the guard frowns at us. 'This is no laughing matter. If you could please return to your accommodations, we need to do a head count to make sure there were no casualties.'

At the mention of casualties, Pris's smile quickly fades.

Chastened, we slip past the guard and make our way to Drow and Heart's suite, sidestepping a surprising amount of debris on the way.

As I follow Pris and Snake along the rubble-strewn corridor, I shove my shaking hands into my pockets. I have never been so scared in my life—not even when I realised Magnus Baaronson had turned me into a cat. My life had not been threatened then.

Thank goodness for the wine in Heart and Drow's suite. I fill three glasses, then gulp mine down in a single swallow. As I pour myself another, I see Snake's hand tremble. I do not have it in me to reassure him that everything will be all right. Fortunately, Heart arrives in time to take the pressure off me somewhat.

'Ah, Princess, you are here. Your grandmother, Princess Petunia, is worried about you, given that you have not shown up in her rooms.'

'I've been with Snake and Percival,' Pris says, not picking up on Heart's actual concerns.

'You left the King in... less than... optimal circumstances,' he says as I hand him a glass of wine. 'Perhaps you would like to return to her suite and let her know you are all right?'

'I am fine here, thank you,' Pris tells him. She does not add that she has had enough of her family for one day—although I sense she wants to.

Heart shrugs. 'It is your call, but I think we should get a message to her. You were the last person unaccounted for, and she was certain something had happened to you.'

'If you think we should,' Pris says, taking a sip of her wine.

Heart presses the buzzer to summon a servant. I am surprised when one appears only a few minutes later. I had assumed they would all be busy cleaning up and that seeing to our needs would be a long way down on their list of priorities.

'Piers, please inform Lady Susan that we have found Princess Pricilla and she is well,' Heart instructs the brownie.

Before Piers leaves, Pris adds, 'And if you can ask her to organise a change of clothes for me—normal clothes, not these archaic dresses—I'd appreciate it.'

Heart raises an eyebrow.

Pris stares him down. 'Susan said we don't have to dress like ghosts from the past when we're not at court. So I assume she'll be able to find me more comfortable clothes.'

Heart's eyes crinkle around the edges when he smiles at Pris. 'You are as feisty as everyone says,' he comments before turning back to the servant. 'You heard the princess.'

'Add me to the list for normal clothes too,' Snake says.

I have no idea why he wants to change. He is very smart in his courtier garb. Why swap that out for jeans and a T-shirt?

The servant darts from the room before we can find anything more for him to do. Thanks to the wine, the slight tremor in my hands finally subsides, and we head for the seats around the fire. We are not long seated when another servant knocks before bringing in a tray of sandwiches and coffee. I had almost forgotten it was lunchtime, but my stomach remembers as soon as I smell the food.

'Cook says the dining room cannot open until evening meal time, so this is to tide you over,' she says before backing out of the room.

We all move to the table, and for a short time, we push our worries aside and eat lunch, happy to be alive.

Snake is the first to break the silence. 'When they say we can't leave our rooms, do they mean we can't go anywhere at all? I'd like to go back to the library and finish our petition.'

Heart answers before I can. 'Most of the guards are holding the outer barrier in place while the magically gifted find and repair any smaller holes. It would not be safe to move too far until they are done.'

At that moment yet another maid taps on the door and enters, carrying Snake's and Pris's questing clothes and footwear. 'Lady Susan sends her apologies. She has not had time to purchase any other clothes for you, and she hopes these will do. They have been cleaned and mended.'

'They are perfect. Can you thank her for me?' Pris says, taking her clothes from the creature. 'Where can I change?' she asks.

'Come, I'll show you the guest bathroom,' Snake tells her, grabbing her hand.

Heart chuckles as they disappear. 'I think there may be a little more than getting changed going on there, eh, Percival?'

'I am certain Snake will be a gentle—'

I do not get to finish as Drow barges through the door, all anger and fury. 'This has got to stop. They have dared to attack the court directly. They would only do so if they believed there would be no retribution.'

Heart, perhaps used to Drow's dramatic interruptions, does not look up from his coffee. 'Will there be? I mean, we have not done anything about the other attacks—not even Tomas's death.'

'A few of the guards have been sent out to hunt down the creatures who did this, and they are on orders to bring them back here. But no, there will be no counterattack and no retribution in the World Below. How can there be when the ones causing the problems act on their own initiative?' Drow drops into a chair by the fire, catches sight of the food, then gets back up to join us at the table.

I wait until he has a cup of coffee in his hand before I say, 'Drow, you do know our only hope is to persuade King Maddox to assist the Queen? Once she is back on the throne, she will be able to deal with these attacks on the court, and magic in both realms will be stronger.'

'You are right, Percival, and I have already thought of a

way to extend the petition to include retribution for the Unseelie Court as being one of the positive outcomes.'

'Do you truly believe we can convince him?' I ask.

Drow grimaces. 'I fear it is not him we need to persuade but Chancellor Rimould. King Maddox has been off his game since Tomas died and relies more heavily on his advisor, who counsels against taking action in this matter.'

I tap my fingers on the table as I force my brain to work the way it used to when I played politics along with the best of them. 'And is he maybe a conservative? I seem to remember Eleanora saying something to that effect.'

'He is, but he can be persuaded to act given the right motivation and if it's in the Unseelie Court's interest.'

As Drow and I talk, it is like we are back in our university days, nutting out a problem together. I stop as a memory dislodges from the recesses of my brain.

'Drow, Effie said a lack of magic has been causing problems, but has someone been recording the incidents like we used to record the effects of the blight?'

'Not officially, but I think there is someone who might be able to help—Tomas's nephew, Dinian, has taken it upon himself to collate what reports we receive. You all head to the library, and I will search him out.'

'Are we allowed to leave?' Heart asks.

Drow pauses on his way to the door. 'Oh, yes, did I not say already?' Then he is gone.

Heart rolls his eyes and turns to me. 'Who is going to tell the lovebirds?'

I sigh as I stand up. 'I guess that will be me.'

CHAPTER 8

Pulling It All Together

S nake has indeed been a gentleman if what I witnessed when I entered his room was anything to go by.

'Oh, you're alone,' I say, pointing out the obvious.

Snake laughs. 'It's difficult to be too romantic when you're worried someone will barge in at any moment.'

'Ah, then how did Pris get out of her dress?'

Snake winks. 'I did say not too romantic.'

The door to the bathroom opens, and Pris enters. She's rather further along in the dressing process than Snake, and as her eyes drift to his bare chest, her cheeks pink up. He slips past her into the bathroom, leaving the door open.

I am getting a definite third-wheel vibe and rush to say, 'I have come to collect the two of you. We are all heading to the library so we can work on the petition.'

'But I haven't had a chance to tell King Maddox that I accept his offer.' Pris says. 'I should go now.'

I raise my eyebrows.

She glances down at her travel attire, then back at me. 'I guess I can't go dressed like this?'

'No, you cannot.' I bite back a smile. 'Perhaps we could

send a servant to request a few minutes of the King's time before the formal dinner tonight. That way you will have time to plan with us and also to dress appropriately.'

'Sounds okay. What do you think, Pris?' Snake says, doing up the last couple of buttons of his shirt.

Pris draws in a breath and lets it out slowly. 'I guess it'll have to do.'

'Fine. I will ask Heart for some paper and a pen, and you can write a request for the King.'

Pris wrinkles her nose. 'I guess I should write one to Susan too, asking her to make sure I'm dressed suitably for a royal consort.'

'How very forward thinking of you,' I tell her with a small smile. She is already starting to get used to how the court works. 'Now I shall wait for you outside. Please do not be long. We have much to do this afternoon.'

Heart is still trying to find a pen when Pris and Snake appear from the bedroom.

'Ah, found it,' Heart says, brandishing an ink pen. He unscrews the bottom and checks the ink before handing it over to Pris.

'This is a bit posh for a quick note,' she says, and Heart laughs.

'This is the Unseelie Court version of a biro. King Maddox likes us all to write with quill pens, but most of us have an ink one hidden away.'

Pris sits at the table and stares at the two blank sheets of parchment in front of her, bottom lip drawn between her teeth. 'So does that mean I have to write differently as well?' she asks Heart.

'The one to Lady Susan should be fine to write normally, but when writing to the King, it is best to use formal language. If you can, make your writing look a little fancy. He will appreciate the effort.'

Snake snorts. 'It's all a bit much isn't it? All this old-world playacting.'

Heart's shoulders tense, and I fear Snake is in for a bit of a dressing down. I am proven wrong when Heart speaks.

'It may be hard for someone with as few years as you have under your belt to understand that sometimes hiding in the past or playing a role can be comforting. And especially so when life has not been kind to you.'

My heart is heavy as my friend speaks. He lost his wife more than forty years ago, and he still misses her. His grief also brings shame to me. Heart cannot be with his wife, but I could be with my bond-mate Nisha, and I have chosen not to be. Still, I am finally on the road to setting things right. It is such a shame that I have waited hundreds of years to do it.

Heart's words must have touched something in Snake too, and he makes his way to his grandfather's side before placing a hand on his shoulder. 'I am sorry. I didn't mean to criticise.'

'It is all right, son. We all mock that which we don't understand. If you think of the Unseelie Court as a bunch of misfits trying to make a place where there is a space for every-one, then you may find its foibles easier to understand.'

'But not the lack of modern amenities,' Snake says, wrinkling his nose.

'King Maddox did start but was forced to slow down because there wasn't enough magic around,' Heart says.

Snake catches my eye, and I sense he's wondering if King Maddox is feeling the impact of a lack of magic, why is he not fixing it? I do not have an answer, so I say nothing.

'I'm finished,' Pris says, waving the two folded documents in the air.

I pull myself away from the touching family scene to join her at the table. 'Would you like me to check the one for the King?' I ask her.

Pris's eyes twinkle with mischief. 'Why, Percival, that is so sweet... or is it that you don't trust me?'

'Rumour has it your last words to him were something about going to hell, so can you blame me?'

She grins as she stands up and tucks the letters into her back pocket. 'While I appreciate your offer, I think I had best deal with King Maddox on my own terms, otherwise he'll never respect me. Now, we'd better get moving, or Drow will have everything sorted, and we'll have to waste time convincing him of any changes we want to make.'

'This should be good,' Heart says to me as we follow the princess to the door. 'If she thinks being there will prevent Drow from putting exactly what he wants in the petition, then she is in for a bit of a surprise.'

I chuckle. 'Or maybe Drow is. Pris is very adept at turning things to her advantage.'

Heart raises his eyebrows. 'Care to place a wager on that?'

I think about it for a moment. Drow and Pris are pretty evenly matched. Still, I think the princess may have a slight advantage. 'You are on. And whoever loses has to endure dinner this evening without the benefit of wine.'

Heart looks pained at my offer of a forfeit.

'Either you back Drow or you do not,' I tease him.

He laughs. 'It is a wager.'

'What's the bet?' Snake asks, dropping back to walk with us while Pris hands her notes to a passing servant.

Heart taps the side of his nose with his index finger. 'Never you mind, young Snake, never you mind.'

I cannot help but smile. I'm enjoying being back with my friends again. My smile fades as I enter the library and see who Drow is sitting with. I remember the elf from my last visit here as a cat. When he thought no one was looking, he played a rather nasty trick on a brownie maid and said nothing when she was dismissed for incompetence.

Drow stands up as we enter and frowns at his companion until he too rises to his feet. 'Lord Dinian, may I present Princess Priscilla, Snake Fieth, and Percival of the Wyld Woods. Everyone, this is Tomas's nephew, Dinian. He has been collating reports of fluctuations in magic for the King.'

The elf pushes a fringe of black hair out of his eyes as his gaze brushes past Snake and homes in on Pris. He glides around Drow, then takes Pris's hand and kisses it. 'I am so very pleased to meet you, Princess. As we are to be working together, may I call you Priscilla?'

Pris's lips tighten a little, and I wait for her to tell the upstart elf her name is Pris.

'You may,' she tells him, withdrawing her hand and tucking it through Snake's arm.

I cough to hide my laugh. The princess has the measure of Tomas's nephew.

As Snake leads Pris to the table, Dinian's eyes follow her trouser-clad figure, and he smiles appreciatively. I want to say something, but fortunately Heart steps in and gently slaps the back of the creature's head. 'Show some respect. She is related to the rulers of both creature courts.'

I expect the young elf to blush or show some sign of embarrassment, but he does not. 'I am beginning to see a reason to move the court towards more modern forms of dress,' he says. 'Perhaps it won't be that long until we can.'

Not only does his leering at Pris confirm my initial impression of the creature, but it also sounds warning bells, although I cannot quite put my finger on why.

'Perhaps we could start,' Pris is saying, and I draw my attention back to the petition. 'I am expecting to be called to meet with the King in a couple of hours, so we need to make the most of our time here.'

'Ah yes,' Drow starts. 'Perhaps if Percival could take the lead on completing the initial outline we had. He knows how these things work, and with Snake and Heart helping, we should have a decent draft ready in no time.'

My heart warms at his trust, and I smile my thanks. Snake is already sliding the books he found earlier down to the other end of the table. I pick up the papers, and Heart and I join him. As we set up, Snake sends dagger glances towards Dinian, who is standing far too close to Pris for anyone's liking.

'I don't like that elf,' Snake whispers as Pris moves away from him and takes a seat, making sure Drow is between her and her would-be suitor.

As we work silently through the texts, Dinian asks, 'How are you enjoying your time in the Unseelie Court?'

'I'm not here for a family visit,' Pris responds in her iciest tone. 'I am here on business.'

Dinian carries on as if she has not spoken. 'It cannot be all business. You must make time for me to show you some of the delights of the court.'

'I know what I'd like to show you,' Snake mutters. 'The business end of my fist.'

'Be calm, Snake. I am sure Pris can more than handle that creature,' I say.

As if to underline my words, Pris says, 'I am here for business and nothing else, and the only interest I have in spending time with you is if you can contribute something to our petition. Now, do you have any information that might help, or not?'

'Of course, Priscilla. Your wish is my command.'

Snake sniggers as Dinian uses Pris's full name, the one she hates with a passion.

The elf pulls a sheet of paper from the pile of documents in the middle of the table. 'This is a summary of the reports below in order of number of reported incidents. I've found the reduction in magic in the World Above has meant healers have not been able to heal some illnesses. Some have even lost their ability to help other creatures and have reverted to using natural medicines.'

'I had no idea things were that bad,' Drow mutters.

'There is more. Additionally, some of the magical races are not having as many offspring—brownies and sprites have been experiencing a steep decline in numbers. Perhaps the worst sign of magic waning is that many creatures report it more difficult to fight human pollution and to counter the damage it does to the world.'

Drow leans forward and picks up the stack of papers. 'This is good work, Dinian. We should slot this in after the legal arguments and our reference to the obligations the crown agreed to—for both monarchs to support each other in keeping magic clean to benefit both worlds.'

'What exactly is the legal argument based on?' Pris asks, and Drow tuts.

He never used to be this curmudgeonly. In fact, he used to enjoy teaching creatures about their history.

He looks down his nose at Pris as he answers her, and I wonder if there is more going on here. Life was so much clearer when I did not have to worry about such things.

'Well, Princess, once upon a time, magic used to flow freely between the World Above and the World Below. When people with magic began being noticed in the World Above, the Queen closed the gates—'

'Between the worlds.... I know that. I also know that magic was tainted in some way by this. I assume the agreement you all keep talking about between the courts came about when some of the gates were reopened?'

Drow locks his fingers together and studies the princess for a moment, as if he is taking her measure. A twitch at the corner of his lips suggests that, contrary to outward appearances, he might actually be enjoying this conversation.

'You are correct. When the council refused to open the

gates to prevent the spread of blight, the dragons intervened. Many were already beginning to feel the loss of magic, the dragons included, and they stepped in. The Queen of the Seelie Court was already bonded to a dragon who boosted her magic in times of need. The Dragon Queen threatened to sever that link if the doors were not opened.'

'I get that,' Pris says, 'and I also know that Queen Ariana was cleaning the flow of magic when she became sick. What I don't know is where the Unseelie Court fits into this.'

Heart leans closer to me. 'Ah, the impatience of youth, eh, Percival?'

'It is indeed wearying,' I respond.

Drow's demeanour has softened, and I can tell he is warming to his subject. 'At the same time, the Queen of Dragons offered to raise the Unseelie Court to the same level as the Seelie one if they promised to work with the monarch of the World Below to cleanse the magical flow.'

'So the King was bonded to a dragon?' Pris asks.

'Yes, he was, as was King Maddox when he was named heir. I believe you met Ed'ruven when you came through the portal.'

Pris smiles. 'We did.' She places her arms on the table and sits forward. 'If I understand you correctly, the agreement with the dragons is what you're calling legal precedence?'

'Correct.'

'So, if everyone was keeping up their side of the bargain, how did magic get in such a bad way? Was someone not doing what they needed to?'

'It is amazing how someone new can size up a situation and cut right to the meat of the thing,' Heart chuckles.

I put a finger to my lips. 'Hush a minute. I want to hear how Drow deals with this.'

'There are many reasons magic has been failing, but I believe the two main ones are that Queen Petunia faced so much political opposition, it took almost all her time and energy to hold on to the throne, so she and her dragon were not as active as they once were.'

'And my uncle?' Pris prompts.

'He decided to move and extend the court and so was perhaps not as diligent as he should have been either.'

'And there was always the problem that when the two worlds were sealed off, some gates disappeared,' Snake adds. 'So magic did not flow as easily as it once did and needs constant attention.'

'Very good,' Drow praises his nephew.

The room falls silent, and Drow leans back in his chair.

Pris stares at the table, tracing the pattern of the wood with a finger. She stops and looks at Drow. 'I disagree.'

'With what?' Drow asks dourly.

'About where to put the impact of the loss of magic,' Pris answers. 'When I spoke to the King, he said he would only consider our petition favourably if it were in the Unseelie Court's interest to do so. I think we show him the impact the loss of magic has, follow that up with the reasons why, and wrap the whole thing up with family and legal obligations.'

The room is so quiet, I expect to see tumbleweeds roll by.

Finally Drow speaks. 'I have years of experience in arguing cases in court, and—'

Pris edges forward on her seat. 'And if this were a court case, it would be based on law, but it isn't. King Maddox is already aware of his commitments, and he has not only refused to meet them, but he's put the court squarely before them. We need to try something different, something that might shake him up a little.'

All eyes are turned to Drow, but he is staring straight at Pris, his head cocked to the side. 'What about his family ties and the fact that his brother is being held in the World Below?'

Pris's brows draw into a frown. 'I will take your guidance

on that. From the little I've found out so far, Uncle Maddox still holds a grudge because my father chose my mother over him. So pressing family ties may backfire.'

Drow blinks, then nods a couple of times. 'All right, we will lead with the impact on the Unseelie Court, using not only the lack of magic but also the attacks because the Seelie Court is weak without the Queen to guide it. We should leave family ties out.'

Beside me Heart gasps, and I chuckle. My wine with dinner is no longer in jeopardy.

'Drow must be losing his touch,' Heart mutters.

'Is there anything we are able to offer from the Seelie Court, perhaps an olive branch that Queen Ariana will uphold?' Pris asks Drow.

'Well played,' Heart murmurs. 'First she beats him with logic, now she draws him back in by asking for his expertise. Drow had no hope.'

Drow smiles, apparently agreeing with Heart's whispered assessment of the situation. 'I like the way you think. One thing you could offer that I believe King Maddox will agree to and that Queen Ariana will jump at accepting. And I also believe her council will not be able to disagree with the collapse of magic at stake. Reinstate Princess Petunia as heir to the Seelie throne.'

'Oh, I like that,' Pris says. 'It closes Bernais down because it gives an alternative to him should the Queen not be able to take up her duties for any reason. And will appeal to King Maddox because it strikes at his enemies in the World Below.'

'And it puts you one step further from the throne,' I mutter.

Dinian leans forward. 'Is that wise? I mean, won't such a strong alignment between the courts mean the attacks will get worse, not better? Won't they try harder to take the Unseelie Court down?'

'I believe it is more likely it will weaken the Baaronson faction and the attacks will stop,' Pris responds.

The set of Dinian's jaw shows he disagrees. He opens his mouth to speak, but Pris closes him down.

'While we appreciate your input, I would like to find out what Snake and Percival think. After all, we three must stand behind this document.'

'You know me, Pris. I'm behind anything that will weaken Bernais and help my mother.' Snake grins.

I take a while to respond. Much as I hate to admit it, Dinian might have a point. Will throwing a spanner in Bernais's works make him even more violent? Given his nature, it is certainly a possibility. Still, if more magic is available in the World Above, then they will be better able to defend themselves. And the threat of persecution could put off some of his more lukewarm followers.

'I do have misgivings,' I start, gathering my thoughts as I speak, 'but I think it is better to offer it rather than leave it out.'

'Excellent,' Drow says. 'We have a plan. Dinian, thank you for your help, but we have it from here.'

It appears as though the elf will object, but he picks up his papers and moves to a smaller table on the other side of the library. Although he seems to be carrying on with this work, every time I glance his way, he is more interested in us than the papers in front of him.

*

Every now and then, Dinian mutters under his breath, as though he wants to draw everyone's attention to the fact that he's still here. His antics make it difficult to concentrate on what Drow and Pris are saying. I want to be able to block him out, and usually I'm easily able to do that, but something about the guy gets right under my skin.

I'm about to say something to him when a knock on the door has everyone falling quiet. A servant enters with a note on a silver tray. He takes it straight to Pris, who reads it and then tells the creature she will be there.

As the servant leaves, she catches my eye. 'I have fifteen minutes with the King in an hour.'

I smile. 'Great. Let's keep working.'

'Actually, we're almost done,' Drow says, putting down the papers Percival handed him before the interruption. 'I think Percival and I can pull this together into a final copy while you go and dress, Pris.'

'I don't need an hour to get dressed,' Pris exclaims.

Drow chuckles. 'Tonight's dinner is a formal meal and is timed to begin directly after your meeting with your uncle. I think an hour will be almost enough time for you to dress.'

The shock on Pris's face makes me laugh too.

'You might well laugh, young Snake, but I requested a suit of formal wear be laid out on your bed.'

Pris smirks.

Okay, now this isn't as much fun. 'Please tell me the outfit doesn't have a fancy collar.'

Drow tries to keep a straight face but gives up. 'No, I got the message when one of the servants found a collar in the pot plant. I have tried to keep it plain and in our family colours.'

'Thanks, unc,' I say, rising to my feet.

Drow grimaces. 'I will never get used to this modern language.'

'We'll see you at dinner,' I tell Percival as I move to join Pris.

At the door, we are met by Dinian. 'Perhaps I can accompany you back to the royal accommodation, Priscilla. I believe you are with Princess Petunia, and my suite is next to hers.'

I roll my eyes. In spite of everyone else calling her Pris, Dinian uses her full name as if it's a privilege she has granted only to him.

'Thanks for the offer, but I'm going to wait while Snake changes, then we'll head to my grandmother's room together.'

Dinian turns to me and takes me in as if it's the first time we have met. His lips curl in almost disgust, but he is too well-mannered to show his true feelings. I raise an eyebrow, daring him to say something, but he schools his face into a polite mask before turning back to Pris.

'As you wish, Pricilla. Please, if I can be of any further assistance to you, you only have to ask.'

I want to tell him Pris will never need his help, but I'm wise enough not to speak for her, aware it will only get me into trouble. Still, I smirk when Pris tells him, 'I can't imagine I will need your help, but I'll keep your offer in mind.'

She slips her hand into mine, holding me back so Dinian can leave first. I wonder if Pris is worried about him following us. There is something off about that guy.

We walk in silence back to my suite, and Pris waits in the living room while I go and change. True to his word, Drow has picked out an almost-black dark-green tailcoat and a slightly lighter-green waistcoat. I have a pristine white shirt to go under them. The top part of the outfit is finished off with a bow tie, which I shove into my pocket to put on before the meal. I send a mental thank you to Drow, as these clothes are positively modern compared to my last outfit.

For the bottom half, I have black knee-length boots to go over stretchy, fitted black pants. I study the pants, which are almost like thick leggings. I can't wear them. They're going to be too revealing.

There's a knock on the door. 'What's taking so long?' Pris calls through.

'Um... hold on, just coming.'

I drag on the pants. I can hold my hands over the front to protect my modesty until we're seated. I pull on the boots, then check myself in the mirror, expecting everything to be on show. The pants are very discreet—so discreet, in fact, that I pull out the waistband to check everything is still as it should be.

I chuckle in relief.

'What's going on in there?'

'Nothing.' I tuck myself back in and run a comb through my hair. It has grown in the past few weeks and could really do with a cut. Perhaps I can—

'Snake!'

No time. Grabbing my jacket, I open the door.

'Mmm,' Pris says, grinning. 'Don't you look smart. Hold on, shouldn't there be a... um... bulge about there?' She points, a cheeky grin on her face.

'I could tell you about that, but then I would have to shoot you,' I quip back.

Pris nods solemnly. 'So, magic it is, then.'

I laugh. 'Come on, let's go and see what Victorian wonder they have for you.'

That soon wipes the grin from her face.

Time is ticking on, so we walk briskly to Princess Petunia's suite. Pris barges in without knocking, only to stop in the doorway. I pile in behind her, almost pushing her over.

'Oh, Grandmother. I didn't think you'd be here.'

'I am surprised you took the time to think of me at all, given that I have had no word from you since you rushed from the court this morning,' a tart voice responds.

Pris colours, and I know she is embarrassed rather than angered because her eye doesn't have that telltale glint.

'I'm sorry, Grandmother. I've been busy working on our petition, and now I've got to dress for my audience with the King.'

The princess's gaze turns to me. 'Are you presenting your petition now?'

'No, Snake is here to accompany me.' When her grandmother does not respond, she adds, 'Because of the attacks on the castle.' When the silence continues, Pris goes for a more formal approach. 'Princess Petunia, may I introduce Snake of the Fieth Clan. Snake, this is my grandmother, Princess Petunia.'

I bow. 'It is an honour to meet you.' When I rise, I detect the tug of a smile at the corner of the princess's mouth, but it is gone before I can be certain.

'I am pleased to meet you. Your grandfather and great-uncle are good friends of mine.' She turns her attention back to Pris. 'Lady Susan is waiting in your room. You had best hurry and get ready while I entertain your friend.'

Pris throws a worried glance over her shoulder as she heads to what must be her room. I smile back at her, showing more confidence than I'm feeling.

'Take a seat, young man. I will not bite.'

I do as she bids, although I'm not sure a bite is the worst to be endured from this woman. The keen-eyed gaze she sends my way sets my stomach churning, and I'm ready to tell her anything she wants just for a moment's relief.

'So, Percival tells me you are quite the musician. Do you intend to become a bard like your grandfather?'

Oh my god, is this a take on 'What are your prospects?' and 'What are your intentions towards my granddaughter?' I hope my face shows nothing of my internal shock. 'Although I love music, I intend to study physics at university. I have an interest in how magic operates in the World Above. I'd like to do everything I can to ensure the flow remains strong and perhaps even remove our reliance on the dragons for help.'

As I say the words, I wonder if any of my plans are still feasible. Magic is waning, and recent events have me questioning whether or not I will ever be able to return home.

Princess Petunia's eyes narrow, and I squirm a little in my seat.

'Is that a job? Can you make money from it?'

My brows draw together in a frown. Mum and I had never had much money, so thinking about my future in terms of how much I can make is a bit of an anomaly. I won't lie about this though, not even to make Pris's family happy. 'I've no idea, you know. Mum discussed it with my uncle, and the gnomes were going to support my research, so I should be fine.'

I wait for her to say something along the lines of 'How will you support a family?'

She surprises me when she says, 'Your family are renowned for looking after the magical community. It is pleasing to see you take after them. Have you thought about asking for sponsorship from the Unseelie Court for your work? I am sure King Maddox would be interested.'

I study the princess, trying to assess whether she has an ulterior motive for bringing this up. Does she want me to become part of the court? Or does she think Pris will be likely to visit more often if we are aligned with the King?

Before I have considered her motives, Princess Petunia laughs. It is more like a bark, but it contains real mirth. 'You have much of Drow in you, Snake. I meant nothing more than to say you could have a position in the court and that it might benefit your studies and your purse to follow this up. It won't hurt that Drow is one of the King's chief advisors and that you are... friends with Priscilla.'

'Pris,' I correct automatically, and the princess laughs

again. She should laugh more often. She is so much less severe when she does.

'Yes, I should remember that.'

We fall silent for a while, and as I fidget a little in my chair, I consider some possible conversation topics to make things less awkward. I come up empty, but it doesn't matter, as Susan soon slips through the bedroom door holding a brush and a hair tie.

'Pris is almost ready,' she informs us. 'She asked me to come out and do something with your hair.'

I blanch. 'You're going to tie it back?'

'Yes, I can do that. Unless of course you would rather restyle it yourself.'

'Restyle it,' I repeat. 'You mean cut it?'

Now Susan and Princess Petunia are laughing, but it's the princess who answers. 'My boy, we are in a magical bubble separated from the human world. The use of magic is not forbidden here. If your hair is not what you want it to be, just envision what you want, send some magic, and it will sort itself out.'

Are they joking? They don't seem to be. I try to imagine my hair as it is after a trim, and I send out a little magic. My hair tingles, and I run my hand through it. It feels shorter, but as there's no mirror, so I have no way of knowing if it's an improvement.

'Much better,' Princess Petunia tells me. 'You are quite the dashing young creature now.'

I'm mortified to feel heat rising from under my collar, and I hope I'm not blushing.

'Indeed,' Susan adds. 'I'll just go and finish sorting Pr—'

The door behind her opens, and Pris, a vision in dusky pink, enters the room. The floaty dress she wears is off the shoulder with a fitted bodice and a bustle thing at the back—

at least, I think that's what it's called, from memory. Pris's hair is up, and the only jewellery she wears is a tiara.

'Wow.' The word escapes my lips before I can put a thought to it.

Pris blushes. 'You like it?'

'It's....'

'What Snake means to say is, it is perfect,' Princess Petunia finishes for me. 'Now, you two had best run along. King Maddox hates it when creatures are late.'

'Thank you, Susan.' Pris gives her old nanny a quick hug while I rise. 'Will I see you at dinner, Grandmother?'

The princess nods.

'Good, I have a lot to fill you in on,' Pris says as she takes my hand and leads me to the door.

'It was nice to meet you,' I say to the princess.

She grins at me. 'Good of you to say so,' she laughs as Pris closes the door behind us.

'What was that about?' she asks as we head down the corridor towards the stairs.

'Nothing,' I say, not knowing if Pris has the bandwidth to deal with my conversation with her grandmother with everything else on her mind.

'You'll tell me later though, right?'

I sigh. 'Of course. Do you want me to come in with you when you see the King?'

'No, I'll be fine,' she assures me. 'If you could wait outside though, I might need some moral support when I come out.'

'Heart mentioned there's a music room across the way from the reception hall. I can wait there for you.'

We come to a stop outside the door to the King's personal study. Pris takes a deep breath, then knocks.

A command comes from inside. 'Enter.'

'Wish me luck,' Pris says before taking a deep breath.

'Luck,' I say as she reaches for the door handle.

I watch her disappear before crossing the foyer to the music room. Wow, they have a grand piano. My eyes slide over the array of guitars and lutes—and even a saxophone—placed around the walls, all shining in the late evening light.

Today it's the piano that calls to me. I sit down and let my fingers glide over the ivory keys as I play a couple of scales to loosen my fingers. The sound is deep and resonates around the room, cocooning me in a bubble of music.

'Ah, you are a court musician like your grandfather. A noble calling, but is it what is right for Priscilla?'

The voice comes from behind me, but I recognise it instantly.

'Dinian, how lovely to see you,' I say as I launch into 'Creep' by Radiohead. It's a message to him to leave me alone, but he either doesn't know the song or is pretty thick skinned, as he doesn't move. It seems I will have an audience while I wait for Pris.

How bad can this be? I ask myself as I open the door to King Maddox's study. Play at being princess for a day, get the King to agree to help Queen Ariana, then I can be done with it.

The study is darkened in the evening light. There is only one lamp lit, and it sits to the left of him on the desk. The King sits a little straighter as I enter, the lamp throwing shadows across his drawn face. Behind him stands the Chancellor, hands loosely clasped in front of his dark robes. He reminds me a little of a pointy-eared Professor Snape from *Harry Potter*.

'Ah, Priscilla, I see from your dress you have come to see things my way,' King Maddox says as I drop into a curtsey in front of his desk. 'No need for these formalities between us. Please, take a seat.'

There is every need for these… formalities, as he calls them. I want to keep this man at arm's-length while I neither know nor trust him. Standing in front of the desk, I unconsciously mirror the Chancellor's stance. 'If this is to be a private chat, perhaps the Chancellor could be excused.' I really don't want anyone to witness what I say to the King. Not least because it will be easier to deny what I have agreed to later.

'He and I have no secrets… but… if you insist.'

'I do.'

The Chancellor sends me a hard stare as if he's trying to assess my motives, then bows his head to the King and leaves via the side door. Once we are alone, I take a seat in front of the desk. The King leans back and waits for me to speak. I need to choose my words carefully. I don't want to lie to him because I might get caught out later. On the other hand, I don't want to sign myself up for something for the rest of my life either.

'I agree to be your consort for the time being, but only until I can speak with my parents.'

A smile tugs at King Maddox's lips. 'You don't trust me?'

This time I have no problem with being completely honest. 'I don't know you, so I have no idea if I can trust you.'

His eyebrows rise, and that almost smile is still there. It's almost as if he is enjoying my discomfort.

'Before I commit fully to anything, I need to understand Mum and Dad's intentions for me. They have always been involved in planning my future, and this never came up.'

This time he nods a slow, thoughtful nod. 'I can agree to that.'

'And in return you will listen to our petition?' I don't want him to forget his promise.

'I only agree to listen—'

'And you will take into account the best interests of the court.'

This time his frown is sterner. 'If you will let me finish.'

'I'm sorry, it's just this is very important to me.'

'I appreciate that, but you must understand that you will be asking me to leave my court in a time of great peril—'

'To try and lessen that danger.'

King Maddox glares at me.

'I'm sorry,' I mumble. 'It won't happen again.'

'I would look at things a little more favourably if my succession were assured, but alas, it is not.'

He can't be thinking of me as his successor, can he? Wait, I'm sure someone mentioned the court is always ruled by a King.

'Have you named your successor?'

'I have. It is to be Lord Dinian.'

Of course, the one person I have met here who makes my skin crawl. 'It's good that your succession is assured. You'll have someone to look after the court while you are away.'

King Maddox continues to stare at me.

'It is good, isn't it?' I ask, a little less certain.

'The creatures of my court will acknowledge him as my successor when I formalise it, but many think I could do better for them by choosing someone who is a little less... self—' He clears his throat. 'Someone who has their best interests at heart.'

He could definitely do better. 'Do they have someone in mind?'

'They do. Petunia's boy, Yves.'

Petunia has a son? I have another uncle? How many more family members are going to be sprung on me?

I hope my thoughts don't show on my face, but the twitch of King Maddox's lips tells me my expression has betrayed me.

'Then why not have him? Is he unsuitable in some way?'

'No, except for the problem of Petunia's role in the succession of the Seelie Court. Were she ever to be forgiven, he would be in the line of succession for the World Below. And then... there's Tomas's wish. He wanted a future for Dinian. I have been thinking about it, and Dinian's position would be stronger if I could announce you and he were betrothed.'

'Absolutely not! No way is that ever going to happen.' The words are out of my mouth before my brain can react to the King's manipulation.

King Maddox leans back in his chair and watches me through hooded eyes. 'Think about it. Not only would it strengthen his position, but I'm sure you could round off some of his rough edges.'

This is the total opposite of what I came in here to achieve. My idea of a short alliance has somehow slipped into a lifelong commitment—and it could be a long life.

'I notice all the benefits are for Dinian and the Unseelie Court. What about me? What would I gain from this?'

'An elevated position in my court. Surely that is enough.'

Flabbergasted. The word pops in my mind and sticks there. I never really knew what it meant before, but now....

'An elevated position? I don't want to be a part of your court—or any court, for that matter.' I spit the words out. 'All I want is to get my parents' names cleared and return to my old life.'

'I see I have taken you by surprise—'

'That's an understatement,' I mutter.

'Perhaps it is best if you take some time, mull things over, and let me know your decision... say, in the next couple of days.'

'I will not change my mind.' I rise to my feet, struggling to contain my emotions. I need to get out of this room and away from the King. 'Will you hear our petition after dinner?'

'I will, as we agreed. But bear in mind, I will not be in a position to consider leaving until things at court are settled.'

My fists clench, and for a moment I imagine myself punching that smug, self-satisfied smirk from his face.

Instead, I don't say anything further as I calmly walk to the door. I can't believe my own flesh and blood is blackmailing me into becoming betrothed to save his court. And to a creature like Dinian!

The door thuds behind me. At least this time I haven't stormed from his presence. I close my eyes and try to calm myself a little as the sounds of a waltz being played on piano come from across the hall. Ah, Snake. My jaw unclenches. He will know what to do. He always has a more balanced perspective than I do.

Before I reach the door, Dinian appears from nowhere, blocking my path. 'How did it go?'

His smile and the triumph sparkling in his eyes hit me. He knew all along. He's been a part of this.

Shooting him a withering look, I say, 'Stay away from me, you... you.... Argh!' I push him aside, which gives me a small amount of satisfaction, and open the door.

Snake is still playing as I enter the music room. I slide onto the seat beside him and lay my head on his shoulder.

His fingers continue to dance smoothly across the keys. 'So, it didn't go well.'

I shake my head, and his fingers pause. 'No, keep playing,' I whisper. 'Dinian is outside, and I don't want him to hear what we're saying.'

The music starts again. 'What is it?'

'King Maddox says that unless I become betrothed to his heir, he cannot leave the court.'

Snake's body tenses, although you wouldn't know it from the music. 'Who is his heir?'

'It's... um—'

'Let me guess… it's Dinian, isn't it?'

I don't respond.

'Of course it is. And that's why he's hanging around. He was waiting for you to come out. I can't believe the one person I would hate to see you with is the one person you must play up to.'

'What?' I ask, sitting upright.

He laughs bitterly, and his tone is resigned. 'You have to play along, Pris. It's all part of the same game we were playing before. You have to find some way to make the King think you are on his side until we have Queen Ariana back on her feet.'

'I don't. We can find another way,' I insist.

'Perhaps if we had time, we could, but time isn't on our side—and I suspect they are better at this game than we are. We have to play along with this in the same way you played along with King Maddox's first demand.'

Frustration is curling like a serpent in my belly. 'Where does it stop, Snake? Where do I draw the line and say I am not prepared to do this anymore?'

He stops playing, then half turns and draws me into his arms. Speaking close to my ear, he says, 'When it gets too much for you, that's when. There is no way you are *ever* marrying that prat.'

I lean into him. He smells of lavender and… Snake. With his arms around me, I am home, and I can't believe everything is conspiring to keep us apart when all I want to do is be with him.

'Do you think you can do it?' he asks. 'Because if you can't, we will find another way.'

I stay where I am, wishing the world away. Then the gong sounds for dinner, and I know I can't stay here forever.

'I can try,' I say. 'But I'm not promising I won't kill him before this is over.'

Snake's chuckle rumbles in his chest. 'Back at ya.'

CHAPTER 9

The Formal Appeal

When I step out of my room, I am surprised to find a servant waiting by the door. When I ask him why he's here, I'm even more surprised by his response.

'The King requests your presence. He has decided to receive your petition before dinner.'

My gosh. We are not ready. My hands shake. My eyes slide to the table where our petition is laid, all ready to be given to the King.

I breathe in through my nose and out through my mouth until the shaking stops. Picking up the documents, I straighten my shoulders. 'All right, lead on.'

When we arrive at the public reception rooms, the servant tells me Drow is already with the King, then he leaves me outside the King's study. I tug at my jacket, checking I am presentable enough. Dinian saunters my way, followed by Pris and Snake a few steps behind.

'Have you any idea what this is about?' Pris asks.

'I believe we are to meet with the King before dinner,' I say.

A frown draws Pris's brows together. 'I wonder why he's moving things up. After our meeting earlier, I can't believe it means anything good.'

I move closer to Pris and Snake as they entwine fingers. My move was meant as a sign of support, but I realise it isolates Dinian, making him an outsider. I cannot say I feel guilty about that. There is something about the boy I do not like.

'I'm surprised King Maddox is still going through the motions of considering your request. The attack today showed how vulnerable we are. The Chancellor is concerned that too many more such attacks will pull the court out of its time and space,' Dinian says.

I study him a little more closely. There is a tone in his voice I cannot quite place. Is it disdain? And is it for the King, or for us?

'Perhaps that wouldn't be such a bad thing,' Pris mutters. 'Not only is this court stuck in the past, but it's also out of touch with the world it sits within.'

Dinian turns a cold gaze her way. 'Do you mean the magical world, or the human world?'

Pris glares back. 'Both.'

Looking from one to the other, it is clear there is something going on here I am not aware of. With everything else happening, I do not have time to sort out their spat. Instead I turn to Pris, hoping to add a little to her understanding of the creatures who live here. 'You need to understand that many of the Unseelie Court's creatures have been persecuted, and to them this is a safe haven. Many find the lack of change here a comfort when so many other things in their lives are uncertain.'

'True,' Dinian says, 'but Priscilla is right about one thing —we could do with modernising our court. Perhaps allow a larger council than the King has at the moment.'

I bristle at the lad's comments. I am aware he merely voices the impatience of youth, but I take offence at his criticism of King Maddox. 'When you are King, you can make all the changes you want. At the moment you are still yet to be formally named heir, so—'

'So I should keep my mouth shut and offer my support.' Dinian's lips are pursed, like he has sucked on a lemon, and his voice drips disdain.

He turns back to Pris, and his demeanour changes. He smiles and winks. 'I'm sure you agree with me though, don't you, Princess. Things will change when it's our turn.'

Snake's jaw tenses. Pris's grip on his fingers tightens as if in warning, and she mutters something under her breath.

Dinian chuckles. What is going on between the three of them? I raise an eyebrow in question. Snake shakes his head and mouths, 'Later.'

I turn my back on Dinian, dismissing him. It is time for us to focus on the task ahead. My voice is firm when I say, 'We must concentrate on the meeting. It is all part of the same problem anyway—freeing the Queen, which will help bring magic back to full strength, then she can put a stop to these attacks on the Unseelie Court.'

'We're with you on that,' Pris says.

Snake is strangely quiet.

'Snake, what is it?' Pris asks.

'I'm wondering about something. If the dragons are so powerful, why haven't they forced King Maddox to help?'

How do I explain the complex relationship between dragons and creatures to someone in the few minutes we have here?

'Dragons are.... Let us say they hold themselves apart from all other beings. They have immense power and could prob-ably rule creatures and humans if they so desired, but they do not.

Dinian perks up at the mention of dragons. 'I bet there is a way to harness their power,' he says almost as if to himself, sending a cold shiver down my spine. I pity the dragon who has to bond with him. I angle my body to cut Dinian from the conversation and continue.

'Although dragons can compel those they call lesser beings to do their bidding, their one guiding principle appears to be to never use their magic to force another being to go against their nature.'

'Not even if magic were to disappear?' Snake asks.

'It appears not,' I confirm.

'We could do with a little less freedom and a bit more governance,' Dinian interjects.

'You want the dragons to lead us?' Pris asks.

'What? No! I meant our court could do with a strong leader—one who is not afraid of imposing his will.'

'A minute ago you were saying the King needs more councilors. Now you're saying he should be more of a dictator,' Pris says, and I am surprised by the scorn in her voice.

'They are not mutually exclusive, my dear Priscilla. Having more advisors does not prevent the King from making a decision, then enforcing it. At the moment this limbo helps no one.'

I am a little disconcerted at finding myself partially agreeing with Dinian. I may not like the lad, but his point about leaving the court in limbo is a valid one.

'Well, let's hope he decides in our favour this evening,' Pris says.

Dinian's brows draw downwards. 'I'm not sure that it is in the best interests of the court to have the King absent when we are under attack.'

'Then it's a good thing you're not invited to this meeting,' Snake snaps.

A smirk tugs at Dinian's lips. 'Oh, but I am.'

Snake and Pris lock eyes, and something passes between them. A sense of unease ripples through me. I wish they had time to tell me what is going on. Before I can ask, the door to the King's study opens, and Drow appears.

'King Maddox will see you all now,' he tells us before standing aside to allow us to enter.

As we cross the corridor, I overhear Dinian muttering, 'Of course the gnome is here. He's virtually running the court. I don't know how Maddox can let a non-elf have so much power.'

I ball my fists as I lead everyone in. Catching Drow's eye, I have no idea whether he has heard or not, but from the cold stare he gives Dinian, I'm pretty sure there is no love lost between them.

There are not enough chairs for everyone to sit, so I stand behind one. Pris and Percival join me, but Dinian slides into the other chair on this side of the desk. The rather dour creature standing behind the King frowns down at him and says, 'Lord Dinian, I had no idea you were one of the petitioners.'

I bite my lip to hide my smirk as the smarmy elf realises his mistake. He rises and follows Drow around the desk. As my uncle takes his position on the other side of the King, Dinian is forced to stand beside him, even further from the action. The scowl on his face tells everyone what he thinks about being relegated to second string.

He stares daggers at me, and I get the impression he believes us to be in some sort of tug-of-war over Pris. Perhaps in some ways we are, but as soon as we get out of this joint, any claim he may believe he has over her will disappear.

Once everyone is in position, Chancellor Rimould clears his throat and begins proceedings. 'Your Majesty, may I present Princess Priscilla, Snake of the Fieth Clan, and Percival of the Wyld Woods as ambassadors sent from the court of Queen Ariana. They request to present a petition on her behalf.'

'Welcome to my court,' King Maddox says as if we haven't already been in his presence today.

Percival takes a step forward, bows, then holds out our document. Everyone in the room seems to hold a collective breath while the King leans back in his chair and stares at Pris. Beside me, Pris tenses, and I suspect she is gearing up to give her uncle a piece of her mind.

I reach out and place a hand on her arm, hoping to remind her we need to show a little restraint here. King Maddox's eyes drop to my hand, then he raises his eyes to meet mine. In the past I would have removed my hand when challenged in this way, but Pris and I have come too far for me to be cowed by the King. I stand tall under his scrutiny, and my hand remains where it is.

Unfortunately, Pris witnesses our silent communication, and it must be the final straw for her. She shrugs off my hand and joins Percival. Taking the scroll from him, she glares at her uncle.

'We had a deal,' she forces out through gritted teeth. 'I am ready to stand by your side before the court tonight. Now it is your turn. Take the petition.' She slams the document down on the desk.

Honestly, Pris is one part magnificent and two parts downright scary when she's like this. The battle of wills shifts between uncle and niece, and I don't like King Maddox's chances of coming out on top.

Chancellor Rimould reaches over and takes the scroll, saving face for both Pris and the King. He unrolls the parchment and scans the document before sending a sidelong glance towards Drow. Rolling it back up, he says, 'Thank you for presenting your argument so succinctly, and so comprehensively. I am sure the King will want a little time to consider his response.'

King Maddox, still locked into a staring match with Pris, grunts something that the Chancellor takes to be assent.

Percival reaches out and touches Pris on the hand. 'It is time to leave.'

'No, Priscilla stays,' King Maddox barks. 'She promised to attend court by my side, and attend she shall.'

Percival does not move. For a moment I think Pris is going to refuse, then she turns to the sprite. 'It's all right, Percival. You take Snake through to the dining room, and I'll speak with you both after we've eaten.'

Pursing his lips, Percival answers, 'If you are sure?'

She nods before turning a pleading glance to me. I smile, understanding it will be easier for her if we do as the King asks. 'Come on, Percival. You might not be starving, but I am.'

I lead the way out, remembering to walk backwards, Percival at my side. Once we reach the door, we bow, and the King nods his dismissal. I'm not completely happy about leaving Pris alone in there, but I have to trust that she knows what she is doing.

When the guard closes the door behind us, I blow out a long, slow breath. 'That was intense.'

Percival nods as he studies the door. 'Something else was going on in there.' He leads me across the corridor. 'Do you know what it is?'

I want to tell Percival about the King's demands, but Pris told me in confidence. Still, I don't like keeping Percival in the dark—we're a team. 'Pris and her uncle are having a disagreement about her role at court.'

Percival strokes his chin. 'Interesting. Given that Pris

cannot be in line to the Unseelie throne, I wonder what....' He stops stroking and raises surprised eyes. 'He cannot.'

'I think he can,' I say.

Shaking his head, Percival reiterates, 'He cannot. She is in line to the Seelie throne. There are protocols.'

'Are you sure?'

Percival simply stares at me until I catch on. Of course there are protocols.

I grin. 'We should tell Pris. She will be so relieved.'

'We will later. It may not do her any good, though, if King Maddox is using her as a bargaining chip.'

I shrug. 'She's already considering playing along for the moment, but I'm sure she'd feel much better if she knew she had an out.'

'Come, we had best head in to dinner,' Percival says as some of the court begin to drift into the dining room beside the music room.

I place a hand on his shoulder. 'Percival, why would King Maddox choose Dinian as his heir? He doesn't seem to be an outcast or have the creatures' best interests at heart, and he also doesn't appear to be close to the king.'

'He is the nephew of King Maddox's husband.'

I nod. 'But I thought the position of King was not hereditary here.'

'It is not, but it does tend to be passed on to close family. Dinian has been here a couple of the times when Eleanora and I visited. He was always charming and the apple of his uncle's eye. I believe Tomas convinced King Maddox that he would be able to breach the gap between the Seelie and Unseelie courts, as he lived in both worlds.'

'I didn't know the court here wished to reconcile.'

'According to Drow, they do not. What they do want is for the two courts to be on an equal footing. And to do that, they want to change the view that the Unseelie Court is comprised of outcasts. King Maddox has taken Tomas's advice to heart and believes the best way for the two courts to live in harmony is to place someone who is not an outcast on the throne.'

'Ah, so their way of stopping the attacks on the court is to go, "See, we're not so different"?'

'Something like that.'

'I don't see it changing the minds of creatures like Bernais. And I don't see Dinian being a fit ruler—he prances around like a peacock. And I'm not sure he has time for anyone who's not an elf. And, most of all, I don't like the way he looks at Pris like she's something to be devoured.'

Percival grunts, and I take that for agreement. 'He is showing a lot of interest in her.'

My hands clench into fists at my sides at the thought of Dinian and Pris spending any time together.

Percival chuckles. 'Are you worried he might sweep her off her feet?'

I laugh, but it sounds hollow.

Am I worried Pris might be attracted to Dinian? To be honest, I'm pretty sure she doesn't like him. What I'm worried about is us not being able to spend much time together while this charade continues. What I'm sure of is that Pris and I have an intense attraction, but with everything going on, we haven't had time to explore what that means.

I run a hand through my hair. If only I were certain of where we stand and could count on us having a future once this is over. Or maybe if Dinian weren't continuously niggling me....

'I was joking, Snake.'

Percival's voice jolts me out of my reverie.

'I know, Percival. It's just.... Never mind. Let's go find the others before I talk myself into believing he might just be able to do that.'

Keeping my face impassive and my back to the door, I wait for Snake and Percival to leave. The snick of the latch tells me they're gone. My palms are slick with sweat, but I rein in my nerves and attempt to appear calm.

'What now?'

I expect King Maddox to answer, but it is his Chancellor who does the honours.

'We will review your petition—although I suspect Drow is fully aware of what it contains—and then decide on how to respond.'

I close my eyes for a moment, wondering if there is a way to have the King step up and do the right thing. I open them again to find King Maddox smiling at me, and his smile offers no comfort.

'Of course, you have it within your power to influence the outcome of that process,' King Maddox says.

I resist looking at Dinian. I've a sneaking suspicion he is in on the King's plan and is happy to get on board with it.

There is a flicker of exasperation in Drow's eyes, and he sneaks a sidelong glance at Rimould, who is too tense and tight-lipped to notice.

'Perhaps we can leave that discussion until later,' Drow says, and I find myself absurdly grateful for his interference. Turning to the King, he asks, 'Would you like me to summarise their petition for you, Your Majesty?'

A brief look of displeasure crosses King Maddox's face, but when he turns to Drow, he presents his usual mask. 'I think that can also wait until later. I believe we will soon be expected at dinner.'

Drow checks his watch. 'We have a few minutes, sire.'

'Very well. Dinian, perhaps you can entertain Princess Priscilla awhile.' The King gestures to two chairs and a table tucked in behind the door.

'But—'

'It is in your best interests to get to know each other.'

I'm not quite sure who the King directed this at, Dinian or me, but I'm sure I have no desire to know the elf any better than I already do.

'I'm fine,' I said. 'I'll read a book.'

Dinian watches the King for a few minutes before returning his attention to me. He clearly wants to be a part of their discussion, but he also doesn't want to miss an opportunity to spend time alone with me.

'Go,' the King says, and Dinian's decision is made for him.

While the three older creatures gather around the scroll, Dinian joins me at the other end of the room. Instead of sitting, I feign interest in the books on the shelf.

'Can I perhaps suggest something suitable for you to read?' Dinian offers.

Never in my life have I needed anyone to tell me what to read. A quick glance at the King tells me he is watching us, so I bite back my snarky retort and say with saccharine sweetness, 'And just what is it you would suggest I read?'

The sarcasm was lost on Dinian. Reaching past me, he chooses a book and places it in my hands.

'I think you will enjoy this. It should give you some guidance on how you should behave while here in the Unseelie Court.'

I look down and find myself holding a copy of Jane Austen's *Sense and Sensibility*. Dinian is attempting to make a statement with his book choice, but I'm at a loss as to what it is.

'I'm not quite sure what you want me to take away from this, Dinian.'

He smiles at me, and I'm sure he thinks it is a charming smile, but it's a bit too practiced for my tastes. 'We expect a certain standard of behaviour at court, and I am sure you can take some cues from this.'

A laugh escapes before I can hold it back, and Dinian's charming expression turns sour.

'Have you read this?' I ask.

'Well, no, but it is set in a genteel time when women knew their place,' he blusters.

I place the book back on the shelf and turn away from him. Let him wonder about Jane Austen's true message—that women should not constrain their behaviour according to societal expectations. I take a seat.

He sits opposite and leans in rather too close. 'You shouldn't reject your uncle's proposal out of hand. Together you and I could be a force to be reckoned with in both the Unseelie and Seelie Courts. And if you showed yourself to be a willing partner, I might be persuaded to ignore your little flings with the lower creatures.'

I can't move. In my mind, I'm raising my hand and slapping Dinian across the face, but I don't move a muscle. He can't possibly be serious, can he? Does he actually think I'm in this for the power? And that Snake is a passing fancy? Is he so totally wrapped up in his own world, he thinks I'll go along with this?

I'm about to tell him what I think of his suggestion when a voice behind me interrupts. 'You two seem to be having... fun, but I am afraid the staff are waiting dinner for us.'

Rimould's voice is stiff and formal, and do I detect a note of displeasure? I risk a quick peek and find him watching Dinian, lips curled in disdain. I quickly look away. Have we got a friend there? Or at least an ally when it comes to Dinian?

Carefully schooling my face into a mask of bland courtesy,

I ignore the elf who intends to spend the rest of his life with me and slip around the Chancellor.

As I wait for the King to join us, Drow places himself in front of the desk. I suspect it's because he doesn't want me to see what they were working on. How can he be so on our side one minute and on the King's the next? It must be difficult. If I didn't know that he believed it was best for King Maddox to help the Queen, I'd be suspicious of his motives.

I'm relieved when the King offers his arm to escort me into dinner. Dinian follows close behind, ahead of Rimould and Drow. I guess it's important to him to show his superior position in court.

When we reach the top table, I am sandwiched between the King and Dinian. My appetite has disappeared. Dinian makes a show of pulling out my chair, and as I sit, he pulls his own chair closer to mine. This should be a fun night.

Once our party is seated, servants start bringing in the food. While one of them places a platter in front of me, I risk a glance at Snake's table. He is sitting beside his grandfather and opposite Percival, with his back to me. Percival catches me staring and smiles. I take that to mean 'you can do this,' and I straighten my spine as I smile back.

I can do this. I mean, it's only for tonight and perhaps tomorrow. How hard can it be?

CHAPTER 10

A Brick Wall

lthough I'm surrounded by friends, family, and well-wishers, without Pris by my side, I feel as if I'm eating alone. I took a seat with my back to the royal table because I didn't want to face her sitting with him. Now I'm wishing I hadn't been so petty, because I want to see her, and I worry she may need my support before the evening is done.

'Bunch over,' a voice says close to my ear.

Heart digs me in the ribs. 'You heard the lady. Move over so she can sit.'

We all shuffle along by one seat, and Lady Susan sits beside me.

'What's up?' I ask her, and she raises an eyebrow in response.

'Well, I'm pretty sure it's not great etiquette to ask us to bunch over,' I say with a smile.

Susan laughs. 'Would you believe me if I said things are less formal in the court at the moment?'

It's my turn to raise a quizzical brow.

'All right. I wanted to warn you guys.'

'Why not speak to Pris?'

Sorrow briefly crosses Susan's face before she tucks it away behind her court mask. 'I don't think she's forgiven me for the things I didn't tell her.'

I place a comforting hand on Susan's arm. 'She will. Just give her time.'

'I hope so. I think it might help when she finds out I've managed to buy some normal clothes for you and her.'

Now I'm surprised. 'How did you manage that? I thought we were in lockdown.'

'We are, but I still have my mobile. My sister and her family are in Inverness, so I got her to shop for me. Your clothes arrived with the food delivery today.' She eyes me critically. 'I had to guess your size. I hope everything fits.'

I want to hug her. I've never been much interested in clothes, but when you have to primp up every day for court, jeans and a T-shirt begin looking mighty good.

'Thank you.'

'You're welcome.'

The conversation fades as a server removes our plates and another one lays the next course in front of us. I expected it to be a main after the Waldorf salad appetiser, but I'm surprised to find a sliver of salmon on a bed of green beans. Yet another server drizzles some lemony-scented sauce over top. When they leave we're free to speak again.

'You didn't make all this effort to tell me about clothes,' I say before my mouth closes round a forkful of salmon. 'Yum, this is excellent.'

'It should be. Our chef ran a Michelin-starred restaurant before returning to the court.'

Susan's face softens as she talks about the chef, and I wonder if there is something more there. I want to ask, but I don't want her to become distracted. She finishes her fish before speaking again.

'There are rumours amongst the servants and ladies-in-waiting that the King is going to betroth Pris to Dinian.'

My jaw hardens at the mention of the King's manipulation.

'Ah, I can tell from your reaction that he has spoken to her already.'

Before answering Susan, I sneak a quick glance to make sure Pris is okay. She is nibbling at her food and looks quite miserable. Dinian leans towards her and says something in her ear. Smiling wanly, she says something back and continues eating. I will her to look at me so I can send her some courage, but she doesn't.

'He has,' I admit.

'And I assume being Pris, she rejected the King outright.'

I chuckle. She knows Pris so well. 'Yes, but he would not take no for an answer. She is "taking some time" to consider her options.'

Susan nods. 'The King wants stability in the court, and for some reason, Dinian has convinced him his marrying Pris will bring that.'

I let her words sink in before blurting out, 'What? This was Dinian's idea? How do you know?'

'Those of us in service to the court know almost everything that goes on within these wards. Also, I've made a point of keeping up on the gossip, and I've been updating Princess Petunia on court goings-on.'

Out of the corner of my eye, I survey the high table. Princess Petunia is chatting with my uncle. They keep glancing up as if to check no one is paying any attention to them. I wonder what they're talking about that they want to keep secret.

'And she needs to be kept up on what is going on because?'

'It's a good thing you're not at court often, Snake, because you'd be eaten alive.'

'Thanks,' I say dryly.

'No, that's a good thing—keeping out of the politics.'

'I'll take your word for it. So why does the princess want to know what's happening?'

'Princess Petunia has been the Unseelie Court's unofficial ambassador to the World Below for years.' Susan's voice has dropped so low, I have to lean in to hear what she's saying. 'Mostly she works through the witches, Eleanora, Euphemia, and Eugenia. They've been carrying messages back and forth for her for years.'

'How have they gotten away with that?' I ask.

'They are responsible for ensuring the wellbeing of the land and the creatures in their areas, and they have quite a bit of leeway in how they do that.'

'I guess that makes sense. But it doesn't explain why you're gathering information for the princess.'

'I was getting to that. Petunia was once one of King Maddox's advisors, but she pressed too hard for him to help her sister, and he cut her out. Now she has had to resort to finding out what's going on by other methods and using her influence with Drow and Rimould to steer the court.'

I chuckle. 'This sounds like something out of a spy novel.'

Susan smiles. 'It sort of feels that way too.'

We wait for another change of food before Susan gets to her real reason for joining me.

'I need you to convince Pris to play along with the betrothal—'

'But—'

'She has to, Snake. Not only will it keep the King happy, but she needs to keep onside with Dinian.'

'We've already planned to do that, Susan. Especially

because King Maddox has said he won't do anything about our petition unless she does.'

Susan blinks a couple of times, then stares at me. 'I didn't know that. It makes it all the more important the King thinks she is going along with things.'

'If I can, I'll weigh in, but you can't expect me to push too hard. I don't want her to end up being forced into marrying that smarmy elf.'

Sympathy clouds Susan's eyes. 'It must be hard for you, but it's not forever.'

I sigh and concentrate on my plate, suddenly weary of court intrigue. I don't want to tell Pris to play nice with Dinian. I want her uncle to do what's right and help Queen Ariana without playing all these games.

I blow out a long breath. Even if that happens, what will it mean for Pris and me? There is something much bigger going on here than the Queen being sick. All we can do is let events play out. Once it is done, I doubt very much if we'll be able to return to our old lives. My appetite has disappeared, and I need some time alone.

'If you will excuse me,' I say to my dinner companions before rising and leaving the room.

A footman closes the dining room door behind me, and I start to head up to my room, then change my mind. I'm almost at the music room when a hand drops onto my shoulder.

'Are you all right?' Drow asks, his voice laced with concern.

'Sort of,' I say without turning. I don't want my uncle to find out how upset I am over what is happening with Pris. We haven't spoken about it, but I'm pretty sure he's not happy about our being together.

'Come, let's sit,' Drow says, using the hand on my shoulder to direct me to the closest chairs.

I shrug the hand off. 'I just need some time alone.'

Drow moves in front of me. 'This must be very difficult for you.'

I raise my gaze to meet his. 'What must be difficult?'

'Coming to court, realising your friend Priscilla has a role to play here—'

'And here I was thinking you meant meeting my family and finding out about their checkered past. And Pris is not just a friend.'

Pain flashes in Drow's eyes, which soon turns to sympathy, and I can't bear it. So I duck around him and carry on to the music room.

Drow's voice follows me as I walk. 'Snake, it is not wise to become too attached to Princess Priscilla. She is not meant for you.'

That's it, the final straw. My whole body tenses as I turn to face Drow and let loose. 'You can't be serious, warning me off Pris. Not you who campaigned for freedom for lesser creatures and creatures' rights. How can you lecture me on who I can and cannot date?'

There is now real pain on Drow's face, and for a moment, I regret my outburst—but only for a moment. As I open the door to the music room, he says, 'I only say this to save you from pain. I can't control the King, and he has his heart set—'

I slam the door, cutting off his last words.

Too angry to play, I pace circuits of the room, waiting for my heart rate to return to normal. I'm almost there when the door swing inwards and Heart's large form fills the opening. Not wanting another lecture, I stare out the small window at the back of the room.

'Those long meals get too much for me too sometimes,' he says.

I stay silent as I watch the people of Inverness wander past the castle. Then the sound of an acoustic guitar being gently strummed fills the room. I lean my forehead against the cool pane and allow the music to soothe me.

'It's been a tough couple of days for you, son, and it's not going to get better any time soon.'

Heart's voice is almost lyrical as he speaks, and I am lulled as he continues.

'I've lived a few years longer than you. And, like you, court is not where I am at home. If you will take a little advice from an old man, I will tell you, all any of us can do is be true to ourselves. Many will tell you what is best for you, but only you know what is in your heart and what you are able to live with.'

I am about to turn and join my grandfather when my heart almost stops. Below, mingling with the locals, are Grossman Green and Giles Regis, the elven representative in the World Above. What is he doing out of London and hanging out with Grossman? The last time I had seen them together was when they were giving evidence against Pris's and my parents. A ripple of fear runs up my spine. This is bad.

· ·✴ 🌙 ✴· ·

Dinner is excruciating. Unlike Snake, I can't leave before the King does, and I find myself angry at him for deserting me. I pick at my food. The King has ignored me the entire meal. He isn't talking to anyone. He just moves his food around his plate or sips his wine, seemingly lost in thought.

I'm left with only Dinian to talk to—and what a joy that is. His conversation consists of sniping about every noble in the place. According to him, he's the only creature at court I can trust. How little he knows me. He has no idea he is making me even more sure I don't want to count him as a friend.

154

The servers bring out coffee and, to my relief, King Maddox leans in and says, 'Would you join me?'

It's not quite a request, but it doesn't sound like a demand either. I rise, relieved at finally being away from Dinian and the critical eyes of the members of the court, and follow the King across the hallway to the audience chamber. Our footsteps echo in the empty space as King Maddox leads me to one of the window bays.

I wait for him to speak, but he simply stares out at the Ness. Then there's a tickle in the air, a light stroke of magic against my skin. The same tickle I feel when I'm talking with Am'ratha, and I realise King Maddox is talking to his dragon. The conversation is obviously private, so I lean against the window ledge and try to contact Am'ratha.

Royal One, I am happy you have called me. Are you well after the attack? I am sorry we could not come to your aid, but flying in broad daylight risks revealing ourselves and the Unseelie's home to the humans. I sensed you were not physically harmed or in distress, so Ed'rathe and I have remained hidden.

The voice in my head brings a smile to my lips. Communing with Am'ratha is like a phone conversation with an old friend.

Am'ratha, it did not even occur to me that you could help or should help, but I appreciate your concern. We're all fine. I'm pleased to find out you are still at the loch.

'I believe King Maddox is talking to his dragon. I have not been given mine yet. Apparently I won't get one until I am formally named heir. Hopefully that will happen after the King announces our betrothal.'

Dinian's voice comes from so close to my ear, it makes me jump.

Excuse me, Am'ratha, someone is trying to get my attention.

How rude. No one should interrupt our conversations. Tell him to go away, Royal One.

'Priscilla, I was talking to you.' Dinian's tone is all impatient command, and it stirs a fire inside I was barely able to keep in check during dinner.

'Firstly, Dinian, I do not appreciate being spoken to in that tone.'

His eyes widen with what I can only assume is shock at the way I'm speaking to him.

'Secondly, I was talking with a dragon, and you've rudely interrupted us.'

'You have a dragon?'

'That's what you take from that?' I seethe.

Dinian's eyes are sparkling and bright with excitement. 'I understand you're annoyed at me, but do you have a dragon?'

Honestly, can anyone be more self-absorbed?

'You don't *have* a dragon. You are paired with one to see if you bond. And yes, I am in the process of bonding with a dragon.'

Let me talk with him, Royal One. I am sure I can convince him to go away.

The threat in Am'ratha's scares me, and I am tempted to let her deal with Dinian.

I can handle him, but I'll keep you in mind should I need to scare the pants off of him.

Am'ratha chuckles. *I am here if you need me.*

'How come you have one?' Dinian's tone is sulky and petulant. He reminds me of an infant who's been told he can't have a toy.

I shake my head. How has no one strangled this creature before now? How am I going to get through the next couple of days without doing it myself?

'As I am in line for the Seelie throne, I have been asked to bond with a dragon.'

Before Dinian can respond, and I can tell from the frown drawing his brows together that it will be something cutting about why he hasn't got a dragon as he is the heir to the Unseelie throne, the King interrupts us.

'My dragon advisor, Ed'ruven, is in favour of your petition, and Drow is leaning that way, but Chancellor Rimould is worried about leaving the court without the protection of both my dragon's and my magic.'

'Surely you cannot seriously be considering abandoning us —not when we need you here at court, sire,' Dinian says.

The dirty, rotten turncoat. Only this afternoon he was helping us with our petition, and now here he is, trying to convince the King to stay. Where does he really stand on this matter? Or is his only position one that benefits Dinian the most? And if that's true, what does Dinian stand to gain by the King staying at court?

'And I worry that the waning of magic needs to be dealt with—but I am still undecided,' the King says, ignoring Dinian.

This lack of action is doing my head in, and—I can't believe I am thinking this—but Dinian might be right: the court is in need of some leadership.

'If you're undecided, why did you ask me to come here?'

King Maddox's eyes drift back to the view out of the window. 'I had thought Ed'ruven would persuade me one way or the other, perhaps even offer a way I could protect the court and help the Queen that I haven't thought of.'

I force myself to take a couple of calming breaths before I respond. 'Didn't your dragon warn you of the dangers of not acting?'

'Aye, he did. And that is the only reason I have not rejected your petition out of hand.'

I'm at my wit's end. 'Then what will convince you to act?'

'I will act when I know my court is safe.' His eyes slide to Dinian, and the implication is clear—the court will be safe when he has his successor in place, and I know what I have to do to guarantee that.

Dinian's smug smile strokes the flames of my anger, and I find myself unable to respond in case I speak my mind and ruin everything.

'Once you take your position at court, I will have my family with me, and I will have a stable succession plan,' King Maddox says, almost wistfully.

'You can have all of that if you help resolve the magic situation,' I tell him.

The King closes his eyes and says nothing. I hope he is considering my words, but when his eyes open, he sets his jaw and says, 'My word is final. This is how it has to be.'

We shall see about that! I silently promise him.

The King turns his gaze back to the river, and I consider myself dismissed. I push myself off the wall and head for the door. Dinian catches me up.

'Let me escort you,' he says, offering his arm.

'I don't need an escort,' I snap back.

Dinian grabs my arm, halting my progress. I spin around, eyes blazing, ready to give him a piece of my mind. The words freeze in my mouth when I find a puzzled look on his face.

'I don't understand why you are so against this. It's not like this has to be a real marriage. After all, the Unseelie Court does not expect its king to provide heirs. And I've already said you can keep your pet gnome—'

I wrench my arm from his grasp, and, seething with suppressed fury, I stride towards the music room, anxious to put some distance between me and the elf who is determined to marry me.

Flames lap at the coals as I attempt to prod the library fire into life. Effie leans in closer, drawn by the warmth.

'If he won't listen to Petunia, is there anyone else who might sway him? Heart, perhaps, or what about Tomas's brother?'

Effie leans back in the chair. 'Heart is an entertainer and a drinking buddy, not someone King Maddox would discuss affairs of state with. And Raymond rarely comes to court now. He did not come often when Tomas was alive. Now I suspect we may not have the pleasure of his company at all.'

I cannot just leave it there, and not just because my future relies quite heavily on King Maddox doing what is expected of him, but because there is something very wrong with magic, and it's affecting the courts and creatures. 'Then it is up to you and me to make him understand. He must listen to you when you have the best interests of creatures as your motivation.'

Effie slowly shakes her head. 'I have tried. Besides, King Maddox is like a caged animal when he thinks he is being backed into a corner.'

I pace the rug in front of the fire. 'I will not give up. There must be something we can do.'

Before Effie can answer, if indeed she was going to, the door opens, and Drow enters. 'Ah, I see we are holding a war council,' he says as he takes a seat beside Effie on the sofa.

I study the two longtime friends who are so relaxed in each other's company and wonder, not for the first time, why they are not together. I worry that they both spend so much time looking after others that they do not take the time to take care of themselves.

Drow sits forward, rests his elbows on his knees, and clasps his hands.

'The attack today was a reminder that the court is vulnerable. He is worried and possibly a little scared. He does not want to be the last King of the Unseelie Court.'

'Of course not, but can he not see now is not the time to hunker down and wait things out?' I ask.

Drow stares into the fire for a moment, as if collecting his thoughts, before answering. 'The best I could do was have him agree to consult with Ed'ruven. Perhaps his dragon can persuade him.'

'Let us hope so,' I say.

'Anyway, fun as it is sitting around the fire with you both, I'm on a mission to find something to help shore up the court's defences. I am sure King Maddox would feel easier leaving to assist Queen Ariana if the court was more heavily protected.'

'A good idea, Drow. Perhaps Percival and I can help you.'

'Thank you both.'

'Also,' I start, but am not sure I should be bringing this up. My friends eye me expectantly. 'I wonder if we should also search for books on battle magic.' They both open their mouths to protest, but I hold up a hand to stop them. 'I know it has been banned, but I would not trust Bernais and his cronies to ignore the edict, and we should be prepared to defend ourselves against anything they may throw at us.'

Effie frowns. 'While it would be good to find something to counter magical attacks, Percival, you know how damaging such magic can be to the environment. Also, I worry that our knowing this magic may increase the probability of it being used.'

'Let us consider that as a last resort, then,' Drow says.

'And perhaps agree we would only use the defensive

elements in response to a magical attack?' I say, not wanting to completely alienate Effie.

Effie reluctantly consents to at least see what is available. With nothing left to say, we disperse down different aisles of books.

Scanning the titles, I quiver with excitement when I come across a tome entitled *A Study into the Establishment of The Unseelie Court*. I reach up and pull it from the shelf, then decide that rather than gathering more books, I will start on this one now.

Effie and Drow have already piled some books on the table, so I move to the end and set myself up, ready to scan the text for information. I have only just sat down when Pris flings open the door. She is followed into the room by an amused Dinian and Snake, who has a face like thunder.

'Hi, Percival. What's happening in here?' Pris asks.

Snake takes a seat beside me, and as he does, he leans in close to whisper in my ear, 'Don't say anything. I don't trust that elf.'

As Dinian approaches I slip the book I was studying onto my lap. Drow appears from behind a book stack and blocks his and Pris's view of the table. 'We were just chatting about old times and got into a bit of an argument about something, and now we are each trying to prove the others wrong. Childish, really.'

Pris glances my way, and I force my shoulders to relax. Heeding Snake's warning, I do not want to give too much away in front of Dinian.

Effie then appears from another stack. 'We have been caught out, boys. Anyway, it's about time we put an end to this nonsense and head for bed.'

There is hurt in Pris's eyes, as she knows us well enough to realise she is being excluded because of Dinian's presence. She tries to catch Snake's attention, but he appears to be busy doing up the buttons on his jacket. I elbow him in the side, and he sends me a look like daggers. I nod towards Pris, and he finally takes the hint.

'C'mon, Pris, time for bed. Unless you want to stay and mediate their argument.'

'Yes, Princess, come. I will escort you to your rooms.'

Dinian holds out a hand for Pris to take. She ignores him and starts towards the door, with Dinian trailing behind.

'Go,' I tell Snake. 'I will catch you up later.'

As he stands up to go after the others, I hear Drow hiss, 'When I told you she is not for you, I was trying to save you from all of this.'

Snake does not even indicate he has heard, and I hope he does not listen to his uncle's advice. Drow may think he is protecting Snake, but he does not understand the deep connection the events of the past few weeks have forged between Pris and his nephew. I know better than most what it is like to be kept from the one you love. I do not wish that sort of heartache for my young friend.

CHAPTER 11

Ultimatums

The walk back to my room is tense. Dinian insists he is more than capable of escorting me without Snake tagging along. Snake's face is thunderous, and I fear he is holding in a storm. Even so, he says nothing. I suspect he's waiting for me to send Dinian away. This seems such a petty thing for me to do, as his rooms are close by mine.

By the time we reach the door to my grandmother's suite, I'm fuming. Snake should have left me alone with Dinian. He knows I can't stand the elf, but surely he knows me well enough by now to trust me not to lose my temper and reveal our plan. If he's going to chaperone us everywhere, then no one will believe we are resigned to our fate.

As for Dinian, for all his assertions that if we were together, he would 'allow' my relationship with Snake, he's certainly getting a lot of pleasure needling him at every opportunity.

If this is what the next couple of days are going to be like, then someone's head is going to roll—and it won't be mine. As I turn the door handle, my frustration is climbing, and have to force myself to slip inside without saying anything to either of my tormentors in case I make a bad situation worse.

The suite is only dimly lit. Grandmother must have already retired for the night. In one way I'm relived I don't have to make polite conversation, but in another, I wish she were up so I could ask her advice on how to best navigate the turbulent waters I've found myself in. Then again, my bed is cosy and calling me. The sooner I'm between the sheets, the better.

As I undress, I go over the events of the day, wondering how I managed to get myself into this situation and if there was anything I could have done to prevent it. I worry we won't be able to convince the King to do the right thing and that my parents will spend the rest of their lives in captivity. My mind is buzzing so much, I'm sure I won't sleep a wink. As my head touches the pillow, my body makes a liar of me.

In spite of my angst last night, I sleep like a log until I hear someone shuffling about in my room. Forcing an eye open, I can't see a thing. So I push my body upright and find Susan placing some plastic bags on the floor.

She sends me a cheery smile. 'Oh, you're awake.'

'I wasn't,' I grumble back.

'But now that you are, I can tell you I've some clothes and shoes in the bags for you and Snake.'

Suddenly wide awake and excited, I throw off the covers and leap out of bed. Susan hands me two of the bags. I open the first to find a couple of pairs of blue jeans, a couple of T-shirts, a purple hoodie, and some socks. In the second bag, there's a pair of purple trainers. I pull them out and squeal.

I throw my arms around Susan. 'You're the best.' Then I remember I'm supposed to be mad at her for lying to me, and I step back.

The grin on Susan's face falters, and guilt sends my stomach churning. Perhaps it is time to put all this behind us.

'Susan, why did you do it? Why did you lie to me all those years?' I ask, as I start pulling the clothes out of the bags.

Susan places a hand on my arm, stopping me. 'Your uncle has requested your presence at breakfast this morning, so you'll have to leave changing into these until later.'

I allow my displeasure to show on my face, and Susan chuckles.

'Trust me. I've found the perfect outfit for you.'

She lays a white blouse on the bed along with a slightly flouncy petticoat and a long purple skirt. The outfit is much plainer than anything my grandmother would have given me. She follows it up with a pair of lace-up Victorian-style boots. She runs her hand over them, and they are purple, a perfect match for the skirt.

As I dress, Susan tidies my room like she used to at home.

'You know I can clean up after myself,' I tell her as I have many times before.

'Yes, but I am still feeling bad about how you found out about being a creature. I never wanted to lie to you about who you are.'

I pause, hoping she will say more, but she doesn't. 'Why did you?'

I hear a sigh, but I remain silent, giving Susan time to answer.

'My parents had been part of the Unseelie Court for years when I arrived—an unexpected late-in-life gift. Dad was the butler, and Mum ran the serving staff. I grew up here, as did many of us who wait on the royals. When I was almost eighteen, my father had a heart attack. When he died, my mother took it badly, and I believe his not being here broke her heart. She followed him soon after.'

I turn to find Susan staring out the window, tears gathering in her eyes.

'I'm sorry, Susan. I had no idea.'

'I don't like talking about it. I still miss them.'

'What happened to you after they passed?'

'My sister offered for me to go live with her, but she had her own children to worry about. Your grandmother suggested I stay at court, and she would train me to be her companion.'

Susan's face softens as she talks about my grandmother. The two must be very close.

'Not long after, the attacks on you started, and both Princess Petunia and King Maddox begged me to go and look after you. They were worried that with your parents being so busy, they would need help. I agreed. Your father accepted my presence in your house so long as I pledged to never, under any circumstances, tell you about your extended family or talk to you about magic.'

'And you agreed.' This was more of a statement than a question because she never mentioned a word about magic —ever.

'I did. At first you were too young to understand and never questioned your parents. As you grew older, I tried to convince them that you had a right to know. Eventually they gave in and agreed to bring you here, but before they could... well, they were taken.'

Although I'm beginning to understand why Susan did what she did, I can't let go of the betrayal I feel.

'Couldn't you have told me anyway? I would have kept it secret.'

Finally Susan looks at me, and I find pain in her eyes. She shakes her head. 'If I had done that, I would have had to go. Magical promises are binding, and I would have had to leave you. By that time we were so close, I thought of you like a younger sister, and I couldn't desert you.'

It takes me less than a second to rush to Susan and pull her into a hug. At first she resists, then she hugs me back.

'I would rather have had you there than the truth,' I reassure her. 'And while I'm not happy about the lies, I will be forever grateful to my Unseelie family for sending you to me.'

Susan squeezes me before stepping away and wiping her eyes. 'Come, we had best go to breakfast. The King wasn't in a good mood this morning, and we don't want to make it worse by being late.'

With the sun streaming through the windows and the tables moved to a more informal setting, the dining room is less glamorous than the night before. It is also not so full of creatures.

King Maddox has foregone the high table to sit with Petunia and Drow. He has left a place for me opposite my grandmother but beside Dinian.

Susan steers me towards it, whispering in my ear, 'I know you want to sit with your friends, but you want to keep your uncle sweet, don't you?'

My uncle doesn't notice my presence as he carries on talking to Drow, but Dinian is solicitous in a rather possessive way, pulling back my chair to enable me to move my skirts around it and then calling over a servant to take my breakfast order. I am about to snap at him that I am perfectly able to look after myself when I catch Susan shaking her head. I bite back the retort, and Susan, happy I received her message, sits down beside Euphemia.

As I eat I try to catch Snake's eye. He is down the other end of the table, eating with Percival and Heart, his back partially turned to me. I eat a couple of bites of toast, waiting for Snake to look my way. He appears to be avoiding me—or me and Dinian together.

I stare at my food, trying to will myself to eat, but my stomach is roiling, and the thought of food is making me ill. Is this what it's going to be like for the next few days? My friends keeping things from me because Dinian is close by and Snake not able to look at me when he is near? Tears well, and I blink them away. I excuse myself by saying I need to go to the bathroom.

I'm leaning against the wall, trying not to allow the tears to fall, when a comforting hand drops onto my shoulder.

My grandmother's voice comes from beside me. 'No one said being a princess was easy.' She turns me around, then forces me into a hug. 'Tell me what is the matter. Maybe I can help.'

'It's just... well, everything, but mostly it's Dinian. King—'

Grandmother steps back and studies me. 'I am aware of what King Maddox wants you to do, and even should you agree, it is not a done deal. You are in line for the crown of the Seelie Court, and that position takes precedence over your being related to King Maddox. The Queen would have to agree to the betrothal before it is formalised.'

I stare down into Petunia's bluer-than-blue eyes, assessing whether she is joking or not.

'I shouldn't have to rely on that to stop this madness. It's the twenty-first century, and people are not chattel.'

A smile tugs at her lips. 'You need to be smarter than that, though, when playing politics. You do not want to anger the King at the moment. So this may be a case of holding your tongue and using what tools you have to negotiate. However, you will always hold the trump card, and that gives you room to manoeuvre.'

She stares at me as if waiting for me to catch on. Then I get it. 'Queen Ariana can't agree to anything in her current state.'

'That's my girl.' She pats my arm.

I bask in her pride for a moment before remembering Snake won't even look at me.

'Snake isn't taking this well.'

'He is playing along with your ruse. Don't expect him to be all sweetness and light when he has to allow Dinian to escort you everywhere. Especially not when that elf likes making a show out of everything.'

Although I'm aware that I was annoyed at Snake last night for not allowing me to just get on with things with Dinian, and now I'm annoyed at him for doing just that, I refuse to let him off the hook that easily. 'Would it hurt him to smile at me occasionally though?'

My grandmother gives me a hard stare, and I bow my head. 'I know, it's probably hard for him.'

She pats my hand. 'You are not alone in this, Pris. I am here for you, and so is Effie. When it all gets too much, come and see us.'

My eyes fill with tears again, but this time it's because of the offer of support and the realisation that sometimes having family is a good thing.

'Are you ready to go back in?'

I nod.

My grandmother links her arm through mine and leads us back into the fray.

What a frustrating meal breakfast is turning into. The King is setting the tone. He is barely talking, and when he does speak, his words are clipped. An air of sadness has settled around him, and he appears not to want to do anything about it. I know he has lost his soulmate, but life has to go on.

I pause a moment, my fork halfway to my mouth. Did I really just think that? I, the sprite who has been mourning the loss of his soulmate for hundreds of years? And Nisha is still alive!

Taking a mouthful of sausage, I chew thoughtfully,

wondering whether Snake is glowering at Drow or Dinian? Or perhaps both? I study him, following his line of sight. No, it is definitely Drow he is shooting daggers at. He is studiously ignoring Dinian and the empty seat beside him.

On the way to breakfast, I tried to explain to Snake that his uncle has seen how love can mess up people's lives. His best friends were banished from the Seelie Court because of the creatures they loved. While I think Snake understands that Drow is trying to save him from heartbreak, he would prefer his uncle to butt out.

'Percival, old man, would you be so kind as to pass me the butter?' Heart asks, pulling me from my thoughts.

I hand him the dish and take an opportunity to study Snake once more. He needs a distraction. Before I can think of a suitable topic, my young friend asks, 'Heart, why has Drow never married?'

Heart laughs. 'I have asked that question many a time, but I have not come up with an answer.'

Effie leans forward. 'It is because your uncle will not let anyone close enough to him to fall in love.'

She should know, I think as Snake speaks to the witch over my head.

'Is it because someone has hurt him? Or is he simply against love?'

The tinkle of Effie's laugh brings a smile to my lips. 'No, Snake, to the best of my knowledge, no one has broken his heart. I think it's more that he is a rational man, and love is sometimes irrational, so it is to be... feared? No, that isn't quite right. I think he avoids it because he cannot explain it.'

'Ah.' Snake nods and returns to his food, then glances up again. 'And yet he chose to leave the World Below with his friends. Is that not a sort of love?'

Heart places his cutlery on his plate and stares at Snake for a long moment before answering. 'It was so long ago, and we were much more passionate about things then. I suspect Drow left as much to make a political point as he did to support all of us.' Heart smiles sadly, as if his thoughts are still in the past, then picks up his tea.

'Given he is so caught up in creature politics, why is he still here when he could be back in the World Below, helping Elias?' Snake asks.

I startle as Drow's voice comes from behind me. 'Because Elias has my family to support him.'

'And because your father didn't want you rocking the boat,' Heart adds around a mouthful of breakfast.

'True. My brother is Fieth now, and he would welcome me home, but I am used to my life as it is. Besides, my friends are here. What sort of a life would I have back home without you all?'

As I listen to my old friend, I realise he no longer speaks with the same fire he did when we were younger. We are all a little older and perhaps not so inclined to be radical, but Drow used to fight vehemently for creatures' rights. It was his passion and, I thought, his calling. He and I had both fought to change our world.

I shift in my seat so I can see Drow, who is leaning on the back of Effie's chair.

'What happened to us, old friend?' I ask him. 'We once pledged to fight injustices and make life better for all creatures in the World Below.'

Drow turns sad eyes to me. 'We did, I remember, but it seems so long ago. I was powerless to stop my friends from being banished, just like I could not save you. I guess I began to question whether or not I was capable of changing anything.'

Effie leans a cheek on Drow's hand. 'You could never get it into your head that you only lost a couple of battles. The war is still there to be won.'

The room blurs as my thoughts turn inwards. Drow and I have both been sleeping, and while we slept, we allowed a war to carry on around us. By withdrawing from the fight, he and I are just as responsible for what is going on with the Unseelie Court as Bernais and his cronies are.

'The war is not lost yet,' I say slowly. 'Nor is the battle for the Unseelie Court. We are back, Drow—and Bernais had better beware because this time I will not leave the field until one of us has lost.'

A slow smile forms on Drow's lips, and a spark flashes in his eyes. 'Percival, your words shame me. How can I not take up the challenge you have thrown down? Once we have finished our work for the Unseelie Court, I think it is time you and I returned to the World Below and offered our talents to Elias.'

Drow holds out a hand, and I shake it.

'I would come with you, but I am afraid my banishment is still very real,' Heart says.

'I'll join your crusade,' Effie adds. 'I believe the welfare of the creatures here in the World Above will best be served by sorting out the problems in the World Below.'

Heart chuckles. 'Is that not what Eleanor came to tell you a few months ago?'

Effie frowns at the bard. 'You know how to take the shine off a declaration of action.'

'Or perhaps it is just that I will miss all of you when you ride off on your crusade,' Heart admits.

'And we will miss you too,' Effie says. 'But we will come back home after, and we will begin lobbying for you and Petunia to be reinstated at court, and this time we will succeed.'

'I hope so,' Heart says quietly. 'I really do.'

Moving food around my plate, I can't raise an appetite, and the conversation at the table doesn't help. I tried to dig up some interest but gave up when my tablemates began to plan their return to the World Below.

I sneak a glance at Pris and Dinian. I know we agreed she should play along with the King's plan, but at the time, I had no idea how jealous I would be. Each time she speaks to him is like a knife being stabbed through my heart.

Okay, I get the irony. At first I let other things get in the way of us, so I have no right to condemn her for playing along with the King's wishes now—especially not when I believe it's the right thing to do. It's just, sometimes you can't help the way you feel.

Dinian catches me watching and smirks. It doesn't help that he loves rubbing my nose in the fact that he's with Pris. Even knowing that the joke will be on him when Pris and I leave before they can be formally betrothed does nothing to improve my mood.

I will get through this. Mum, I hope you appreciate what I'm doing to free you.

'So, Snake, what are your plans for today?'

Maybe Heart is at a loose end at the moment too.

'I don't know,' I answer, drawing my eyes back down our end of the table.

'Perhaps you and I could finish off what we started last—'

Crash! My head jerks up in time to catch the main doors violently swinging open. Standing in the entranceway are Grossman Green and Giles Regis, smiling bold as brass.

A collective gasp fills the air. How did they pass through the wards closing off the court? With magic waning, they shouldn't have had the power to do that... unless they are pooling magic... or they have help... or they're drawing it illegally from lesser creatures. The thought of them using creatures for a magical boost sickens me. Someone must have let them in. I scan the room, trying to identify the culprit. No one is smirking. Every creature here appears as shocked as I am at the intrusion. Perhaps I'm wrong, and they made their own way inside.

Pris's hands are balled into fists on the table, and I hope she doesn't do anything hasty. As far as everyone in the World Below is concerned, she and I are still on our quest, so it is best if we keep out of sight. Fortunately she remains in her seat, shielded from view by Dinian. The elf stood up when the king did, ready to face down Giles and Grossman.

'What, no welcome for your brother creatures, King Maddox?' Giles sneers along with the last two words, turning the King's title into a farce.

Two guards belatedly appear behind them, swords drawn, but when they attempt to get close to the interlopers, they are thrown back—there is obviously a shield around the two creatures. The guards can do nothing except stand there helplessly. Another pair of guards slide into place, flanking the King, ready to give their lives for him.

'No need for all this aggression,' Giles drawls, a supercilious smile on his face. 'We have only come to serve a warning from the Council of the World Below. Stay out of matters that do not concern you, or we will pull down your court. What you saw the day before yesterday was a small demonstration of what we can do.'

King Maddox draws himself up, and for the first time since we arrived, I see him for the leader he is. There is an aura of power around him that is undeniable. Euphemia appears from nowhere and begins an incantation. How did she do that without being noticed?

'On whose authority do you send this threat?' King Maddox asks, his voice calm and commanding. I can't tell whether he is playing for time to give Euphemia a chance to use her magic or if he is gathering information.

'Bernais, the newly elected head of the Council of the World Below,' Grossman Green announces, initiating another communal gasp.

King Maddox glares at the intruders, his jaw clenched. When he speaks, his words drip with ice. 'I do not believe you or Bernais Baaronson speaks on behalf of all creatures in the World Below. So you take yourself back to your puppet master, and tell him he can take his demand and shove it—'

'Guards, remove these creatures from the court,' Euphemia commands, and the guards snap to attention. They grab the two creatures. With their shield countered, Green and Regis have no option but to move.

'You have until sundown tomorrow to change your mind, or watch your court crumble,' Giles yells as he is hauled out.

The room is silent.

King Maddox turns his gaze to Euphemia, and I wonder what the punishment is for interrupting a monarch. His voice is low when he speaks. 'Thank you, Euphemia, for dealing with those two and for—' He pauses for a moment. '— preventing me from losing my dignity.'

'My pleasure.'

King Maddox straightens his spine, and I don't quite know what he does, but it is as though I can see the crown on his head when he next speaks. 'Guards, ensure everyone returns to their rooms. The court is in lockdown until tomorrow morning.'

The king makes a dignified exit, followed closely by Euphemia, Drow, and Rimould.

For a moment everyone is frozen in place. Then it is as though someone says, 'Go,' as they all move at once.

'I guess our music session is cancelled,' Heart says as he rises to his feet.

I glance at Percival, not wanting to waste a whole day locked in our suite—away from Pris. 'Do we really have to spend all day in our rooms?'

'I guess we had better do as the King commands, for the moment,' the sprite says. Then he smiles. 'You go on ahead with Heart, I have to stop by the library on to pick up some things.'

Heart smiles. 'Come, young man. If Percival can take a detour, so can we. Let us go and help ourselves to a lute and a guitar or two as we make our way back to our rooms.'

My spirits lift at the thought of a day of music, but they plummet again as Dinian escorts Pris and her grandmother out.

She glances back over her shoulder as they walk towards the door, and her look clearly says, 'Save me.' It is wrong of me, but I'm a little happier knowing she's not enjoying spending time with Dinian.

As we leave the dining room. I ask Percival, 'Why did they set the deadline as sundown tomorrow? I mean, why not lunchtime, or the usual twenty-four-hour threat?'

'Because if they manage to pull the castle out of time, the resulting wash of magic and the influx of strangely dressed people into Inverness is easier to hide at night.'

'Oh,' I say. 'Can they do that—pull the court back into time and space?'

Percival shakes his head. 'I have no idea, but let us hope not.'

CHAPTER 12

And It Changed in a Heartbeat

I roll over and press my face into the pillow. Susan is moving about, making enough noise to wake me, but I want to stay here—hiding. I'm not sure I can stand another day of playing nice with Dinian while the King stays holed up in his study.

The only good thing about yesterday was that the guards would not give in to Dinian's request to spend the day with Grandmother and me. He stormed off in a huff, saying he would have it out with the King.

When Euphemia dropped by later in the afternoon, she told us King Maddox would not admit Dinian to his office and had sent a guard to see that he remained in his rooms as ordered. That was the brightest spot in the day.

Susan brought us food and gossip but nothing more tangible. Even Euphemia, having spent the morning in his company, could not anticipate what the King was going to do.

Grandmother and I spent some time discussing how Bernais had managed to get control of the World Below's council, and came to no conclusion. That he poses a real threat to the stability of the creature world is obvious. The conversation raised concerns about her family, and she asked her dragon, Am'ralla, to join the others at Loch Ness to protect her husband.

Am'ralla agreed to keep an eye on her family but unfortunately didn't have any news about what was happening in the World Below except to say that it appeared to be chaos.

With no information, my main worry was what Bernais being in charge will mean for my parents and Snake's mother, but after fretting the morning away, I came to the conclusion that I can't do anything about their fate. Nor am I able to influence anyone to help them. All I can do is carry on trying to convince the King to go to Queen Ariana.

Besides, Grandmother reminded me that it would take time for Bernais to consolidate his power in the World Below. Until he did, our parents would be relatively safe.

'How come?' I'd asked.

'Because they are from prominent families. Bernais will have to ensure everything is done by the book with them, or he risks losing what support he has. Besides, if he touches a hair on my daughter's head, he will have me to contend with.'

My fears somewhat calmed, I'd thought I would go and share what Grandmother had said with Snake. Only, I hadn't been able to persuade the guards to let me leave our suite, let alone the corridor. Maybe with the curfew being lifted, I can do so today.

'You can't hide in there forever,' Susan says.

'Who says I can't.' I speak into my pillow. 'Besides, I'm not hiding, I'm thinking.'

'Of course you are. Would it help if I told you the King has called a gathering of the full council, and you're invited?'

I sit bolt upright.

'Ah, so that got you moving.' She chuckles.

'I'm so stupid.'

'What?'

I *am* stupid. There was one creature who might be able to provide some information about unrest in the World Below. *Am'ratha, are you there?*

Yes, Princess.

Are you able to tell me what has been happening in the World Below?

'Pris, come on, you're going to be late.'

Hold on a mo, Am'ratha.

'Shh,' I tell Susan, 'I'm busy.'

She raises an eyebrow, a look I well know means don't cross me.

'I'm trying to get an update from the dragons,' I tell her.

'Okay, you have a couple of minutes.'

There is chaos in the World Below. The palace is under siege, and a shadow council backed by local garrisons has taken control of the Capitol.

Oh no, it's worse than we thought. It sounds like the beginnings of a civil war.

Do you have any news of my parents? Or of Snake's family?

As far as we can tell, your parents and Snake's mother are still in the castle, along with Elias. They are protected by the Queen's Guard. Many creatures still support him, but calls for the Queen to appear and put a stop to all this nonsense are growing louder.

Dammit, I thought we still had a few days to change the King's mind, but we've run out of time.

Am'rathaa, does anyone there have a plan?

Elias has admitted that the Queen is sick from cleansing the flow of magic, Royal One. Yesterday he told the people she will appear in ten days' time, which is when the doctors have said she will be well enough to walk.

So, he bought us some time.

Yes, a little.

No pressure, then.

Yes, Royal One, there is much pressure on you to make the King change his mind.

Note to self: dragons don't get sarcasm.

I am not sure if the King will hear what I have to say. He is wrapped up in grief and focused on protecting his people.

If he stays away and the Queen does not appear, Bernais will take over, and any chance of healing the breach and fixing magic will be gone.

Am'ratha, he says if I marry the heir to the Unseelie Court, he will help heal magic.

In times of need, we all have to make sacrifices.

I expected a little sympathy because of our growing bond, but her response is delivered in a matter-a-fact tone, which irritates me.

Why can't he make the sacrifice?

Am'ratha does not answer.

Maybe the threat of his court being ruined will be enough to motivate him.

Perhaps, perhaps not.

My head is spinning, trying to figure a way through this new mess. *Hey, if the problem with magic will get worse if Bernais is crowned, does that mean he doesn't have a dragon?*

He does not. He was just a baby when his family was removed from the royal line. The bonding process will take time, then he would need to be trained to work with his dragon to cleanse magic. Why?

What happens if he declares himself ruler without the support of the dragons?

The sacred bond is broken, and the dragons will have to try and keep magic going by ourselves. We will be fine, but it will not be the same in the human and creature world.

Would we lose our bond? I'm surprised to find that the thought of losing Am'ratha makes me feel sad.

No, Royal One. Those of us with existing bonds will keep them. And the ruler of the Seelie Court will still bond with a dragon so we can keep lines of communication open.

What about the Unseelie Court?

No, once the sacred bond is broken, the Unseelie Court will lose its special status, and those who come after King Maddox will not have access to our magic to protect them.

Does Bernais know this?

I believe he does, Royal One.

Oh my god, does Bernais hate the creatures of the Unseelie Court so much, he's willing to risk magic in both worlds to ensure its downfall? This is madness.

Another thing you should know, Royal One. Bernais's mother is in our world, the World Between, begging for an audience with our Queen. We believe she wants to reinstate their line as heir to the throne and is asking for dragon support.

That news strikes at my heart more than everything else I've heard. Not only do the Baaransons want to be rid of the Unseelie Court, they also want to overthrow the monarchy in the World Below. I freeze as icicles of fear tingle all over my body. These are the creatures who thought transforming Percival into a cat was a reasonable punishment—and they did that when they weren't even in charge.

Our last hope is getting the King to come and help us, isn't it? I ask my dragon, my thoughts conveying my growing dread.

Yes.

Thank you for your help, Am'ratha.

Tread carefully, Royal One. A lot rests on your shoulders.

Great, the fate of two worlds is in my hands. My course is clear. Dinian is smarmy and possessive, and I'm not sure I can hold my temper around him, but I must keep up the ruse even though I can see how hard it is on Snake.

I take a deep breath and slowly let it out. Snake looked so lonely yesterday, and I've not been able to update him about anything I've learnt. The burden is too heavy for me. If I could just see him and share the load....

'Come on,' Susan urges me, swatting the bed to get my attention.

I launch myself into motion. I'll be damned if I will fall completely into line. I dress in jeans and a white T-shirt before lacing my trainers and throwing on the purple zip-up sweat-shirt. Susan doesn't even comment on my outfit choice. She just leaves me to finish off and plait my hair.

There is no one in the sitting room when I finally emerge. Tiptoeing, I open the door to the corridor, determined to see Snake before breakfast.

I am stopped by a guard before I reach the end of the hall.

'I'm sorry, Princess, I have orders from the King. Your breakfast is on its way up, and after you eat, I am to escort you directly to his study.'

'Where's my grandmother?'

The guard frowns at me. 'I am not sure I'm supposed to—'

I glare at him, and he shifts uncomfortably from foot to foot. I guess being royal has some perks.

'I believe she is breakfasting with Lady Euphemia. I am to pick them up on the way downstairs.'

I'm about to tell him what the King can do with his plan

when Dinian's head pops out of a doorway further down the corridor. He turns his head, sees me, then grins.

'I'll tell you what,' I quickly improvise, 'I'll go back to my room and not cause any problems if you promise to keep him away from me.'

The guard's face splits into a smile, and he says, 'It will be my pleasure, Princess.'

I let the princess thing go in the spirit of conspiracy and return to my grandmother's suite. While I wait for my meal to arrive, I spend my time wondering why the guard was pleased at being able to thwart Dinian's plans and thinking how I might arrange a meeting with Snake before the council.

I sit down at the table in Effie's sitting room, again finding myself between the witch and her friend, Princess Petunia. It is not the most comfortable position to be in, especially not when the two are in planning mode.

And make no mistake about it, they are clearly up to something. The fact that they are meeting away from Pris signals that more than anything. They too have been invited to the council this morning, and they are strategising how best to make the King understand that this battle will be fought and won in the World Below.

'I do not know why you are even bothering with the meeting today, Petunia,' I interrupt. 'Surely you would be best deployed using your dragon to return to the World Below to fight Bernais for the throne.'

Petunia stops mid gesture and turns to me. 'You think I have not already considered that option, Percival? All it will do is give Bernais someone concrete to direct his ire at, and I will not be able to help with the battle up here.'

I lean my elbows on the table and steeple my fingers. 'That is likely true—'

'You agree she should stay?' Effie asks.

I shake my head. 'No, she should definitely go. If you are there, it is likely the dragons can be persuaded to grant you Queen-in-Waiting status regardless of what the creature council wants. Even if you could not take the throne, you would have access to the magical flow, and you could carry on cleansing it. That would help reinforce magic in both worlds, and the creatures here would be better able to fight off their attackers.'

My theory is met with stupefied faces and silence.

Petunia sighs. 'That is a possibility, but there are still problems with your plan. The Queen's Guard is sworn to her until she dies, so while she lives, they cannot protect me. In fact, given that I am not the named heir, they would have to treat me as they would Bernais—as a usurper.'

I am still not convinced. 'That would only be if you took the fight to the Capitol. There is still support for you in the countryside, and the people there would protect you.'

'True, but it won't be enough. Only Queen Ariana can rally the people who are undecided, so we need her to be there to challenge what Bernais is doing.'

'That would be the best-case scenario,' I concede.

'And, even if the dragons accept Petunia as heir, she will still not be connected fully to the magical flow. That means there is a possibility she will only have a small impact on the waning magic. You of all people should appreciate how that will limit her abilities given your current state.'

I remember back to the night Magnus cursed me, and how Petunia, with the help of her mother's dragon, tried to heal me. It had only been a partial success, but I always thought that was because the Dragon Queen required some punish-ment to stand for my misdeeds.

'I am not sure that is true,' I say. 'My punishment is the result of my actions, not of Petunia's inability to access the full magical flow.'

Petunia reaches out her hand and takes one of mine. 'So we were told at the court hearing, but I have always wondered if I had been bonded to my own dragon and given full queenly access, would the outcome have been the same?'

Petunia's eyes well with tears. I had not realised that even after all these years, she still blamed herself for not being able to fully reverse the spell.

'I am sure it was through no fault of yours,' I reassure her.

She shakes her head. 'I am not so certain. We were told you had to face some punishment for thoughtlessly spreading the blight—but three hundred years, Percival. That is too long. I fear I should not have interfered that night.'

I squeeze her hand. 'Petunia, I am forever grateful for all that you did for me then and after. Anything beyond that is on my head.'

'You are sweet to say—'

'Goodness, you two, leave the past in the past. We have enough to worry about without bringing up history.'

Effie's words have the desired effect. I withdraw my hand and smile. My witch friend is right. We have to decide the best course of action for now.

'Need I remind the two of you, Am'ralla informed me this morning that Elias has promised that the Queen will be back at court in ten—'

'Nine now,' I correct.

Effie's brow draws down in a frown, and I find myself squirming a little in my seat.

'That means there is only one way we are going to sort this mess out,' she says.

'I agree,' Petunia chimes in. 'We must persuade the King to intervene.'

They both turn expectant gazes towards me. 'What? Do you think I can persuade him? If no one else has been able to, what can I do differently?'

'You can have words with that granddaughter of mine and persuade her to do whatever it takes to get King Maddox to help Queen Ariana, short of betrothing herself to that nincompoop, Dinian.'

'I believe she is doing that already, but we should not place all our eggs in one basket.' I say. 'We need a plan B.'

'Percival, it will not do for me to go Below and declare myself heir. I have been away too many years, and it will take time to get enough people to support me to make a difference.'

Effie sits forward on her seat. 'Pris might be able to do it though.'

Is this the type of conversation that got Pris and Snake caught up in this in the first place? Pushing responsibility onto the two of them because we are too tired or too scared to fight?

'Yes, that would work, Effie. Percival, you should—'

'No, I will not speak to her about it. These problems we face are not of her making, and we should not sit here comfortably by the fire and throw her to the wolves.'

After my outburst, Effie and Petunia appear confused. 'You don't think Pris will be able to mobilise support?' Effie asks.

I bow my head for a moment. 'What happened to us? We were so full of fight when we were younger. We were prepared to take on the world.'

Effie places a hand over mine. 'We were younger then. We had much less to lose. Fighting is for the young.'

I remove my hand from under hers and stand up, staring them both in the eye. They are quite content sitting here, moving pieces on the chessboard. I find myself appalled by their lack of action.

'We know how difficult it is to fight for change. Goddess knows we made little impact when we were younger. Perhaps if we had some of the elders onside back then, helping us, even, we would not be in the position we are in now.'

The fire crackles behind me as Effie and Petunia consider my words, but I am not done yet.

'Our worlds have been on shaky ground for a while, and all we have done is chip at the edges, perhaps even destabilising it further. You must decide here and now if you are happy with how things are turning out, or do you want to make changes for the better? None of us have the luxury of sitting on the sidelines anymore—the time to choose a side in this battle is here.'

'I think you are over—'

'No, Effie, Percival is right. When we cleansed the blight against the orders of the council, we began something—we were just too young to see it.' Petunia rises to her feet and begins pacing. 'We challenged the old guard, and when they slapped us down, we accepted our fate, giving power back to them. And they have used that power to shore up their position, and now they are wanting to drag creature-kind back centuries.'

'That may be so,' Effie says, 'but I do not see what we can do about it—not when magic is tainted.'

'As Percival says, we need to plan.'

I smile. This is the Petunia I remember. She has a fire in her belly and is ready to lead us all to battle. Effie and I watch her as she paces, knowing that while she walks, that brilliant political mind of hers is working.

She stops abruptly and turns to us. 'Let's get the important things out of the way first. Percival, will your family be safe?'

This was the same question I asked myself last night, and raising it again also raises my anxiety. Sprites are pacifists by nature, and they tend to stick to their groves. However, that will not prevent them from being drawn into the coming battle. At the moment I have to trust that Ellie would find some way to get a message to me if they were in any danger and that we have enough friends who will protect my clan.

'I do not know. They are still in the grove, mourning the death of my father. Ellie is close by in the village with your mother, Effie, so I believe my family will be protected for the moment, especially while all unrest is focused on the Capitol.'

As I answer something tugs at the back of my mind— something important to this discussion. The wizards!

'And Ellie is in touch with the wizards, or at least with Mandor. She persuaded him to participate in our maze trial.'

Petunia taps her index finger against her lips. 'Interesting.' She begins pacing again.

'Right, we have Pris and Drow working on King Maddox. It is now more essential than ever that he agrees to help Queen Ariana. Not only will his intervention hopefully enable her to return to her duties, but it will reinforce relations between the courts. Both outcomes should give those attacking the Unseelie Court something to consider.'

Effie and I exchange glances. There must be more to come.

'Percival, you and Effie should continue trying to find a way to protect the Unseelie Court from attack. If we can take that worry from King Maddox, he will be more inclined to leave. Also, once the court is protected, the rest of us can return home and see what we can do to help.'

'Not much of a plan,' I say, earning a scathing look from the princess.

'Until we know exactly what is happening, we cannot be precise. If Drow, Heart, Effie, and I go to the Wyld Woods, we can offer support to Eleanora. I am sure she, Elias, and Fairburn already have some plan of action, and we would be better served to strengthen their efforts than do something that might run counter to them.'

I open my mouth to speak, then close it again. While I would love to have a more solid plan of attack, Petunia has agreed to leave the court and return home to fight. That is a massive concession.

'All right,' I say before asking, 'Petunia, what about your husband, daughter, and son? Will they come with us?'

Petunia closes her eyes, but I catch a glimpse of pain in them before she does. She turns away from us before answering. 'When we stayed at the castle, we took on a sacred duty to maintain the portal between worlds. They cannot leave, but they will be safe. Because the portal is also an entrance to the World Between and also bypasses the usual gatekeeper from the World Below, the minotaur, the dragons will not allow anything to befall its defenders.'

It will be difficult for Petunia to fight this war away from those she loves most, but war ofttimes splits families and friends. We will be there to support her, and her family will be safe. That is what matters.

A gong rings, summoning us to King Maddox's study.

'Well, this is it. Make or break time,' Petunia says as she leads us out.

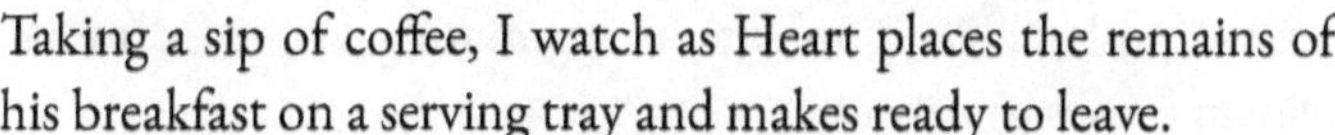

Taking a sip of coffee, I watch as Heart places the remains of his breakfast on a serving tray and makes ready to leave.

'Are you coming to this morning's council?' I ask.

Heart smiles and shakes his head. 'Court bards do not get

invited to councils, no matter how good a friend they are to the King.'

'But wouldn't you want friends amongst your advisors? At least you can trust them.'

Chuckling to himself, Heart does up the buttons on his jacket before answering. 'Snake, if I were on the council, I would have to care about all the minutiae of court life as well as all the big issues, and that would leave me no time for making the music that soothes everyone after they have dealt with those things. Besides,' he says as he opens the door to leave, 'Maddox already knows what I think on the matter.'

Heart closes the door behind him, and I finished my coffee, wondering to myself if Heart hadn't perhaps got it right. Look where getting involved in politics had gotten me: eating my breakfast alone while the person I most want to be with is spending time with someone else.

My fork is halfway to my mouth when there is a knock at the door. I consider the bacon and egg and wonder if I have time to eat it before answering it when the decision is taken from me. Pris sweeps in, her face like thunder. Following close on her heels is Dinian. So close, in fact, she almost shuts the door in his face.

'I thought I was escorting you to the council,' he tells Pris brightly, ignoring her slight.

'Wait for me outside, then,' Pris snaps back at him.

Dinian's only response is to grin more widely.

Pris glares at him, but he doesn't move, so she turns her back to him.

I place my fork back on my plate before taking a rueful look at the remains of my breakfast. I guess I'm not going to get to finish it. As if intent on aggravating Pris even more, Dinian moves to her side.

'Why are we here?' he asks.

Pris rolls her eyes as she answers, 'I'm here to discuss

tactics with Snake before we meet with the King. Lord only knows why *you* are here.'

'We are a team,' Dinian says. 'Where you go, I go.'

This finally gets a rise from Pris. She turns on Dinian, hands on hips, and lets him have it. 'Snake and I are a team. Percival, Snake, and I are a team. My dragon and I are a team. You and I are....'

Okay, time to put a stop to this before Pris says something she'll regret later. She doesn't have to be friends with Dinian, but our plans require us to keep him onside. I push my chair away from the table, stand up, then walk the couple of steps to Pris's side. Placing a hand on her arm, I lead her away from Dinian before she uses some of her advanced karate on him. Fortunately, Dinian has taken her words to heart and is staring out the window as if ignoring us.

When we are far enough away that Dinian cannot hear us, I whisper, 'What's up?'

Pris turns angry eyes on me, and slowly they soften. She takes a deep breath as if to calm herself before she answers, 'Nothing.' She rubs her hands over her face. 'Everything.'

I wrap my arms around her, and she leans into me.

'I'm tired of having a shadow. I'm tired of being relegated to the role of "princess," and I want to be with my friends—with you.'

I know what she means. Having her in my arms feels so right, and all the tensions of the last few days begin to melt away. I want to tell her how much I have missed her and how hard it has been seeing her with Dinian, but I don't. I don't want Pris dealing with my crap while she's so close to the edge, dealing with her own. Unfortunately, my body has other ideas, and I am no longer able to hide the effect her being this close is having on me. She raises her head and smiles.

Boy, do I wish we were alone so I could—*no, stop that.*

I lean in until my lips are close by her ear. 'It's only for a couple more days,' I whisper.

She tenses in my arms, and I realise I've said the wrong thing. Then again, I don't know what the right thing to say would be under the circumstances.

'It's all right for you,' she hisses. 'You get to spend time with your family and Percival while I'm primped and pampered and pimped out to the most irritating person I've ever met.' Her eyes flick to Dinian, and she shudders, emphasising her distaste.

'Elves can be rather supercilious creatures.' The words are out before my brain connects with my mouth. Then I follow up with strike number three. 'And you aren't too primped today.'

Like me, she is dressed in the clothes Susan's sister smuggled in, and she appears much like the Pris I met in London less than a month ago.

As she steps away from me, I know I'm going to pay for not connecting my brain before I spoke. I brace myself for an earful, but what I see in her eyes is pain, not anger. That changes my entire perspective. Hard though this not being together has been for me, I have had friends and family for support. She is doing this alone.

I touch my forehead to hers. 'I'm sorry. I'm an oaf. It's just... I don't know—'

'I miss you,' she whispers, hugging me closer.

My heart thuds in my chest, and I pull her closer and lean my cheek against hers, savouring the few moments we have together. 'I miss—'

'Although I am enjoying this little love fest, that sound a few minutes ago was the bell calling us to council,' Dinian says. From the tone of his voice, he appears pleased that Pris and my time together has been short—and chaperoned.

I press my lips to Pris's forehead, holding her to me a

moment longer before reluctantly releasing her. With one last look at my barely touched breakfast, I take Pris's hand, and we follow Dinian to the court rooms.

Outside the doors to the room where the King holds court —I guess it's something like the throne room—we find Petunia, Euphemia, and Percival already waiting. From the music room, I hear Heart picking out something on the piano. How I wish I could miss this meeting and spend the rest of the morning playing with him.

Instead, we join the others, and Pris lets go of my hand. Dinian manoeuvres himself so he is between Pris and me. I lean around him to catch Pris's eye, but she is staring intently at the door, already getting into character for the meeting ahead.

The doors are thrown open, and a guard steps through to usher us in. Dinian holds out his arm, and Pris places her hand on it, then the two lead us inside. I smirk at what an odd couple they make right now—Dinian in his Regency finery and Pris in her jeans and jumper.

We enter as a group and bow to the King. He is sitting at a round table. How very King Arthurish! In Arthur's court the table was intended to signify that all voices were equal, but with the King flanked by Drow and Rimould on one side and Dinian and Pris taking the seats on the other, it is easy to see where the power lies here.

I slip in beside Drow, which places me almost opposite Pris. Percival sits beside me. Petunia sits beside Pris and takes her hand, offering her a smile of support before looking up and acknowledging me with a slight nod. I smile back, grateful Pris has the support of her grandmother. Euphemia is the last to take her seat, at the end of the table opposite the King.

Chancellor Rimould clears his throat. 'Now that we are all here, we can begin. We are here to decide whether or not King

Maddox should grant the petitioners from the World Below their request to have him aid Queen Ariana.'

While his Chancellor speaks, King Maddox's eyes remain fixed on a point at the opposite side of the room. His face is grey, and his eyes are tired and drawn, as if he's been up all night. If the time when Drow returned to our rooms is anything to go by, he was working for at least a good part of it.

When the Chancellor finishes speaking, King Maddox raises his head and scans the creatures seated around the table. 'After the discussions last night, I believe my duty to the sanctuary that is the Unseelie Court must remain paramount. Like the captain of a ship, I must defend what was entrusted to me, so I deny your petition.'

My head is ringing, and my hands form two tight balls.

Someone gasps, 'No.'

And all I can think is, he can't do this. Not only is he endangering his own people, but he is allowing magic to disappear from both worlds, and he is sentencing my mother to banishment.

Before I can voice my objections, Princess Petunia stands up. 'You stubborn old goat. You have allowed the bigots to scare you into inaction. And in all this time, you have not realised that the Unseelie Court is not a place, it's an ideal. It's where those of us who don't fit traditional society can band together. Your job as our leader is to fight for us and what we stand for, not to hide away and wait for things to blow over.' She speaks with passion and fury, and I couldn't have said it better myself.

King Maddox and Princess Petunia are locked in some staring contest, and my eyes move from one to another. The princess appears determined, and the King.... I'm not certain what he is. Princess Petunia's words appear to have rattled him, but I'm not sure he has it in him to rise to her battle cry.

It is the King who looks away first. 'I will not abandon my people.'

'Then at least let me send out a call for those who want to come and defend the court to join us,' Petunia counters.

King Maddox sighs. 'They will not arrive in time. Those who wish to may stay and help defend the court. Anyone who wishes to leave should do so as soon as possible.'

Pris leans around Dinian to plead with her uncle. 'Come with us and—' Pris starts.

King Maddox holds up his hand to stop her. 'No, Priscilla. I must see to my court first. When this current threat has been dealt with, then perhaps we can help with the problems in the World Below. Now, I have to prepare for the coming battle.' He turns to Rimould. 'You will see the announcement is spread?'

Rimould's face is as inscrutable as always. 'Of course, sire.'

I scan the faces around the table. This wasn't a council, as there was hardly any debate. It can't be over.

The King rises and exits the room. Every single eye follows him. When he is gone, Pris pushes her chair back and bangs her fist on the table as she glares at Drow and Remould. 'How can you two allow him to do this? He is sentencing this court to death and all but ensuring magic will die out in both our worlds.'

Dinian places a restraining hand on Pris's arm, and she turns her anger on him. 'Don't touch me!'

The elf appears unperturbed by her outburst. 'There is nothing you can say here that will change anything. You must petition the King again.'

If looks could kill, Dinian would be flayed alive.

'If you will excuse me,' Rimould stands, 'I must see if the King needs anything.'

'He needs something, all right,' Pris spits. 'A backbone.'

'Priscilla, enough.' Princess Petunia's tone is steely, but I detect a flicker of approval in her eyes.

Pris drops into her seat.

'Your anger will change nothing. We must now put all our effort into a plan B, as Percival would put it.' The princess turns her gaze to Dinian. 'Do you not have somewhere else to be?'

Ignoring the dismissal, Dinian says, 'No, I don't,' and leans back in his chair as if to emphasise his point.

Before anyone can eject him, the door opens, and Heart joins us. 'I have just been updated by Rimould. I've come to say my good-byes.'

'Good-byes?' I repeat as Heart joins us at the table.

'Yes, lad. I have hidden away here for too long. I will try to go home to my family in the World Below. I want to make sure they make it through the coming conflict, and I need to see what I can do for my daughter.'

It takes a moment for the enormity of Heart's words to sink in, then I find I'm too choked up to speak. Tears make their way down my cheeks, and I finally manage to say, 'You're going to try and help Mum?'

Heart drops his hand onto my shoulder. 'Yes, lad. It is about time I did something for her. Will you come with me?'

I glance over at Pris, trying to work out what is going on in her mind, but she is staring out the window, her thoughts elsewhere.

'I understand, lad. I have some packing to do. You still have an hour or so to make your decision before I leave.' He turns to go, but I tug at his sleeve. In a moment I am standing up and drawing him into a hug.

'Thank you,' I mumble into my grandfather's shoulder.

He pats my back. 'No, son, I should be thanking you for reminding me I have a family and friends. And for helping me realise I have been in mourning for too long, and it is high time I returned to the land of the living.' He pats my back once more. 'We will do what we can if you feel you are needed here,' he says, then he is walking away.

'Wait up, Heart,' Drow says. 'I will come with you. There is little left for me to do now, and I fear that my family will need me if we are to free your daughter and Pris's parents while preventing Bernais from taking the throne.'

It's like we have all been held in suspension, waiting for the King's decision, and now that he's made up his mind, we can all act.

What will I do now that the King has stated he won't be going to the World Below with us? My eyes trail after my uncle and grandfather, torn between leaping up and going with them and wanting to stay with Pris.

Beside me, Percival rises to his feet. 'Well, Petunia, what is our plan B?'

'It seems I will have to return to the World Below and petition for my place as heir to be reinstated, after all. What about you, Effie?'

'I am tempted to come with you, but while we are under attack, my place is here, protecting the court and the creatures in Scotland. I will go back to the library and continue our search for something, anything, that might help shore up the court's defences. When it is time to fight, I will stand alongside King Maddox.'

'I will join you in the library, Effie—at least for a while, as I have very little in the way of possessions to pack,' Percival says. 'I have decided to journey to the Wyld Woods to help protect my family and to join those working to prevent Bernais from taking the throne.'

The sprite turns to Pris. 'Will you come with us, Pris?'

Pris drags her gaze back to the room and wipes a tear from her eye. 'No, Percival, I can't go. Much as I want to be there for my parents, I don't believe there will be a Word Below or an Unseelie Court unless the King works with the Queen to fix what is happening with magic. I'm afraid I have to stay.'

As I process Pris's words, my heart pounds in my ears, and I'm not sure whether it's because I feel her pain or because I'm disappointed—no, I'm angry—I'm completely gutted she made this decision without even talking it through with me first.

She stands up and rounds the table until she is beside me, then she speaks to me like there is no one else in the room. 'I'm sorry, Snake. I don't see any other option for me. I'd be no use in the World Below, and I still think there's a chance the King might be persuaded to change his mind.'

Her eyes show the depth of her pain and uncertainty but also her determination to do what she believes is right. She reaches out and touches my arm, begging me to understand, melting my heart as she does.

My insides feel like they're being pulled apart. My path is not as clear-cut as hers—this is not a political decision for me but a personal one. I want to do everything in my power to save my mother, but the thought of leaving Pris to face what is coming alone tears me up.

Percival joins us and takes hold of my hand. 'Stay with her, Snake. You know we will be doing what we can for your mother. She has family and friends working on her behalf. And Pris, well—she needs allies here. She needs you.'

I stare into Pris's eyes. They ask what she will not put into words. They plead with me not to leave her here alone.

'Okay, I'm staying for as long as Pris needs me.'

Somewhere in the background Dinian snarls, I'm sure he thought he was rid of me. I dismiss him from my mind. All I'm interested in is being here for Pris.

CHAPTER 13

Preparing for Battle

Tears flow unchecked down my cheeks as I hold Snake's gaze. It is like we are suspended in time, and I want to stay there with him forever, but the noise in the room soon comes back into focus, and reality takes over.

'Thank you,' I mouth, not trusting my voice.

He smiles, then reaches up to brush away my tears.

I want to say more. To tell him I understand what he's giving up to stay here with me. To explain to him that everyone else has a purpose now, and this is the only place I can be useful. All too soon, though, he is hustled away to the library with Percival and Euphemia, and the moment has passed.

Dinian mutters something under his breath. I'm too emotionally drained to take him on, so I ignore him and ask my grandmother, 'What do we do now?'

She doesn't answer. Instead she stands up and strides over to the door leading to the King's study. She knocks firmly, and the echo fills the room. The door opens a crack, and she speaks to someone—I assume it's Rimould, as I can't imagine King Maddox is in any state to do anything for himself.

Grandmother's footsteps clip-clop over the floor as she returns. 'Rimould has informed the King that we are waiting to speak with him, but he does not think the King will see anyone before the deadline.'

My head drops and my shoulders slump. Of course the King won't see us. I doubt even promising to marry Dinian here and now will change his mind. Is there anything that would alter that? Perhaps there is.

'Grandmother, how many people in the court would likely favour the King saving magic over the court?'

Her eyes widen with surprise. 'You're thinking of calling for a vote?'

I nod. 'I'm not—'

Dinian's chair scrapes back, then crashes to the floor. 'You cannot call for a vote. The King's word is absolute, and I will not let you do anything that might change that.'

I study the elf for a moment, wondering about his motivation. Of course he sees himself as leading the court one day, and he therefore wants to ensure his own power will be absolute... but there's clearly more to it.

'Perhaps you can worry about the future of the Unseelie Monarchy once we have ensured the court will live on after today,' I tell him, not bothering to hide my distaste. With King Maddox having made up his mind, I see no value in keeping up the charade.

The annoying elf is not cowed. A sly smile tugs his lips into a sneer before he quickly hides himself back behind the courtier's face he normally wears. 'I do not think I need to worry about that either way.'

What does he mean by that? I'm about to ask him when the doors crash open, and Snake rushes in. 'Pris, Princess Petunia, you need to come quick. Percival and Euphemia think they've found a way to save the court.'

The three of us start to follow Snake out of the room

when I step in front of Dinian. My unease about his last comment is still fresh, and I decide he should sit this out. 'Sorry, Dinian, we need someone to stay here to find out if the King will see us and to come and collect us if he will.'

He stares at me, and I wonder if he senses that I don't trust him. 'What if I can help?'

'Then someone will come and get you,' Snake tells him.

'Please, Dinian.' I hope a little pleading will flatter his ego. 'We will only be gone a little while, and I'll fill you in when we get back.'

He huffs out a breath and says, 'All right, but if you are not back in an hour, I will come and get you. I'm not sitting here by myself all day.'

I beam a smile at him, hiding my dislike perfectly. 'Thank you.' I rush to catch up with the others before he changes his mind.

'I don't know how you can be so nice to him,' Snake says as we race up the stairs.

'Me neither.' We slow our pace as we approach the library, and I ask, 'Do you guys think Dinian would work against the King and the court?'

Grandmother stops in the middle of reaching for the door handle. 'Why do you ask that?'

'I don't know, it's just a feeling.'

'Well, I don't trust the guy.' Snake manages to instill a whole heap of feelings in those few words.

'That may be jealousy talking, young man, but I know what you mean. While I don't think he would actively work against the court, he's certainly known for looking after number one at all costs,' my grandmother declares as she opens the door.

Once we are all seated around the large table in the library, Euphemia briefs us. 'We believe we have found a way to counter the magical attacks on the court, but we will have to act fast.'

'Effie,' Grandmother interrupts, 'slow down. Start at the beginning.'

Percival leans forward and butts in. 'I picked up a book yesterday which told how the Unseelie Court was built and managed. On our way to the library I was telling the others about it.'

'And he said the Kings of old used to place the court in stasis—in a sort of a protective bubble—when they departed on a royal tour.' Snake carried on. 'Everyone would leave the court except for the castle caretaking staff, and the building would be placed in stasis so it would not drain magic unnecessarily.'

'Cool,' I say.

Percival smiles. 'We talked about it and thought maybe putting the Unseelie Court in stasis might be an answer to our problem. The court would be safe, and King Maddox could concentrate on saving magic.'

Petunia leans in. 'I am sensing a "but".'

'There always is,' Euphemia laughs. 'The spell requires a lot of magic. Magic has been waning since the times of the blight, and this spell was last done centuries ago, when magic was in abundance. Also, it has only ever been done to Urquhart Castle.'

Percival points at the page of the book in front of him. 'It takes an elf, a gnome, and a witch to join magic and cast the spell of protection.'

I stare at the sprite, sensing there is a problem but not seeing what it is. 'We have enough of those types of creatures to do that. In fact there's enough of them here that we could have two or three of each combining their magic—if that's a thing.'

'It is a thing, but that is not our problem. We need to find somewhere that has enough magic for the spell,' Percival says.

Okay, now this is more like it—some action we can take to get things sorted. 'I take it there isn't enough in Inverness?'

He shakes his head. 'There are very few places in the World Above or Below that would have the amount of magic we are talking about.'

'Okay, you need Snake and me to find the magic? We'll do it, won't we, Snake?'

It's Euphemia's turn to shake her head, and Percival leans over and takes my hand. 'No, Pris, we need Snake and Petunia to go. Your job is still to stay here and convince King Maddox that we can protect his court and get him to leave with you before the castle is placed in stasis.'

I stare at him, not sure I've heard him correctly. I look at Snake. 'You don't want me to come?'

He sounds torn when he says, 'Of course I want you to come, but you're also needed here.'

Percival squeezes my hand. 'Apart from ensuring the King leaves before the court is sent into stasis, we still need some creatures with strong magic to stay and shore up the wards.'

'What happens to the court when it goes into stasis? Will the people left behind be able to carry on as normal?' I ask.

'From what we can tell, it will be like in the story of *Sleeping Beauty* when the court sleeps—'

'Or like cryogenics,' Snake expands on Euphemia's explanation.

'So we really don't want to be here when that happens,' I say.

Percival nods. 'The risk of staying is twofold. If the barriers fall before we can put the court to sleep, then anyone who remains will be at risk. Because of that, we have suggested all vulnerable creatures leave before the deadline tonight.'

'The other risk is to those who are caught in the stasis

spell. They will not be released from suspended animation until the spell is reversed,' Euphemia finishes.

'And what will happen if magic disappears completely?'

I think I already know the answer, but I have to ask anyway.

'They are as good as dead,' Percival tells us.

I don't want to dwell on that thought for too long. 'Will the creatures who need to leave be able to get away in time?'

Euphemia's face breaks into a grin. 'Many of them have already left the Unseelie Court and are blending in with the people of Inverness. I believe they have a few surprises up their sleeves for our attackers.'

We sit there in silence, and I know they are all waiting for me to support this plan.

My fingers twist into knots, an external visual of what is happening to my stomach. 'I can't do this,' I tell them. 'I can't be the one who is responsible for getting King Maddox out.'

It's Petunia's turn to take my hand. 'You can, you know. You are the last hope for the Unseelie Court to be saved and keep the balance in our two worlds.'

All the fears that plagued me when using my magic in the minotaur's maze return in a rush. 'We're doomed if I'm the one you're all relying on.'

'You won't be alone. You will have Am'ratha and Ed'ruven to feed what magic they can. And they will be there to help you escape,' my grandmother tells me.

'Ed'ruven?' Snake asks.

'King Maddox's dragon,' she tells him.

'What about Ed'rathe?'

Euphemia answers. 'Am'ralla, Petunia's bonded one, and Ed'rathe will be needed to transport us to the source of magic we are to use to cast the spell.'

I don't know why, but I blurt out, 'Dinian is going to be so pissed that Snake's riding a dragon.'

There's a moment of silence before everyone laughs, and the tension in the air dissipates. I check around the room and see that we appear to have consensus on a way forward. 'I guess this is our plan B, then?'

Those around the table nod their agreement.

Percival catches my eye. 'Pris, a lot of responsibility rests on your shoulders. Once the court starts going into stasis, you will have only moments to get out. If King Maddox does not come with you, he will play no further part in this conflict.'

I try to make light of it. 'So, no pressure then.'

'Yes,' he says, straight-faced, 'there is pressure.'

I smile at him. 'I know, Percival.'

'Ah, sarcasm.'

I nod, and he smiles.

'The only thing I worry about is, how will King Maddox and I know when to leave?'

Petunia answers, her lips curving in a wistful smile. 'We can communicate via the dragons, just like the leaders of old did.'

The room falls silent for a moment, then I realise there is something we've forgotten. 'Who's going to inform King Maddox of our plan?'

⁕

Escape into music has always been my refuge, and I find it calms me today as all around me is in chaos. When I walk to the music room, I feel a little guilty—I should be preparing to leave like everyone else. Well, almost everyone. This time Pris will be staying, or more accurately, I will be leaving her behind.

The guitar is my go-to instrument, but today the piano is calling. I warm up with a couple of scales before starting

Ludovico Einaudi's 'Walk.' I'm a little rusty, but soon I'm lost in the flow of the music.

I sense Pris enter. She hovers in the doorway, listening until I finish playing. As the last notes linger in the air, she joins me on the piano bench.

'That was beautiful.'

'I'm not a pianist, but some pieces of music are just made for the piano.'

She leans her head on my shoulder. 'I've missed your music—and you.'

I lean my head against hers. 'Stay a while, then.'

She draws in a breath, and I know this will only be a stolen moment.

'Let me guess, you have to rush back to the King and Dinian.' I try to say the words in an even tone, but my hurt leaks out.

Pris places a hand on my thigh. 'Please don't be angry with me, I can't bear it. It is difficult enough not being able to spend time with you, but being forced into Dinian's company makes it all the harder.'

I place a hand over hers. 'I'm sorry. I've missed you too, and it's driven me a little crazy.'

I attempt a smile when I find that her face reflected in the dark wood of the piano is serious—almost haunted.

'King Maddox is still waiting for an answer about Dinian. For a while during the council, I thought I'd been let off the hook, but now we still need the King onside, and....' She sighs. 'And while I put off talking to him about it, Dinian is behaving like we're already betrothed. I feel like the two of them are herding me like a couple of sheep dogs.'

I knew the charade had been hard on her, I hadn't realised how hard. My heart aches for her, and I feel... sad. I don't know what to say to make things better. 'Have I lost you?' It's all I can come up with.

'To Dinian?' Pris scoffs. 'Hardly.'

I'm not ready to laugh yet. Her relationship with Dinian is not my main concern. 'I'm more worried that I may have lost you to the duties you'll be compelled to fulfil as part of the royal line,' I admit quietly, hating the fact that Drow has managed to get under my skin.

She slides her arm around me. 'You will never lose me to that. I just have to find a way to get out of this without alienating King Maddox. We can worry about what the Seelie Court expects from me later.'

In an uncharacteristically fluid movement, I stand up with her in my arms as the piano stool scrapes across the floor. I'm not gentle when my lips find hers as all the pent-up emotions of the last couple of days break through the wall I built around them. I slip one of my hands down her back and rest it on the curve of her hip, pulling her close to me.

A moan escapes her lips as her fingers entwine in my hair, and she pulls me closer. My world shrinks to the feel of her body against mine and the heat and need that is threatening to overwhelm me. There are too many clothes between us. I slip my hand beneath her T-shirt and the feel of her smooth skin sends another wave of desire through me.

I raise my head to suggest we find somewhere more comfortable, but it's as if that move in itself breaks the spell. As her fingers trail down my face, her eyes catch mine, and mixed with the smoke of her desire is regret.

'You didn't come here for this.' My voice is husky, and I struggle to control it—and myself.

Her lips curl into a wicked smile. 'Well, no, not exactly, but I can't say I'm disappointed.' She pulls my head down, and this time her kiss is sweet and teasing.

'Pris,' I groan, 'if you don't stop....'

She smiles wistfully. 'I don't want to stop... but we have to. We both have things to do.'

I take a half step back. With her body moulded to mine, the blood my brain needs to function is in the wrong place. It takes a minute for my body to settle and my head to kick into action.

'Don't we always?' I ask.

'Yes, only this time there is a battle looming, and goodness knows what we will find when we return to the World Below'.

I entwine my fingers with hers. 'I wish we were able to face this together.'

Pris gives my hand a squeeze. 'Me too, but at least with you gone, Dinian will stop trying to one-up you.'

'And you being with Dinian will keep King Maddox happy.'

Her laugh is deep and throaty. 'No, me agreeing to marry him would make King Maddox happy, but at least he will be distracted by what is coming.'

I pull her to me, but she resists. 'Snake, we can't.'

'Because someone might see?'

She shakes her head. 'No—well, yes, but that isn't what I was thinking of. Petunia and Euphemia are explaining our plan to King Maddox. When they are done, you and Percival will be leaving with them.'

'I could stay, you know. Drow or Heart could be the gnome.'

'Euphemia says Heart's magic hasn't been the same since he lost his wife. Besides, Drow and Heart have already left.'

'So soon?' I ask, surprised at how disappointed I am that I didn't get a chance to say good-bye.

Pris leans in and hugs me. 'They left a letter with Percival for you, but they couldn't wait. The guards are closing off the doors any minute now.'

A door bangs in the corridor, followed by the sound of two familiar voices.

'That's it,' I say. 'Time to leave.'

Pris hugs me tight. 'Percival said to tell you your questing clothes are clean and in your room.'

I don't want to let Pris go, and I hold her for a moment longer before pulling away.

'I don't want to leave you.' I lean forward and brush my lips against hers. 'But this is only good-bye for now. We will hurry back and meet you in the World Below.' I kiss her once more, and it's a kiss full of the promise of things to come.

I walk away without looking back, because I know if I do, I will not have the strength to leave.

·˙*˙🌙˙*˙·

Lady Susan leads us out of the castle through an underground passage. It is dank, and wet, and it smells like a disused sewer system. Footsteps echo off the walls, interspersed with sloshing water and an almost constant scratching.

Something runs over my foot. I sweep my torch downwards and up again quickly. Our pathway is scattered with rats. Not the harmless rats found at home in the Wyld Woods, but mean and hungry rats that look as though they would eat you alive given half a chance.

Finally we reach a ladder that Lady Susan says opens into an alleyway not far from the castle. She climbs up first, and once she's checked there is no one around, she motions for us to join her. As Effie spells the stench and sewerage off our clothes, Lady Susan starts back down the ladder.

'You're leaving us here?' I ask.

She nods. 'I let Pris down once before. This time I will stay with her. Besides, this is my home. No one is going to chase me from it.'

'But you risk getting held in stasis,' I say.

She shrugs. 'Perhaps, or perhaps we might get enough of a warning to get out. Now go, the lot of you, before someone realises you're here.'

The manhole cover clangs as she drops it back into place, startling us enough that we move towards the alley opening. We are just about to step into the street when Snake motions us back into the shadows.

'There are an awful lot of lesser creatures around—more of them than normal.' It is the voice of Grossman Green. 'Do you think some of them may be getting out from the castle?'

Whoever he is talking to answers, 'They can't be. We have all the exits covered. No one is getting out.'

'I am not so sure...,' Green starts to say, then trails off as if he has become distracted.

'Perhaps they are lesser creatures come to help defend the castle from the outside. They will make little difference in the long-run.'

'Say, where has Bernais disappeared to? Wasn't he supposed to join us? We will need his magic if we are to drive the Unseelie from their court once and for all.'

'Never you mind. Just keep an eye on your part of the plan.'

Once the creatures have passed by us, Snake leads our small group back onto the road and round some back streets. The plan is to walk to where Petunia has asked the dragons to wait.

'Hey, look!' The call comes from behind us.

'Go!' Snake hisses.

I glance over my shoulder.

Grossman Green is less than a block away, pointing at our retreating backs. 'I told you they were getting out somehow. After them,' the goblin says over the sound of running feet.

We speed up and make it to a busy main road before our pursuers almost catch us up. Petunia waves down a taxi, and we all pile in. As Petunia reels off the address, the taxi door locks just as Grossman Green grabs for the door handle. The goblin bangs the window with his fist as the taxi takes off.

'Would you believe the nerve of some people?' the driver says. 'Think they own the world, they do.'

The taxi pulls into traffic, and the driver checks his rearview mirror. 'They'll have a bit of a wait for another ride this time of day. You all going to some fancy-dress thing?' he asks as he moves through the traffic.

I frown. Snake, Petunia, and Euphemia are in trousers, shirts, and jackets, and I am in my normal black trousers and jumper. I think we look pretty normal, but apparently not.

'Sort of,' Snake tells him. 'We are going to a Dungeons and Dragons party.'

The taxi driver nods as if this is normal. Moments later he turns into an industrial estate and pulls over.

'Are you sure it's here?' he asks doubtfully, scanning the deserted street.

'Yes, this is perfect, thank you.' Petunia pulls out some cash and pays the driver.

I am surprised as I catch a glimpse of the bundle of human money she has stuffed into her inner coat pocket. She catches my eye. 'Just in case,' she whispers. 'You never know when you might need a little ready cash.'

'Have you not heard of banks and plastic cards?' I ask as we get out of the car.

'Of course.' Her tone is haughty. 'However, if I want a little something while I'm at court, I need cash.'

We make our way between the industrial units to a field behind them. Once the taxi is gone, there is a rush of wind, and the dragons land.

Hurry, Ed'rathe says. ***We cannot hold the invisibility spell for long, there is not enough magic here.***

Snake climbs up onto his back, then gives me a hand up to sit in front of him.

'I will feel better with you where I can see you,' he chuckles, no doubt referring to my fall last time we travelled by dragon.

I want to answer back with a snarky comment, but I am not looking forward to riding a dragon again, and I do feel much safer with Snake in behind me.

As we take off after Petunia's dragon, Am'ralla, my stomach lurches, and I grab hold of one of Ed'rathe's scales.

Flying high above Inverness, Petunia asks the dragons to do a loop of the city. From our vantage point above, we spot a number of creatures gathered in groups at what they believe to be all the castle entrances. A shimmer of magic pulses over and around each group. There are a lot of them, but not as many as I had imagined. Perhaps the rebellion is not as widespread as we first thought.

I am also able to make out lesser creatures setting up wards and traps around the castle. Inverness Castle itself shimmers as the creatures still inside weave their own wards of protection.

'I hope they can hold out for long enough,' I say.

The word is out, and any creature nearby who is true to the court is coming to help.

I hope they get there in time, Ed'rathe rumbles.

'Where are we heading?' Snake asks as the dragons climb and swing away from Inverness.

'The Isle of Skye,' Percival says.

'That's where we're going to find a store of magic?'

'Of course. The Old Man of Storr should have all the magic we need to work the spell.'

I lean back into Snake and try not to let my terror at the speed we are travelling and the height we are flying turn me into a total wreck.

CHAPTER 14

Saving the Unseelie Court

I must have dozed off, as I awake to Snake prodding me gently in the ribs.

'We're here,' he says, his voice close by my ear.

From the position of the sun, I think it is midafternoon-ish, and we are flying over the Skye bridge. The dragons land near the rocky pinnacle that towers high over the west of the island. There are a smattering of tourists on the path, so they use the magic that shrouds them to make it appear like we are walking out from a patch of mist.

As we walk, Effie says, 'Legend has it that the Old Man of Storr was a giant who lived on Trotternish Ridge. When he was buried, they could not cover his thumb. This small part of the giant still juts out of the ground, creating the famous jagged landscape.'

Snake smirks. 'But you're going to tell us that the legend is actually true.'

'Young man, I don't like your tone of voice,' Petunia tells him, and when Snake blanches, she winks. 'But you are right, of course. It is more than a legend dreamt up to bring tourism to the area. One of the ancient giants is sleeping here and has done so for many years, ever since magic in the World Above dropped below the levels needed to sustain such an enormous magical creature.'

'What they got wrong, though,' Effie butts in, 'is that the giant is a woman, not a man. And as she sleeps, she gathers magic into a power stone in case of great need.'

'Cool,' Snake says, then his brows draw into a frown. 'If she's been building the magic for perhaps hundreds of years, do you think she's going to give her magic to us without a fight?'

'Well,' Effie says, 'I am sure if we ask in the right way, she will. We simply find a way to explain that this is a time of dire need.'

Now Snake's eyebrows go in the opposite direction, and his voice drops with sarcasm. 'Of course she will, because everything since I got caught up in this crazy mess has gone to plan.'

I turn to tell Snake to stop being so negative, but I swallow my words when I see a tightness around his eyes and mouth. He puts on a good front, but these last few weeks have taken a toll on him. I am sure he is worried about Pris, about what will happen to her if this does not work, as well as his own role in casting this spell.

'She will be all right,' I try to reassure him. 'King Maddox's magic is strong, and she has Am'ratha with her.'

He forces a smile, perhaps acknowledging my effort at support. 'I know, but—'

'But you will not be there to make sure?'

He nods. 'And she doesn't have full control of her magic yet. So I'm not sure how much she will be able to do.'

'Then we need to be successful here,' Petunia says brusquely.

Sometimes when Petunia cuts straight to the point, she can be abrasive, but today I welcome her certainty.

Effie leads us away from the main body of tourists, and we three make a barrier so no one can see what she is doing.

Snake leans down and whispers, 'Percival, how are we supposed to get to the magic?'

Surely he heard our plan, then again perhaps not. We did a lot of fine tuning while he went to get Pris. 'A simple exposure spell should reveal the power source.'

'It can't be that simple, can it?' he asks.

I straighten my spine, pulling on the role of advisor, and I have so often had to with him. 'No, it is not. The real trick is convincing the giant to let us access the magic she has tended for hundreds of years.'

'Do we have a spell for that?'

I snort. *Where does he get these ideas from?* 'I believe we should leave that bit to Effie, as she is more experienced in talking to a wide range of magical creatures.'

Snake stares at me, as if he does not believe what I am saying. 'So you're telling me this whole plan relies on Euphemia convincing the giant to give us her magic?'

I nod.

Beside me Snake mutters, 'If I had known how flimsy our plan was, I would never have left Pris alone to face the upcoming battle.'

Too late now, I think as Effie begins to chant the reveal spell to open the earth and expose the stone containing the giant's magic. As the music increases in intensity, the tingle of magic fills the air, and the ground beneath our feet shivers.

'It is done,' she says, and we turn as one. It will take all of us to lift the stone into the open.

Finding a grip on the stone is difficult. It's not just that the stone is relatively smooth, but it is also dirt-encrusted and slimy. Once we all have a hold of part of the stone, we heave. Nothing.

'How about if we all push from one side,' Snake says, 'you know, laws of physics and all that.'

We all move to one side and crowd together, and push. It doesn't budge an inch. We try again, giving it all we have, but it will not move. Euphemia tries another release spell, but the giant will not let go of her treasure.

Petunia's eyes glaze over as she asks her dragon for help. 'Am'ralla says there are too many people around for them to come. Hold on, the Queen of Dragons wants me.'

Closing her eyes, Petunia speaks with the Queen. Minutes later she sighs and opens them. 'It seems the dragons and the giants have a pact. Neither the dragons nor the giants will interfere in one another's business. If we want to use the stone, we must retrieve it ourselves.'

'Of course,' Snake mutters, 'and for our next trick, we'll find the needle in a haystack.'

His shoulders are hunched, and he stares despairingly out to sea. My poor young friend is losing heart. That is a worry because this is only the beginning of what we must face if we are going to ensure creatures remain free and equal in the World Below.

I for one am not prepared to give up. Too much rests on us saving the courts, not the least of which is my future. For the first time in hundreds of years, I now believe I have one, and I will not let it go that easily.

I make my way to his side and pat his arm. 'Come, Snake, we must continue fighting.'

'Why?' he asks, his voice bleak.

I wish I could tell him it is because if we carry on challenging the Baaronsons and their people, life will get better. He is my friend, and I cannot lie to him. 'Because the alternative is too horrendous to contemplate.'

Snake laughs, and some of the tension leaves his shoulders. 'Not much of a pep talk, Percival.'

It may not be, but it has worked. Snake turns back to the stone, and I ask, 'What now, Effie?'

The witch turns and walks towards the outstretched fingers of the giant's hand, then places her palm on the rock before pressing her forehead against the stone. We all go silent.

'Come, sister, do not guard your secret so well. There is unrest here in the world of humans, and magic is waning. It is time to use what you have stored to benefit the two realms you used to protect.'

It is mine and it keeps me warm while I slumber. It is so cold here, sister, and I am so lonely. Come lie with me.

The last sentence has some compulsion behind it, and I find myself considering how I might lie down with the giant. Fortunately Effie appears not to be affected.

'I cannot, sister. And you need rest for only a little while longer. Soon your work will be done and you will find peace with your kinfolk.'

'What does she mean?' Snake asks.

'If what Effie believes is correct, once we take the magic she has stored, she will no longer have a purpose and will join her kin in their own realm.'

Nothing happens for a moment, then the ground appears to roll like waves in the sea, and the stone is free. At the same time, a group of tourists rounds the headland.

'Hey, what are you doing? Anna, something's not right here—where's your phone?'

A woman stops and stares open-mouthed while she fumbles in her backpack. I cannot help with the spell, but I can help with this. I walk towards the group as my companions move into position around the stone.

'There is nothing to see here,' I tell them. 'We are just carrying out some routine maintenance.' I put some glamour behind the words, reinforcing the idea that there is nothing unusual going on.

'Bobby,' the girl named Anna says, 'you had me worried. It's just maintenance workers.'

A frown furrows Bobby's brow. He has seen more, so the magic is taking a little longer to work on him.

'You were having a little bit of a joke,' I suggest to him. 'Now you want to return and find somewhere to warm up.

His face clears. 'Don't get huffy, Anna, I was just mucking around. Come on, we've seen the stones. Let's go and have a pint somewhere warm.'

The group heads back the way they came, and I stay on the path, ready to deter anyone wanting a closer look at the Giant of Storr. I half turn so I can watch both the path and my companions. The three greater creatures are holding hands in a circle around the stone. Another tingle of magic reaches me, pricking my skin, telling me they are ready to begin casting.

· · ★ · ☾ · ★ · ·

My mother often talked of spells worked with the power of three. I've never seen a spell cast this way because in the World Above, we try to keep magic hidden from mortals. Humans are able to explain away small magical feats as tricks—they do it every day.

However, magic on a large scale would be difficult to ignore. Not just because three chanting creatures would make a spectacle but because magic on this scale would have an impact on the physical world. The world would be drained of magic and would soon show signs of decay.

As I take the hands of a royal princess and the Witch Protector of the north, the enormity of what I'm about to do hits me. I can't believe I'm about to cast a major spell with two of the most notorious creatures of our time. Me, the gnome who tried to stay hidden most of his life, to blend in, to not cause ripples.

I breathe in through my nose and out through my mouth, attempting to calm the panic rising from my gut. If this is to work, I need to focus on saving Pris and the Unseelie Court. I push away my awe of working with these two women and just concentrate on the magic pulsing from the stone, tasting the feel of it and steeling myself not to recoil from its intensity.

Euphemia squeezes my hand, and I turn my attention to her. 'All right, listen carefully to the words of the spell. You need to memorise them.'

'What we need is to get a move on, or there will be no court left for us to save,' Princess Petunia says dourly. She reminds me so much of Pris, my heart aches.

'Hush, this will take as long as it takes. Now listen:
Out of time, it doth reside,
In dire peril, heart and mind.
To save it all, the court must hide,
One point in time must we bind.'

I repeat the words in my mind, my experience learning song lyrics no doubt helping me memorise them quickly. I nod when I'm ready. Princess Petunia is still mumbling, but a minute or two later, she tells us, 'I am good.'

'We must repeat this out loud while holding the court in our minds.'

'Sounds easy enough,' I say.

Euphemia shakes her head. 'Not so easy. We must sing it to this tune to use the stone's power as well as the magic around us.' She hums something that sounds a little like 'Greensleeves.'

I can't help the grin that splits my face. Finally something is going my way. This will be much easier than parroting the words.

Princess Petunia tugs at my hand. 'It is nothing to smirk about, Snake. This is a serious business.'

'But it's "Greensleeves,"' I say, stupidly pleased.

Her frown softens, and she smiles slowly. 'I believe it is. Well, that will make things easier.'

'Are you two ready?' Euphemia asks.

Princess Petunia says, 'Yes,' but I ask, 'How long will we need to sing—I mean, how will we know if the spell has worked?'

Princess Petunia smiles again. 'The dragons are communicating. Am'ratha is circling Inverness. If the spell works, the magical light of the Unseelie Court will begin to dim to a blue glow. This is the sign for her and Ed'ruven to fly Pris and King Maddox out of the castle. Once they are free, or when the court is fully in stasis, she will tell us we can stop.'

The princess's words have a sobering effect. Pris could well be stuck in the court should things not go to plan. I suck in a deep breath in an attempt to calm my nerves, then slowly let it out.

'Are you ready?' Euphemia asks again.

'As ready as I'll ever be.' I draw in a breath, filling my lungs in readiness for a long singing session.

'Right, prepare yourselves. Draw on a little magic, and let us begin.'

We link hands and draw on magic. My hands tingle, and I almost fall to my knees when the magic the others are drawing rushes through me. Combining the power of three intensifies the levels, and I am vibrating to my very core. It is all I can do to hold myself together and maintain the circle.

'Snake, concentrate. Do not lose yourself to the flow, or this will never work.'

Petunia's tart tones act as a beacon grounding me. I focus on her, and it helps me find my sense of self in amongst the magic.

Euphemia starts singing the spell, and we join in. I hold Pris and the Unseelie Court in my mind while also trying to keep myself whole as the magic intensifies to a whole new level.

As the magic increases, I can sense every individual molecule in my body, and it feels like they are unbinding. I struggle to maintain my chanting while channeling the magic and keeping myself whole. I miss a word, then I hear Ed'rathe in my head.

You are almost there, Snake. Don't let go!

I hear his words and wonder who Snake is. Am I Snake? Yes, I am Snake. It is as simple and as difficult as keeping that name in my head while I work the spell.

Well done, my friend. I would hate to lose you as my creature just when I am getting used to you.

Ed'rathe's my dragon. The thought sneaks into my mind as I repeat the spell. I'm not going to be able to keep this up for much longer. All my worry is for nothing because at that moment, Euphemia's hand slips from mine, and the circle is broken. I stumble to my knees and lean forward onto my hands, panting, trying to draw breath.

Did we do it? I ask Ed'rathe as the stone swims before my eyes. Then the world goes black.

· · ✦ 🌙 ✦ · ·

I study the sprites and hearth elves outside the window of the court audience chamber as they shore up the wards around the castle. Apparently they're laying a few nasty little traps. King Maddox paces behind me, muttering under his breath. Dinian is slouched over a chair, reading a book, completely disengaged.

'Shouldn't we be doing something?' I ask, running my sweaty hands down my trousers. I changed into my questing clothes to be ready for action, and here I am, twiddling my thumbs, waiting while others work.

King Maddox stops. 'We are to stay here and stay safe, for the court is as much about us as it is about the place.'

'What a waste of our skills,' I say.

My uncle studies me, a quizzical expression on his face. He's trying to work out if I'm being serious. This is confirmed when he speaks, his voice taking on a lecturing tone.

'No, we are preserving our magic. We are the last line of defence. When everyone else has fallen, it is up to us to protect them and escort them to safety.'

'Oh.' Not a great comeback. Then again, I'd thought King Maddox was hiding out here, making like nothing was wrong, so I'm thrown a little off balance by his explanation.

'Only problem is, I don't know how to use my magic well enough to do that.' Deep down I'm embarrassed to admit this, but I hold my head high—after all, it isn't my fault I never learned.

King Maddox stares at me, almost as if he is seeing me for the first time. He sighs as if all of this is too much for him. Or perhaps it's me who is adding to his burden. 'Of course not knowing about us would mean you did not grow up with magic. You will be of little use to us now.'

I close my eyes and absorb this blow. I am sick of creatures dismissing me because I know nothing about their world or because I can't use my magic. I want to scream, 'It's not my fault! You were all part of the conspiracy that kept me from my heritage.' The only thing that stops me is that we have bigger things to worry about.

My uncle resumes his pacing just as the door to the chamber opens, admitting Susan. I still can't call her Lady.

Then again, I can't get my head around my being a princess either.

She bobs a curtsey. 'They made it out, Your Majesty.'

'Excellent,' King Maddox says and continues pacing. 'Now we must wait.'

Susan starts walking backwards out of the room.

'Wait,' I say. 'What are you and the others doing now?'

'We are strengthening the internal wards. It should help with staving off the attack, but we also need strong wards to protect the court in case it's in stasis for months rather than days.'

'Oh. I'm not sure my magical abilities are quite at that level yet.'

'It is not difficult. I can teach you. You're a quick learner, and you come from two lines of powerful elves. And if you can't master the technique, I can use your magic to bolster mine.'

'She is needed here,' King Maddox says.

Why is he being so difficult? It makes me all the more determined to go with Susan.

'You won't need me until the attack begins. I will return as soon as it starts.'

He flicks his hand in a shooing motion. 'Go. Perhaps you will be of some use in defending the castle after all.'

The anger I have been keeping under control while we waited threatens to bubble up and overflow. I half turn, ready to give him a piece of my mind, to remind him it is not my fault I was kept from my true heritage. The only thing that stops me is Susan. She places a hand on my arm and shakes her head. I follow her out of the room, and as the guard shuts the door, she says, 'He is worried for his court and his people.'

'I know, but that doesn't excuse how mean he's being,' I tell her.

Susan's smile is sad. 'It is not you he is mad at, it's your father. Family is everything to King Maddox, and it broke his heart when your father stayed in the World Below with your mother. He visited, of course, but it was not enough. King Maddox made the court his family, and now he's worried he will fail us.'

'If he had helped Queen Ariana sooner—'

I stop mid-sentence. If my uncle had helped sooner, would the attack on his court never have happened? I was no longer quite so certain about that. Bernais and his cronies were too well-organised, and they had quite a following. They and their creature purist cronies must have been planning the overthrow of the two courts for some time. Queen Ariana's absence is merely a convenient opportunity for them to launch their attack.

'So, how do we do this?' I ask, changing the subject.

She leads me through the hallways and shows me how to look for weaknesses in the spell weaves—it's kinda like blurring your eyes, and anything that's clear holds a weakness. It's a slow process, and I find my mind drifting. Then I see it. I see the molecules moving and how Susan pulls the rents together and adding more molecules to strengthen it, sort of like darning.

She draws so little on my magic as she works that I'm sure she asked me along just to give me something to do, and my heart thaws a little more towards her.

'King Maddox sent me to care for you when you were little. He went a little mad when the love of his life died. Then your father went missing, and he called me back with a message spell. It was only when I arrived back here that I realised he had meant me to bring you too. By that time, you had disappeared.'

'But the lasagna? You knew you were going?'

'No, I was meant to be out that night at a birthday party with a friend.'

Steeped in the memories of that night, it suddenly strikes me. 'You're friends with Giles Regis's daughter?'

'Yes, Verona and I've been friends since we were children.'

'But you're—'

'Older? Only by a few years, which is no time at all in our lifespan.'

'I meant—'

'That I'm a gnome? That has never mattered to Verona, and in the World Above, her father has had to accept my presence, although there has always been an underlying hostility.'

'And now—'

'Giles Regis and I find ourselves on different sides. Verona's and my friendship will not stop me from giving that creature exactly what he deserves should he and I come face to face.'

Susan stops what she is doing and studies me. 'Are you ready to try now?'

'I... How did you know?'

'I have watched you learn things over the years. You get a certain look when something clicks with you.'

I find the next patch and give it a go. I stare at the ward, going almost a little cross-eyed, until I can see the particles that make up the shield and the extra particles floating around in the air. I will the stray particles to fill in the gaps. They wrangle with me a little, but eventually I will them into place.

The end result is not as tidy as Susan's, and I expect her to smooth it over for me, but she smiles and says, 'That'll do.'

My heart is lighter, and we work through the corridors, mending as we go, and I am soon working as quickly and neatly as Susan. Not long after, the light above us blinks out, and the ward I'm working on trembles.

Susan covers my hand with hers. 'The battle has begun. You must return to the King now.'

I don't move, reluctant to leave the fighting to others. 'So I can hide away during the battle?'

'No. I told you, he wants to protect us. Also, I shouldn't tell you this, but he holds the thread that keeps the court out of time. He will need your strength to keep it there.'

'He has Dinian. Let me stay and fight with you.'

'That elf is no better than he should be and will be very little use.' Susan places her hands on my shoulders and pushes me back towards the audience chamber. 'Go, help your uncle. Whatever you may feel about him, he is very important to all of us—he literally holds the wellbeing of my world in his hands.'

I do as my old nanny requests, her words ringing in my ears. My uncle could not be all bad if someone like Susan respects him.

CHAPTER 15

The Battle Is Won

By the time I reach the audience chamber, I feel like I'm wading through a balloon being collapsed from the outside. The air is thick, and it's difficult to breathe or move. Having focused so intently on the wards to strengthen them, I can almost see them bend under the external pressure, then move inwards.

When I enter the room, I find Dinian still slouching in the chair, reading. I storm over to him and grab the book from his hand.

'We're under attack in case you haven't noticed,' I snap. 'Why aren't you doing something to help?'

He raises an eyebrow. 'I am holding myself in reserve. If the King fails, it is my job as heir to take over.'

I follow his gaze as he checks on King Maddox. Framed by the window, his forehead leaning against the glass, he appears to be watching the activity below. On a closer inspection, the lines of strain around his eyes stand out—eyes so very like my father's.

I stride over to him and place a hand on his arm. 'Use my power.'

He turns his head towards me, his eyes two pools of sadness. 'No, girl, this is my duty.'

'And you are to be my wife, so you should wait and share your power with me when the King is depleted,' Dinian says from behind me.

Does he sound almost gleeful at the prospect of the King collapsing? What am I missing here? Is he hoping the King will die in his attempt to keep his court and people safe? Does he want to be King that much?

I throw Dinian a disdainful look, drawing my lips back in a sneer. 'I'm not your wife yet, and if I have any say in the matter, I never will be.'

I move closer to my uncle. 'King Maddox, Uncle, take my power. Your people need this place to stay where it is, and you need to keep it here for them.'

The plea on behalf of his people works. King Maddox reaches out and clasps my hand. His palm tingles as it touches mine, followed by a gentle tug. I almost swoon as my blood sings in response to his call. I'm locked in place by the spell, but it is working. The tension around the King's mouth lessens, and I sense the palace stabilising as the wards repulse the worst of the attack.

'I do not think I can hold this for much longer,' King Maddox whispers. 'Your power is helping, but they are strong.'

'So are you and your people,' I tell him. 'And don't forget, we don't have to hold this forever—just long enough for the others to cast their spell.'

While my words bolster the King, my own fears grow as the edges of the magic holding the court out of time begin to fray. At the same time, something else tugs at my senses. It is like a slow, warm wind heading towards me.

Crash. I jump as the window beside us caves in. Is this it? The end of the court?

A dragon nose appears. ***Come, help the King onto my***

back, Ed'ruven says. I lead my uncle to the opening, and, after making sure no sharp edges will cut him, he hauls himself out and slides onto his dragon's back.

In a moment Am'ratha takes his place. ***Your turn.***

I move to slide across her neck, but I'm tugged back into the room.

Dinian holds my wrist in a vicelike grip, and his lips curl into a snarl as he says, 'You are mine. Do not ever forget it. You will stay with me, or take me with you.'

I twist my arm out of his grasp and snap, 'I am nobody's, and I thought the plan was for you to stay here so the people would have a leader when they're brought out of stasis.'

His lips curl again, baring teeth. 'I am not spending my time sleeping. Who knows when we will be awakened. I come with you, or you don't go.'

Am'ratha's voice rumbles in my head. ***Come, Princess. We have little time.***

I glance towards the other side of the room. A light film is advancing towards us at the pace of a man walking.

Bring him, Royal One. Your people will need you in the coming battle, and I can carry two.

Against my better judgement, I allow Dinian to grab hold of my arm, and we jump onto Am'ratha's neck together. As my dragon shoots into the sky, the filmy wave touches the window, and I breathe a sigh of relief. I settle in for the ride to Loch Ness and survey the town as we fly over. No one would know a battle is waging—or is it?

Something itches at the back of my neck, and it isn't Dinian. Grossman Green and Giles Regis easily breached the wards yesterday, and yet they did not make it in today. Also, even though the castle is being held in stasis, smaller battles would still be occurring outside. Why aren't we seeing more fighting? I want to talk to the King about my concerns, but his dragon is too far away.

'This is so amazing, my first dragon ride,' Dinian almost purrs in my ear. 'I cannot wait until I get my very own dragon.'

I shudder as he leans his head against mine. I can't pull away without unseating us, but I send an elbow backwards, digging him in the ribs.

'Ouch, what was that for?'

'You're too close,' I tell him.

I can ditch him in the river if you want, Am'ratha sends for my ears only.

Best not, I tell her, although I'm sorely tempted.

In the moments before we left the court, Dinian had shown himself to be a selfish, self-serving git. Not only am I more determined that I will never marry him, but I'm also not prepared to keep up this sham of friendship, not even if it keeps my uncle onside. I wriggle forward, trying to put as much distance between us as I can.

'You should be nicer to me,' Dinian says, his voice taking on a threatening tone. 'You never know when it might be useful to have me as a friend.'

I suppress another shudder. I would rather kill myself than ask Dinian for help.

Hold tight, Am'ratha says, *We are almost at the loch.*

·· *' ◟ ,*· ··

As the sun begins its descent over the Isle of Skye, the air around me thickens with magic. It is like being enveloped in a wet blanket. Then, all of a sudden, it is gone.

I walk the few paces back to where the others had stood around the power stone. The ground has closed back over, and all sign of the stone is gone. Around the place where it had appeared, Effie, Snake, and Petunia lie, limbs akimbo.

The ground is cold, and I rush over to check that they are still alive. My heart thuds in my chest as I try to find Effie's pulse. It is there. That gives me hope for the others. I take my time checking Snake and Petunia. They are alive. Shaking each of them in turn, I try to wake them. They remain asleep. I will have to move them somewhere warmer so they can recover.

Ed'rathe, I call, *I need your help.*

We cannot come, Dragon Friend. You have taken all the magic, and there is not enough left to make a glamour. We are forbidden from revealing ourselves to mortals. I will find a place close by where we can draw on magic, then let you know where you can find us.

I am on my own. Should I go for help, or wait until they wake up? The chill in the air bites at my face, and I fear if I leave them for too long, they may still die. I reach for Effie's and Petunias' hands and send what little warmth I can into their bodies. I keep a little magic in reserve for Snake.

They are going to die of exposure, I tell Ed'rathe. *Are you able to help in another way?*

Give me a moment, Dragon Friend.

'Ugh. What happened?' Snake is slowly pushing himself up off the ground.

Thank you, I tell the dragon.

Snake stands up, surveying the scene in a bit of a daze.

'Snake, we need to move the others to somewhere warmer where they can recover.'

'What?' He shakes his head as if trying to clear it.

'Can you help Effie and Petunia to that bench by the path while I search for some food?'

'Ahh.' He turns his eyes to me, though I am not sure he actually sees me. 'I guess.'

I leave them and head for the lights of the township. The

smell of fish and chips wafts towards me, and I increase my pace. Without slowing, I reach into my pocket and search around the supplies I left at Eleanora's place in the World Above. I touch something papery. No, that is my stash of books. And that hat is the bell Eleanora's daughter put out for me to request tea. I pause. Tea would be nice. No, I need to concentrate on hot, warming food.

Ah, there it is. I grasp a wallet filled with money Eleanora insisted I have. At the time I had laughed because money is only useful in the World Above, and I was going on a quest in the World Below. Besides, in the World Above, I am a cat. What use would a cat have for money? She simply smiled at me and said, 'You can never predict what will be useful and what will not. Best to be prepared for every eventuality.'

Now, as my hand comes back through the portal and I draw the wallet out of my pocket, I am ever so grateful she ignored me and left it anyway.

Half an hour later, I am walking back to the spot where I left the others, my mouth watering at the aroma of freshly cooked fish and chips wafting from the parcel under my arm. The three of them are huddled together on the bench, sharing their body heat and looking like they have not eaten in a week. I open the parcel, and the hit of salt and vinegar is heaven and sets my taste buds tingling. They fall on the food like ravenous beasts.

Finally they slow down, and I step forward to take my share.

'We should be going,' Snake says. 'We should call the dragons.'

'There is no magic left in the area to hide them,' Petunia says.

Alarm flashes on Snake's face. 'But how are we going to get to Loch Ness?'

Petunia shrugs. 'There is no rush. Our task was to put the court in stasis, and we have done that.'

'I need to go to Pris and make sure she is okay.'

'Ah, the impatience of youth.' Petunia smiles.

'The boy is in love, Petunia, cut him a break,' Effie says. 'Besides, don't you want to go to Loch Ness and check up on your family?'

I wipe my fingers on a napkin. 'Snake, I think the next bit is up to you and me. I don't like doing this, but needs must.'

He looks at me suspiciously, not getting my meaning at all. When we arrive back at the town, I lead our team away from the main street into a residential area. It is not quite dark enough for this, but I think I still have enough magic left for an invisibility spell.

We find a quiet street, and I have Effie and Petunia wait at the corner. The first house has a car, but we walk until I find a dwelling with two vehicles parked in the driveway. 'We need to break into the house and steal the keys,' I tell Snake. 'This is where your skills come in.'

'I can do one better.'

He tests the doors, and to my surprise, the driver's door of the second car opens. 'Always worth a try just in case.' He smiles crookedly.

'We still need to get it going,' I whisper.

'Hop in,' Snake says. He slides into the driver's seat, reaches under the dashboard, fiddles with some wires, and the vehicle sparks into life.

'How?' I ask

'Dad taught me when I was little. In the magical object retrieval business, it was always important to have getaway options. I never needed to use it, but he and Mum both made me practice.'

We back out of the driveway and onto the road before stopping at the corner. Effie and Petunia shuffle across the back seat. Once Snake has convinced them to buckle up their seatbelts, he directs the car towards the bridge to the mainland.

'I hope the dragons aren't far,' Snake says, pointing at the petrol gauge. 'I don't want to have to explain a hot-wired vehicle to a service station attendant.'

He smiles, and I can't stop myself from chuckling at the thought as we make our way across the bridge to the mainland.

The car hurtles across the causeway. I'm not used to driving on the open road, and my knuckles whiten as I grip the wheel. My stomach is churning. Initially I think it's because I want to get us to the dragons as quickly as possible, but as we leave Skye, the certainty that something is not quite right begins to grow.

'Are you sure the court is in stasis?' I ask.

'Am'ratha reported it was and that the King and Pris were on their way to Loch Ness,' Princess Petunia tells me.

Ed'rathe, are you there?

Yes. Am'ralla and I are settled in a field outside a place called Boardford.

I check the next signpost. *We are a little over ten minutes away.*

Your time means nothing to me, Noble One.

We will be there soon.

I focus on the road and try increasing our speed. I almost roll the car as I take a corner too fast, and I ease my foot off the accelerator a little. Arriving a couple of minutes earlier is not worth risking our lives.

The car is silent as the others rest. Although I try to calm myself, my anxiety grows. I can't shake the feeling that something isn't quite right.

Ed'rathe, can you ask Am'ratha how much damage was done to the castle at the Seelie Court?

Certainly.

It seems like a lifetime but is probably only minutes later when the dragon gets back to me.

Am'ratha said the castle took very few blasts and remains intact. Only a few of the attackers managed to force their way inside. Also, she carries Dinian as well as the princess.

Thank you, Ed'rathe.

So the slimeball wouldn't stay and protect the court—typical, but I am sure that is not what has me even more worried than before.

'Are you all right, Snake?' Percival asks.

'I'm not sure,' I answer honestly. 'Something doesn't feel right.'

'What do you mean? Everything is going to plan.'

Percival has hit the nail on the head. 'Yep, and that's the problem.'

The sprite shifts in his seat, and a sideways glance shows his concern for me. 'You are not happy our plan is working?'

'It's all been too easy, Percival. I worry that we're missing something, because when have things ever gone right for us?'

As the words leave my mouth, it hits me like a punch to the gut, and my dinner threatens to make a reappearance.

'Percival, when we placed the court in stasis, we locked a large portion of the Unseelie guard in the castle.'

'Of course. They remained to defend the court and any creatures who decided to stay.'

'Ed'rathe told me that when the court was frozen, only a few of the attackers were caught inside. And if none of the court managed to escape before the spell took....'

Out of the corner of my eye, I see Percival blanche. 'That means Bernais's cronies are free to carry on the fight while many of our team cannot help until we find enough magic to restore the court.'

I nod. 'Even worse, though, I fear it means they knew our plan. Only a dozen or so people were aware of what we were doing. So, that means there is a mole in our midst.'

The car falls silent as everyone comes to terms with our betrayal. I press my foot to the floor, and the car lurches forward. Now that Pris might well be in danger, every second counts.

'What is going on?' Effie asks as she grips the seat in front of her.

'We have to get to Loch Ness and warn the others. We had a spy in the court,' I tell her, 'and I think he escaped with Pris.'

My heart is pounding so loudly in my ears, I almost miss Princess Petunia saying, 'Why not just tell Ed'rathe to contact his sister and have her warn Priscilla and King Maddox to be careful?'

Of course, what was I thinking? Obviously I wasn't thinking at all. If we're to help the others, I need to keep my cool.

Ed'rathe, can you please pass a message to your sister? They might be heading into danger and—

She says they are just coming up to Loch Ness, and.... Hold on, Noble One.... I have lost contact with her.

Euphemia leans forward. 'Do you really think it might be Dinian? Or are you letting your dislike cloud your judgement?'

'I don't know,' I tell her as I take the next corner at breakneck speed, and someone in the back gasps as they are flung across the seat. 'But I do know someone leaked our plan.'

'We will be no use to the others if we die,' Princess Petunia says sharply as she pulls herself back into a sitting position.

It is all I can do to keep the car on the road, so I don't comment. We turn another corner, and I can make out the dragons resting in a field. Well, perhaps not resting, as they appear to be eyeing up the Highland cattle in the next paddock.

There is no time for eating, Ed'rathe.

I am sure I hear him humph as the car screeches to a halt by a wooden gate set into a hedgerow. Everyone tumbles out, and I remind them to lock their doors so no one else steals the car. Princess Petunia reaches into her pocket and then throws a handful of notes onto the back seat. When she catches me watching, she smiles and says, 'That should compensate them for their trouble.'

Damn straight, it should. I counted at least half a dozen £50 notes.

Any update? I ask as I run across the paddock towards the dragons.

No, Noble One. We cannot contact either of the two dragons meant to be at Loch Ness.

Is that normal?

No, Noble One, it is not.

Percival and I climb onto Ed'rathe's back and wait while Princess Petunia and Effie settle onto Am'ralla. The wind rushes past as Ed'rathe pushes into the air. Unfortunately, he doesn't have an accelerator, and all I can do is will him to go faster and pray we will be in time to rescue Pris from whatever is happening at Loch Ness.

CHAPTER 16

Or Is It?

With Dinian's arms wrapped around my waist, I try to put as much distance between our bodies as I can without falling off Am'ratha. I tolerated him while we were in court, but now that he has shown his true colours, I no longer want to be anywhere near him.

Every time he touches me, I suppress a shiver, and he does it so often, I can't relax and appreciate the spectacular countryside we fly over. I begin to suspect he is enjoying my discomfort.

I work at blocking him out because at the back of my mind, a kernel of a thought is growing into a big problem. Something feels wrong about the attack on the castle. There was no great storming of the battlements as Giles and Grossman had promised, and there were very few creatures fighting in the streets. In fact, most of the creatures I saw outside the wards were standing round, chatting. As we flew over Inverness, I found very little magical activity anywhere, and not even any human type fights.

My unease increases as we leave the city behind. Finally I have to admit that what went on in Inverness felt less like a siege and more like a feint. If that was the case, what did Bernais have to gain?

'This is amazing.' Dinian's voice comes from close by my ear. 'When I get my dragon, I will fly everywhere.'

As you can imagine, my brothers are queuing up for the honour, Am'ratha says.

A chuckle escapes even though I try to bite it back. *I thought dragons couldn't do sarcasm.*

You have a lot to learn.

'What are you laughing at?' Dinian asks, his voice suddenly cold and hard.

I don't answer. It's none of his business.

'You do not take me seriously. When we are married, that will change.'

That's it, the final straw. It's time I put the elf in his place. My only regret is that I can't deliver the words face to face so he can see how determined I am.

'Dinian, you need to get it through your thick head that there is nothing on heaven or earth that would make me marry you.'

'I have been promised your hand, and I will have it,' my would-be husband says from behind me. 'If not with your permission, then by force if need be.'

Gone is the charming courtier, and I find myself sharing my ride with a petty tyrant in his place. In my head I'm ready to tell him I don't believe for a moment that my uncle would force me down the aisle kicking and screaming. Besides, as an heir to the Seelie Court's crown, I require the monarch's permission to marry.

Fortunately I don't open my mouth, because I suddenly realise that this high in the sky, I do not trust Dinian not to lash out when he is faced with my particular reality.

I would drop him and rush to save you, Am'ratha reassures me.

Tempting, but no. I need to handle this myself when my feet are firmly on the ground. And I might just deliver it with an un-princess-like punch, I promise myself.

Am'ratha snickers, *I can hear you.*

I know.

It seems an age before I can make out the crumbling ruins of Urquhart Castle in the distance as dusk begins to dull the sky. Almost safe. As we approach the castle, Am'ratha sweeps in a circle to find the best place to land.

Perhaps you should let the dragons in Skye know we have arrived.

When we are on the ground, Royal One. There is some unrest down there I do not like the look of.

I can't make out anything, but then again, my eyesight isn't as good as the dragons'. We drop and begin our approach towards a flat piece of ground near the castle. I catch a glimpse of a small cohort holding off a larger group of creatures by a cattle grid on the road into the lake. That must be what Am'ratha saw.

Are some of Bernais's followers trying to get back through the portal? I ask. *And is Petunia's husband holding them off?*

Perhaps. Am'ratha sounds less certain, and I wonder what she can see that I can't.

Why didn't they simply go through the fields and wait until night? I wonder. *They could have snuck through to the portal under the cover of darkness, and no one would ever have known.*

Royal One, we must change our plans. We cannot wait here for the others, but it is too dangerous to fly directly to the portal, as our undersides are defenceless. Ed'ruven commands that we land until the path is clear.

Am'ratha's tone tells me there is no room for argument here.

'What's going on?' Dinian asks as the dragons land behind the defenders.

I dismount as quickly, wanting to get as far away from Dinian as possible.

'Should we help out, or stay with the dragons?' I ask the King.

He doesn't have time to answer as bodies emerge from nowhere, and we are embroiled in a two-pronged attack with the dragons at our backs.

I take my defensive position, ready to fight, but neither King Maddox nor Dinian has moved.

'Shields,' King Maddox barks as something whizzes past me.

'What the hell was that?' I shout.

'Magic,' my uncle answers. 'Raise your shield.'

'I don't know how to,' I admit.

King Maddox mutters something under his breath, then the air around me thickens. 'Move away from the dragons. We do not want them hurt by a stray pulse.'

'Perhaps we can join up with the portal guards,' I suggest.

'Good thinking,' the King says, and I'm pleased I'm finally good for something.

Moving slowly as a group, we inch closer to the guards, but our attackers figure out what we're doing, and they stop us a few feet from our target.

'If we all stand back-to-back, we can concentrate on maintaining a forward shield only and save our energy,' King Maddox commands.

We move into position, and I feel a little more secure. Something pings off the shield level with my face. 'Aren't we going to fight back?'

'Using magic to harm others is outlawed. While I believe that will not matter to these creatures, there is still a chance they may stop short of hurting us,' King Maddox warns.

Another shot pings by.

'Are you sure we shouldn't attack?' I ask.

'Yes, niece. Let's save our strength. Besides, I think I see reinforcements arriving. They may think twice about attacking Petunia and Euphemia.'

I hope so because I fear I am not going to be much help in a magical battle. I glance over my shoulder, relieved to see there are indeed two dragons heading our way. We may just get back to the World Below in one piece after all.

· ·*· ☾ ·*· ·

Wind whips through my hair, but Ed'rathe is flying so fast, I daren't let go to hold it back. When this is over, I really need to get a haircut—if it is ever over. I'm beginning to feel I will be trapped in this nightmare forever.

I don't have time to wallow in my self-pity because, in what seems no time at all, the dragons are circling above Loch Ness, allowing us to observe the scene below. Pris, Dinian, and King Maddox are surrounded by a handful of creatures, and they're standing back-to-back, ready to fight. I peer down. There is a small knot of creatures, perhaps dwarves, hiding behind a hillock, waiting to attack.

Behind the royal party, a small contingent of creatures is holding back a larger group from entering the fight, keeping them on the other side of a cattle trap. They can't help the royal party, but at least they are preventing them from being over-run. Am'ratha and Ed'ruven wait beside the ruins of the castle, seemingly watching the action.

I gesture to the two of them, *What are they doing? Why aren't they helping?*

Unless the flow of magic is threatened, we stay out of

directly involving ourselves in the affairs of men and creatures, Ed'rathe informs me.

'But you took us to Skye and then back here,' I argue.

Yes, because you were trying to save the Unseelie Court so King Maddox could concentrate on his duty to clean the flow, Nobel One.'

My hands ball into fists, and I resist the urge to pummel the dragon's hide—we are still too high for me to survive the fall should he decide to eject us. How can they stand by and do nothing? Is there another way they can contribute?

Is there anything you dragons can do?

The air thrums, and I recognise this as the dragons talking to each other.

We can protect King Maddox if his life is threatened. He is the one tasked with protecting the magical flow, so he has special consideration.

And if he dies? I press.

He does not have a confirmed heir, so we would have to go to our Queen for direction.

This is so maddening. What is the point of having dragon allies if they can't do anything to help? Ah.... If they can help King Maddox, perhaps they can also help Pris.

Ed'rathe, Pris appears to be Queen Ariana's only heir. With the Queen held between life and death, Pris is, in effect, the leader of the Seelie Court.

Interesting. I shall find out what I can, Noble One.

I sense the dragons talking again.

Ed'ruven believes we are obliged to protect the princess as well as the King.

That's at least something, I guess. Surveying the scene below, I consider our best options for joining the fight—not that I really have any training. Petunia's dragon swoops down and lands. When the princess and Euphemia are on the ground, she takes to the air and circles the skies. I watch as the dwarves hesitate for a moment, allowing Euphemia time to join the royal party and Petunia to go and assist her husband.

'Why aren't the dwarves attacking?' I ask Percival.

'I think the brains of the outfit are in the group trying to get over the cattle stop. Either that, or they are tasked with making sure none of the Unseelie Court get through the portal.'

'Or perhaps both,' I say after watching them a while longer. 'What do you want to do? I'm going to help Pris, but Ed'rathe could still take you to the World Below.'

'We fight. There is no point going back home if we leave King Maddox behind.'

Ed'rathe drops to the ground, and we slide from his back. He bows his head and says, ***Fight well, my friends. I would be sad to lose you when I have just broken you in.*** Then he smiles, and I wonder which is more terrifying, him or the battle we are running headfirst into.

Thanks for the confidence boost, I tell him as he rises to join Am'ralla.

There is no reaction from the dwarves as we join the others. Now that I'm on the ground, I quickly realise there is a battle going on, it's just that the fighting isn't physical. The air around us is thick and shimmers slightly with magic.

'What are they doing?' I ask Percival.

'From what I can make out, everyone has erected personal shields, and they are testing each other out to find a weak spot.'

'Pris doesn't know how to do that.' Come to think of it, nor do I.

'I think King Maddox has her covered.'

'How do we probe a shield?'

'You send finger bolts of power at the creature, targeting different areas around them.'

My eyebrows almost fly off my head. 'But we're taught

that directing magic at another creature is a grave sin. From what I've heard, it's somewhat like getting an electric shock. Misdirect it, and it can be fatal.'

Percival turns a fierce face to me. 'This is a war we are fighting, Snake. There will be casualties.'

My mind can't process what Percival's saying. Creatures are at war? We are actually going to be attacking each other—with magic. I shake my head. Of course we are, and we must use magic too, otherwise the war will be lost before we start.

It started when Grossman and Giles used magic to enter the castle. If I hadn't known it then, the lesson is driven home when a shot of energy clips my ear a moment later.

'Raise a shield,' Percival commands as I reach up to touch the wound, and my hand comes back down bloodied. In seconds I'm following Percival's instructions and surrounding myself with an energy shield.

'We will not let any of you back into our lands. You are not welcome,' one of the dwarves says, and it is as if what he says lets loose the others.

Where the fighting had been controlled before, now the dwarves are attacking with everything they have.

'The royal party have combined their shields,' Percival says. 'We should too.'

In moments Percival and I are sharing bubble.

'You're stronger in magic than I am, so I will maintain our protection, and you concentrate on attack,' he says as a small contingent breaks away from the main group and heads towards us.

I am sending out shards of magic, fearful one might strike, but also afraid none will, when everything stops.

'I have Priscilla. Stop now, or I will kill her.'

I know that voice. My worst fears are confirmed when the dwarves part, and I see Dinian is holding Pris from behind with a knife at her throat. Of course, it makes sense now. Nothing would be able to penetrate a bubble maintained by King Maddox and Effie. The threat would have to come from within.

Beside me, Snake tenses, and I move quickly to grab his arm. 'You can do nothing from here. You must play the long game.'

'I knew that slimy elf couldn't be trusted,' Snake snarls. 'I will break every bone in his body when I get my hands on him.'

I understand his anger, I feel it too, but I need to calm him if Pris is to get out of this alive. 'You might have to wait in line,' I tell Snake. 'If looks could kill, King Maddox would have taken Dinian's life already.'

His body relaxes a little, but the tension around his lips tells me his mind is still working through possible scenarios to rescue Pris. The fighting around us has stopped for the moment while everyone waits to see how this plays out. Perhaps we can use this to our advantage.

'She can take care of herself,' I remind him. 'What we must do is be ready to react when she makes her move.'

'Can't the dragons help in some way?' Snake asks.

'Not while Pris has a knife to her throat.'

'Of course not, so what do you suggest?'

Now I have his attention.

'There are too many of them for us to win in a straight-out fight, so at some stage, we have to make a break for the portal to the World Below. While they are watching Dinian and Pris, we have the best chance we're going to get to take them by surprise.'

'Okay....'

'Can you speak with Ed'rathe and have him ask the others to be ready to make a run for the portal on my command?'

Snake studies me, a thoughtful expression on his face. 'Percival, who knew you were such a great tactician? We really could have used your help in the minotaur's maze.'

'You're wasting time,' I tell him impatiently, not used to accepting praise, but feeling pleasure anyway.

'Done,' he tells me, and I know the others understand when King Maddox sends a subtle nod our way.

Then it happens almost as if in slow motion. Pris moves a fraction, and she jolts her head backwards into Dinian's face, then, almost too fast to see, her knee comes up and she stamps down hard on Dinian's foot. As his hold on her loosens, she elbows him in the stomach and turns so that as he bends slightly in reaction, she kicks him in the shin.

It isn't as pretty as the kata I have seen her practice, but it is effective. Dinian releases his hold, and she turns and swings an almighty punch, landing it right on his chin. Dinian, not having expected her to be able to defend herself, staggers back as Pris pulls back for another punch, but King Maddox grabs her arm and drags her away. Then, as one, Pris, King Maddox, and Effie run through the gap towards us.

'Now,' I yell as loud as I can. 'Meet us by the loch.'

The air thrums as King Maddox puts up a new shield around our group, and I turn to head for the water. Snake does not move. His eyes are fixed on Dinian, who has recovered and is running after Pris, calling for the dwarves to support him.

It is as if Dinian's voice alters reality, and everything moves back into real time. Still tracking Dinian, Snake sends out some bolts of magic, aiming for the ground, and the dwarves hesitate, allowing Pris, Maddox, and Effie to run past us. Dinian is close behind, and as he reaches out for Pris, Snake steps out of the protection of the circle, draws back his arm, and punches the elf, his fist landing full force on the backstabbing elf's jaw. As Dinian collapses to the ground, Snake turns to us, a self-satisfied smile on his face.

'Snake, watch out!' Pris rushes towards him and knocks him out of the way of a magic bolt.

Snake stumbles to the side, and Pris falls at his feet. Am'ratha's roar fills the air, signalling that Pris hasn't fallen over Dinian as I first thought but that she's injured. Snake is staring at the scorch mark on her back.

I freeze, all thoughts gone from my mind. King Maddox rushes back and picks up Pris.

'Run,' he yells as he sprints towards his dragon.

Next thing, Snake has my hand, and he is pulling me and Effie towards the water. Without dragons, the only way to get to the portal is to spell the water under our feet. Effie takes the lead and transforms the water. I am in the middle, keeping up the shield. Snake takes the rear, sending out magical bolts to keep the dwarves at bay.

The dwarves are in disarray. They do not appear to be able to walk on water and keep up a shield at the same time. Working as a team, we are pulling away from them. In front of me, I see King Maddox's dragon enter the portal. Sanctuary is but a few feet away now. Am'ratha and Ed'rathe follow the older dragon.

Effie stumbles in front of me, and I almost trip over her.

'Not far now, old friend,' I tell her. 'You can do this.'

My heart is racing, filling my ears with its thudding. We are so close.

King Maddox is standing at the entrance of the portal. 'Hurry, the dragons are getting ready to close the door. They will not allow fighting so close to their home.'

What does he mean? The dragons never close their portal.

Then the whole pathway in front of us firms up as if there is a barrier between us and the water. King Maddox holds out his hand, lending support to Effie. We speed up. Effie is running full force, and I turn to grab Snake's arm.

'We must run,' I tell him.

He sends one last bolt of magic at the dwarves, swings round, and dashes towards us.

In front of us, the edges of the portal are shrinking inwards like someone is tightening a knot. Snake makes a dive for the shrinking hole, dragging me behind him. I look over my shoulder just in time to see the portal disappear completely.

I suck in great gulps of air. We have made it. No, hold on —where is Petunia? I look this way and that, dread clouding my senses. We have left her behind. Who will lead the rebellion now?

Effie places a hand on my arm. 'It was her choice. She wanted to stay with her husband and protect her home.'

'But what about our plan, Effie?'

Snake stands and dusts himself off and stretches his limbs. 'In all the movies, they say the first casualty of any battle is the plan.'

Effie pats my arm. 'We will regroup and do the best we can with what we have.'

Snake stills for a moment. 'Am'ralla's told Ed'rathe that Princess Petunia and her people made it safely to the castle while the attackers were distracted. They are as safe as any creature can be in these times.'

I slip to the floor, exhausted, but still aware this is not an ending but the beginning of something much larger.

CHAPTER 17

The War Truly Begins

S nake slips down the wall beside me, and I lean into him. I do not like personal contact but, after the turmoil of the last few hours, his presence is comforting. He is not restful though. His head turns this way and that as he scans the cave.

'Where is Pris?' he asks, his voice shaky with panic.

'Don't worry, lad, Am'ratha has taken Pris to safety so someone can tend to her wound.' King Maddox sounds weary, almost like he has had the stuffing knocked out of him.

'That is good,' I say. I mean it, but I do not feel it. I am numb. What started as a personal quest to stop Bernais from playing havoc with my world has now turned into creature fighting creature.

If I am honest, there has been something bubbling in the creature world for the last few hundred years, ever since Petunia and her followers were expelled.

We lost many potential leaders as others chose to support her by leaving too. Still, I always thought we would find a solution without coming to blows. Most creatures do not like change, King Maddox's court is a testament to that, but we have to bend or we will break, or so I believed until now. Never in a century would I have thought we would choose to break.

'Percival, are you okay?' Snake's voice washes me with concern.

I suck in some air and breathe out slowly. Now, there is a question. Am I all right?

'It is a lot to take in, Snake.'

'It is,' he confirms. 'I'm feeling a little overwhelmed too. I keep telling myself what my mum always says—when you are asked to eat an elephant, the only way to do it is one piece at a time... or something like that.'

I cannot help but chuckle. 'I understand what you are saying. This is huge, but all we can do is take one step at a time.'

'Yes, and that first step must be to go save Queen Ariana.' Effie's voice comes from across the cavern and bounces loudly off the stone walls. 'Moving forward will be easier with her on our side. Not least because she and King Maddox can begin restoring magic, which will appease some of Bernais's current supporters.'

'I guess now that I am here, I may as well go and see what I can do to help.' King Maddox's voice booms in the confines of the cavern.

'About time,' Snake mutters under his breath, and I snort, trying to hold in my laugh.

King Maddox sends a look that under any other circumstances would have me shaking in my boots. Now I am too tired to react.

'No time like the present,' Effie says, pushing herself to her feet.

I follow suit, but Snake says, 'I'm not going—'

Effie does not wait for him to finish speaking. 'We haven't time to argue. Come, King Maddox,' she commands. 'This madness has gone on long enough. Time to put an end to it before anyone else gets hurt.'

I smile at the King's back as he simply obeys. Ed'ruven allows them onto his back and waddles towards the opening. There is a gust of wind, and they are gone, leaving us behind.

'Ed'rathe, will you take me to Pris?... What do you mean, if you're able?'

The air buzzes with their conversation. While they work out what they are going to do, I think about where I want to go now. I had thought we would all stay together once we left the World Above, but obviously we're not going to. Now I must decide where to best focus my efforts.

Even though I am concerned for her, going to check on Pris does not seem like the best use of my time. Then again, neither does going to the end of the maze to help the Queen. In either place I will just be a spare part, and I am no longer satisfied with the role of bystander.

'Ed'rathe says Pris was taken to their home, the World Between, and he must ask their Queen's permission to bring us there,' Snake says.

The air tingles with magic, and Ed'rathe drops to the ground for us to mount.

I have permission for both of you to enter our lands.

I do not even need to think about it. 'Thank you for your invitation, but I am afraid at this moment, I have other commitments.'

The Queen thought you might refuse, Dragon Friend. She gave me leave to take you to where you need to be. And you are welcome to join us any time you feel the need.

'Thank you, Ed'rathe, and you too, Snake. If you do not mind a diversion before heading to your home, I would like to go to mine.'

'Are you sure, Percival?'

'Very. I need to check up on my family and say a final farewell to my father. Then I must consider where I will best be placed to help with the coming battle.'

Snake smiles. 'I will miss you.'

'And I you. Pris not so much.'

A chuckle erupts from Snake. 'Percival, you wily old fox, you've been hiding a sense of humour all this time.'

Ed'rathe inclines his head, and Snake and I climb on his back, Snake still laughing to himself. The dragon stands up and moves to the entrance, and a cool wind brushes my face as he takes flight.

He flies out from the cavern for a few wingbeats before banking left. In the distance I can just make out Ed'ruven as he swoops down over the minotaur's maze. Ed'rathe glides over the maze before peeling off and dropping down on the outskirts of the Wyld Woods, just in sight of the village.

I scramble down and bow to the dragon. 'Thank you.'

Snake leans over Ed'rathe's neck. 'I can't believe this is good-bye, but I understand—family is important.

He is right, family *is* important, and I have neglected mine for long enough. Still, that is not my only reason for coming here.

'I have a suspicion that Eleanora will need my help over the coming days, so no doubt we will meet again soon.'

What I do not add is that for the first time in a long time, I am ready to do more than follow orders; I am ready to fight. It will be strange without Pris and Snake, but we each have different paths to follow now.

'It will be weird without you—without your guidance,' Snake says. 'If you get a chance, do you think you could.... No, you will have enough to worry about.'

'Of course I will see what I can find out about your mother and Pris's parents' too.'

'Thank you. Not just for that, but for everything.'

His words make my chest squeeze. I dip my head and offer him a smile.

'Now go, look after Pris. She will need your support to get through these next few days. Many will have expectations of her, and it will be difficult for her to decide which path to take. Farewell, my friend.'

'Good-bye, Percival. Stay safe.'

I watch Ed'rathe take off, and continue to follow his flight until he and Snake are almost out of sight, the empty feeling in my stomach increasing with each wingbeat. Taking in a deep breath, I tell myself it is time to look forward, not back, and start towards the woods, only to find two figures walking towards me.

As they get closer, they materialise into Eleanora and her sister Eugenia. Their faces are pinched and grim. I hasten my steps towards them, knowing I am not going to like what they have to say but also knowing I am no longer the sprite who hides from the truth.

· · * 🌙 · * · ·

I force open an eye and close it immediately. We are high above a mountain range, and I hurt so much, I can't even cling to Am'ratha's back. She must be keeping me on with her magic. I don't like this lack of control, but I'm too sore and groggy to do anything about it. Everything blurs, and I let go, knowing Am'ratha will keep me safe.

The air is warmer. We must be close to or on the ground. *Landing,* I guess as I am jolted, waves of pain sent through my shoulder and arm. The world swims again as hands help me off her back.

Be well, my friend, Am'ratha's voice hums in my mind as I descend into full darkness.

At first I thought I had passed out for a long time, but I open my eyes to find myself being carried on a stretcher down a long, dark corridor. Who is transporting me, and to where? My heart is pounding, and I try to sit up, but I'm forced back down by a wave of dizziness.

I breathe in and out, slow and steady, until my heart calms, and I'm able to think. Am'ratha would not take me anywhere I would be in danger, I trust her to keep me safe, so all I need to do is wait and see what happens. This is so against my nature. However, I force myself to relax.

Finally we arrive at a huge cave. The ceiling is so high, I can barely make it out. Globes hover high above me, generating enough light to see by—barely. I try to twist, but just that slight movement sends burning pain through my body. As my stretcher bearers make their way forward, the room is silent except for the occasional shuffle as someone changes position.

It seems like hours later, but is probably only minutes, when my stretcher is placed on the ground. Again I try to sit up, but my head swims. I slowly and gently turn my head towards the direction I was travelling and gasp in a breath.

If I could move my arms I would rub my eyes, but I have to settle for blinking a few times to make sure I'm truly seeing what my brain is telling me I am.

A deep velvety voice engulfs me. ***Ah, Priscilla Crown, we meet again.***

I can barely comprehend the enormous ruby glow of the dragon's scales or the deep unending black of her eyes. She fills the cavern with her presence, and even without looking directly into her eyes, she has me in her thrall.

Still, I have the presence of mind to say, 'Again?'

The room shakes with a rumble, and I realise she is laughing. I am injured, lying on the ground with no dignity, and now I am being laughed at.

Little one, all those of royal blood are presented to me when they are first born so I can confirm they are worthy to be included in the line of succession.

Little one? Seriously, I am over this, but I can't find the will to do anything about it.

Careful, little one. I will forgive some things, but outright disobedience in my court will not be tolerated.

Of course she can read my mind!

And you need to learn to control your thoughts. Now, lie back and relax. The magic has damaged the muscles in your shoulder and has given you a mild heart attack. If you will allow me, I can repair the damage.

Magic. Someone hit me with magic!

You can rant, or I can heal you.

I close my eyes and try not to think anything uncomplimentary the Dragon Queen might hear. 'Healing, please.'

This may hurt a little.

That was an understatement. Fire burns through my muscles, and I bite back a scream as pain wracks my body. I hold it in. I won't show weakness in front of my unknown audience. Who knows what they might do if they believe I am not strong.

The white-hot pain disappears and is replaced with a cool soothing flow. Then there is nothing but numbness. I lie back, exhausted.

When I wake, I've been moved to the side of the room. I have a much better view of the Queen of Dragons, and it is just as shocking as the first time I saw her. She is at least the height of a three-storey building, and her head is as large as a lorry. She reclines sideways on a chaise lounge carved out of the rock and is by far the most magnificent thing I have ever seen in my life.

That is the glamour talking, Royal One.

I turn my head to find Am'ratha beside me.

She is glorious, but she does like to use the glamour to invoke awe.

'Thank you for coming back for me.' I am voicing my relief. 'And for bringing me here.

I was summoned, otherwise you would not have been allowed here, she says pragmatically.

Alarm bells ring in my head. 'Why?' I whisper.

Princess Adina and her dragon, Am'nera have been waiting to petition the Queen. Our Queen would not grant her an audience without both sides of the conflict being represented. Now you are here, the princess has been summoned.

'Wait. What? I've just been injured and healed. Now I'm expected to what? Represent Queen Ariana in the Dragon Court?'

Yes.

I flop back on the stretcher. Just when I thought things could not get any more ridiculous. I've been betrayed, shot at with magic, and now appointed as a royal ambassador for a second time! Seriously?

Can you stand?

'Sorry?'

Can you stand? Princess Adina is not the type of creature you want to give the upper hand to. You will want to meet her on your feet.

I struggle to stand up and look down at my clothes with dismay. I look like I've been dragged through a hedge backwards before being shot at with magic.

I cannot do anything about that in the time we have, but I can make it so creatures will not notice what you are wearing.

I smile at Am'ratha. 'Thank you.'

You are welcome. Come, we must approach the Queen.

'Wait,' I say as my friend steps forward. 'Who exactly is Princess Adina?'

Am'ratha's large saucer-like eyes regard me, and I imagine I see pity in there.

She is your great-aunt, Prince Bernais's mother. She has petitioned our Queen to appoint her Queen of the World Below given that Queen Ariana is missing and has no named heir.

The world shifts, and I sway on my feet. I knew there was a battle to be had, but I didn't think it would be here so soon, or that I would be alone when it happened.

You are not alone, Royal One. I am with you and will remain by your side.

We reach the podium in front of the Queen just as a blue dragon peels off from a group at the side. I expect a snarl and am surprised by her polite nod.

Am'ratha chuckles. ***We are not like you creatures. Manners and respect are everything in this court—something you would do well to remember.***

Point taken, I tell her.

The woman who joins us moments later obviously did not get the message. She glowers at me as she moves beside her dragon. I would have reacted except I'm so taken aback by how much she looks like a tall, angular, pinched version of my mother, I'm momentarily shocked into silence.

Welcome back to my court, Adina.

'Your Majesty, thank you for seeing me. If I could—'

This is your niece, Priscilla. Priscilla, this is your great-aunt, Adina.

Remembering Am'ratha's warning, I school my voice and say, 'Pleased to meet you, Aunt, and you too, Am'nera.'

The dragon inclines her head, acknowledging my greeting. My great-aunt studiously ignores me.

You may proceed, Adina.

'As my emissary outlined, the people of the World Below grow restless. Queen Ariana has not been seen for months, and our world is in disarray. She has not named a new heir, so I request you name me Queen in her absence. Once that is done, I will name my son my heir, and I would request that he is paired with a dragon as a sign of his new status.'

She has been rehearsing that, I send to Am'ratha, who bites back a snort.

The Dragon Queen's eyes swivel to me. ***Have you something to share, Priscilla?***

She is so reminiscent of one of my schoolteachers, I instantly feel chastened. Then I realise she is actually inviting me to speak. This is my moment, and I've not prepared anything. Taking a deep breath, I marshal my thoughts. This will not be perfect, but I put all those years of debating into practice and start.

'I saw Queen Ariana myself, just a few days ago. I can assure you, she has not disappeared. She is merely ill from cleansing the magical flow.' I cross my fingers superstitiously behind my back. 'I have just returned from the Unseelie Court with King Maddox. He has come to help restore magic to all of our worlds. Once the core of magic in both worlds is repaired, I am sure Queen Ariana will return to the Capitol and ease everyone's worries.'

The Queen of Dragons lowers her head, accepting my words.

'How do we know she speaks the truth?' Adina almost spits the words out.

The Dragon Queen tenses, and I get the impression Adina has moved beyond impolite to rude. The Queen's cold tone when she next speaks confirms my suspicions.

You question whether or not I can read truth in the words of a creature?

Adina hastily recovers. 'No, of course not. It is just we cannot go on like this forever.'

True. I will give Queen Ariana and King Maddox ten days to sort out the problem with magic. By then, if the Queen has not returned to the Capitol, we can consider other solutions.

'On that matter, she has no named successor, Your Majesty.'

I do not take a hand in creature affairs, as you well know, but as I am aware, there is a line of succession already. Princess Petunia is the named heir and was never formally removed from the line of succession when she chose to exile herself. If the Queen does not return to the Capitol, and Petunia returns to the World Below in the next ten days, she will be Queen-in-Waiting.

'But she has been exiled and cannot return here,' Adina says.

Then as, I understand it, with Princess Cecily having renounced her claim to the throne, Princess Priscilla is next in line, and she appears to be in good enough health to appoint or produce her own heir.

The air around us thrums with tension. Adina turns to me, and there is so much hatred in her eyes that Am'ratha shuffles between us.

I'm torn. There is no way I want to be Queen of the World Below, but I can't let Adina know that because she'll use it to her advantage. However, I need to know my options before I make a decision.

'Can I please check something with you, Your Majesty?'

You may speak.

'If Princess Petunia is physically back in the World Below, then she is still next in line to the throne.'

That is correct.

Adina sniggers. 'Good luck with that. My son is in control of the council and will never overturn her banishment.'

I ignore my great-aunt's vitriol and carry on.

'Do you know if my mother can resume her place in the hierarchy?'

Perhaps. As far as we are concerned, she is still a Princess of the Royal Blood. She and her dragon still maintain contact.

Wow, another thing I never knew about my family. They just keep stacking up here.

As far as I understand it, there is an agreement between your mother and Queen Ariana. Cecily would raise you in the World Above, but she could return at any time and take up her duties, thereby resuming her place in the succession.

'Over my dead body,' Adina hisses.

I would love to arrange that, I think. I'm circumspect enough not to say it, but I'm pretty sure Am'ratha and the Dragon Queen can hear me, as Am'ratha snorts in agreement.

I tire of this creature mess. I will not see either of you again for nine days. If Queen Ariana has not appeared by then, you may both approach me.

We are definitely dismissed. Even though I am mentally spiralling, I keep my back straight and my head high as Am'ratha leads me out of the cave and into the fresh air. I expect Adina to follow and brace myself for a confrontation, but by the time we reach the entrance, she has not emerged.

Your great-aunt waits in the chamber, hoping our Queen will speak with her alone.

Of course, I should have expected something under-handed from Bernais's mother. 'Should I go back?'

No, our Queen has spoken, and she will remain bound by her word. Come now, I will take you to the creature guest quarters where you can clean up and rest.

Both those things sound really good right about now.

· · ✦ · 🌙 · ✦ · ·

Ed'rathe skims long snow-topped mountains before spiralling down into a valley surrounded by tall peaks. He stops on a ledge outside a cave opening and lets me down.

You have been allowed into the World Between, but you must not leave the creature compound without a dragon escort, Noble One, he explains.

'Is this where Pris is?' I ask.

I am not sure. I think not though. I must return to my home now. The others here will tell you all you need to know and make sure you are settled.

He spreads his wings and glides out into the valley. I watch him for a while. He is truly magnificent and more so as the sunset bounces off his scales. A blast of cold wind buffets me and reminds me I'm not dressed for altitude. I turn to seek the shelter of the cave.

As I enter, warm, soft light bounces off the smooth walls, highlighting that it is so much more than a simple cave. About ten feet in, I push back a heavy curtain to find myself inside a huge, cosy cavern. A fire roars in a central pit surrounded by scatters of cushions and thickly woven rugs.

Three corridors lead off from the main room. From the one directly to my right, I hear voices, and the smell of food wafts towards me. Following my nose along the dimly lit tunnel, I find it opens up into a dining room filled with around twenty or so creatures from a variety of races. I'm surprised to find a face I know in the crowd. She breaks away and joins me by the door.

'Priscilla Crown's guard. I'm surprised to see you here,' Verona says as she greets me, her face beaming.

'Not as surprised as I am to see the daughter of Giles Regis,' I respond wearily.

Verona grimaces, then shrugs. 'If my father had not wanted me to make friends amongst the creatures in the World Below, he shouldn't have banished me here as a punishment.'

'Yeah, then again, how was he to know you would meet so many handsome and interesting creatures?' a blond sprite says as he joins us. 'I'm Fergus,' he says, holding out his hand.

'Snake,' I respond, grasping it.

For a moment the room falls silent, and it's as if everyone is frozen in place. Next thing, I'm surrounded by creatures, and everyone is asking about our quest and wondering where Princess Priscilla is.

Verona catches my eye, then takes me by the arm and hauls me back towards the central room, announcing loudly, 'This guy looks and smells like he needs to wash up and get into some clean clothes. While I show him the amenities, perhaps someone could rustle him up some clean clothes and a bowl of stew.'

Clearly used to her bossing them about, the others melt away and she pulls me down the opposite corridor.

'Thank you, that was getting a bit intense.'

Verona smiles and leads me deeper into the cave.

'Okay, baths are that way. It's a hot mineral pool really, but it's amazing. I'll get someone to drop some clothes inside the door. The third room on the right is free. We are two to three to a room, so you'll have to share with someone at some stage, so don't spread out too far, as some more of us are arriving in the next couple of days.'

I laugh. 'What you see is what I have with me, so there's not going to be a problem there.'

She smiles. 'Many of our numbers are refugees from the fighting. We are well provisioned, so we can set you up with everything you need.'

I'm weary, and the baths are calling me, but I'm not too tired to ask, 'And who are the "we" you refer to?'

She laughs. 'Don't worry, you're amongst friends here. We are a loose affiliation of groups who have been fighting for equal rights for all creatures. With the change in the makeup of the council, there have been crackdowns on our activities, and the dragons offered us sanctuary of a sort.'

I nod, storing the information away to process later.

'So, just to clarify, you and your dad....'

'Are on opposite sides. Look, go clean up, eat, and grab some rest. And don't leave your room until you're up to being questioned.' She smiles and winks at me. 'Although... before I go, I have to ask, is it true you and Priscilla went on a quest to the minotaur's maze?'

I nod wearily, and she literally claps her hands together in glee. 'Man, I can't wait to hear about that! He was so imposing when he tested us as we came through from the World Below that he's become a little bit of an idol. Now go.' She pushes me through a door.

The room she sends me into has a floor of polished rock, and in the middle is a sort of roundish pool of water bathed in a cloak of steam. I stumble in the rush to remove my clothes and sink into the bath. It is bliss, and I can't stop myself from groaning as I submerge myself in the pool's soothing depths.

I'm in spa heaven. My aches and pains slip away, and I even feel the tension in my shoulders ease. Finally hunger forces me from the water, and I dress in the simple linen trousers and shirt someone has left for me. I pad barefoot to the room Verona said I could use.

It is a simple affair, containing two beds covered in home-spun blankets, each with a chest at their foot and a small bedside table. On one of the tables is a steaming bowl of stew. I wolf it down, barely tasting it, before lying back on the bed, my hands clasped behind my head.

Sleep is calling, and every muscle in my body feels like it weighs a ton, but I can't relax until I know where Pris is. I'm not sure what the protocols are here about contacting him, but if I don't try, I'll just worry.

Ed'rathe, do you know where Pris is?

To my surprise he responds. ***She should be with you, Noble One.***

The words spur me to action, I push myself up and swing my legs around just as the door is gently pushed open. I've never been so happy to see someone in my life. Pris stands in the doorway, dressed identically to me and carrying her own bowl of stew. Her eyes catch mine, and she smiles, tucking a stray strand of white hair behind a pointed ear.

No sooner does she put her food down than I sweep her into my arms. She melts into my embrace, and everything else leaves my brain. I hold her tightly as if I never want to let her go. Then I remember her injury, and I gently remove my arms and step away.

'Your wound?'

She smiles before snuggling back into my embrace. 'I've been fixed—by the Queen of Dragons, no less.'

There is a story there, and part of me wants to hear it, but mostly I want to hold her. She tilts her face, and I respond to her invitation, crushing her lips with mine. As one, we move back until I can feel the edge of the bed. I draw her down with me, and for a while there is nothing in my head but the two of us. We have waited so long for this moment, to be together alone, and I'm not going to let anything come between us.

Sometime later, she is wrapped in a blanket, leaning against me, and picking at her lukewarm meal. Drawing on some magic, I heat it for her, and she smiles appreciatively. While she eats, she tells me about her meeting with the Dragon Queen. I listen, but am too exhausted to even comprehend the meaning.

'What do you want to do about it?' I ask.

She puts her bowl on the table and snuggles back into me.

'I'm not sure. There is so much we still don't know.'

I lean my cheek on her hair, and the smell of her sends a pulse through my body. I pull her closer.

'There is one thing I know,' I say.

'Yes?' Her voice is low and seductive.

'Whatever is happening, it can wait for one night.'

I turn her towards me, and she leans to plant a sweet kiss on my mouth. 'It most certainly can.'

Acknowledgments

I have taken some time off work this year to deal with some health issues. This has allowed me time to to follow my dream of becoming a full time writer. My journey has been shared by Trouble and Lola, who have kept me company and listened to my ramblings.

I've been very lucky to once again work with an amazing team who helped turn my story into something others would want to read.

Thank you to the team at Creating Ink, especially Sali Benbow-Powers, whose feedback added the texture to my story. And to McKinley Hellennes Krantz and the team at Hot Tree Editing, making the words flow.

As always, my love and thanks to my moral support Jim and Sam for putting up with me when when I lose myself in a fantasy world, and being there when I finally emerge.

Finally, thank you for reading my musings. If you enjoyed The Unseelie Court please some time and let me know what you thought of the book by leaving a review on your favourite book site.

About the Author

Vivienne has been writing books since she was fifteen years old, but only friends and family were allowed to read them. Forced to give up work because of family commitments she was encouraged by friends and family to finally put some of her writing out there for others to read.

Born in Invercargill (New Zealand), she has lived in; Dunedin (New Zealand), London (England), Petersfield (England) and currently lives with her husband and son, their dog Trouble and cat Lola in North Sydney (Australia).

When not reading or writing she can be found walking, crocheting, knitting and watching movies.

For future releases and current news you can find Vivienne at www.viviennelfraser.com.au where you can also join my newsletter.

If you enjoyed The World Below, why not try The Guardians of Time Series Time Travel Adventures?

The Time Guardians Omnibus

In the shadows between history and time a secret war is waging—a war where the stakes are the future of humanity.

On one side are the Time Fixers, often called the Time Wreckers by their enemies. They believe fixing past wrongs will pave the way for humanity's salvation.

On the other side are the Time Guardians, who fight for history to remain as it has always has been, believing humankind will find a way to save themselves.

Time Guardian Sigma has pulled together a team of would-be guardians to help him keep history in line; John the pragmatist, feisty Barabal, Alain the inquisitive, and Stanislaus the loyal.

As his team portal through time foiling Time Fixer plots, Sigma is worried they may be winning battles, but they are losing the war—and that's not just because Time Fixer Isolde has been getting inside his head.

Will the Time Guardian's win the war? Will humanity survive the battle? More importantly, will Sigma be there at the end?

https://viviennelfraser.com.au/time-guardians

Or if you enjoy Fantasy Adventure why not try

The Wizard and The Warrior

Centuries ago prophets predicted the rise of a great wizard and a formidable warrior who would save the people of their land. Now an invasion fleet is heading for Aria, is it time for the Wizard and the Warrior to arise and save them all?

Runaway bride Aliah wants to be more than someone's wife. Fleeing his destiny, Seamus has no idea what he wants from his future. Thrown together by fate, the two journey to the nation's capital; one to warn the king of an impending invasion, the other to do the unthinkable—train to be a wizard.

Their chance encounter takes them on a wild adventure where they must face their pasts and decide their future, all while helping Aria prepare to defend itself.

However, fate has not finished with Seamus and Aliah. In an unexpected twist, they are placed at the very centre of the conflict facing their home, and must decide whether or not to take up the challenge.

With the gods on their side, it should be easy for Aliah and Seamus to identify and locate the real power behind the invasion and find a way to defeat him; all while pulling together a support team and having mid-night lessons to learn how to use their newly acquired magical tokens. Well, it would be if the gods weren't hiding more than they shared.

Aria's future hangs in the balance, can two runaways tip the scales?

What one reader on Amazon said: Great book - it might

be targeted at youth readers, but even as an adult, I was hooked on the storyline. Can't wait for the next one!
https://viviennelfraser.com.au/wizard-and-warrior-one